One Man Against The Mountain

The story of a quest to survive winter alone in the Big Horns

Based on the the true-life survival saga of Danny Longwell

By
Mary Jo Mosher
with journal excerpts and photos by Danny Longwell

Published by

STUDIO SEE
622 S. Thurmond, Sheridan, Wyoming 82801
www.studiosee.com

If you purchased this book without a cover, you should be aware that this book may be stolen property. It was reported "unsold and destroyed" to the publisher, and neither the author nor the publisher has received any payment for this "stripped book."

All rights reserved. No part of this book may be used or reproduced in any manner whatsover without written permission of the publisher, except in case of brief quotations embodied in critical articles and reviews. For information, contact Studio See, 622 S. Thurmond, Sheridan, WY.

This is a work of part fiction, part fact. It is the slightly embelished and fictionalized story of one man's true-life solitary struggle for survival in a brutal, unrelenting winter atop the Big Horn Mountains in northern Wyoming. Some names have been changed and events left out in the telling of this story.

Actual journal entries by long-time Wyoming resident and game hunter Danny Longwell (printed in italics) punctuate this re-creation of his quest to prove that he could survive anything the mountain could dish out.

Publisher's Note:
Danny Longwell, even twelve years after his quest on Walker Prairie, still gives full and grateful credit to his dogs Spuds and Misty for keeping him alive and "somewhat sane" during his five-month winter stay in the Big Horns.

Third Studio See paperback printing: January, 2009

*Printed in the United States of America
by
Econo Print
3211 1st Ave.
Billings, Montana*

Acknowledgments

Many thanks to Dan Longwell for sharing his journal and offering me the opportunity to write a story based on his experiences. Thanks also to my husband, Robert Dingmann, for bringing Dan's request to my attention and to Michelle Havenga for acting as messenger between my publisher and me. Last, but most important, this book would not have been possible without the ability and insights God has given me to write it, for I feel that all gifts come from God.

— ***Mary Jo Mosher***

Dedication

This book is dedicated to my daughter Stephanie Mosher for her persistent support of my writing endeavors, and to author Gail Frazer for her friendship, encouragement, and enlightenment.

Chapter 1

SETTLING IN

Dan Longwell stood looking toward the hill at the string of hunters on horseback, jacket collars pulled tight around their necks, hat brims collecting large heavy snowflakes that were growing thicker. The horsemen struggled around and through three-foot drifts, hoping to make distance before dark with packhorses in tow. Hoping the narrow, sometimes treacherous trail along the mountain's edge wouldn't be snowed in by the time they got to its beginning. Hunting season was over. It was time to leave the mountain to Mother Nature's unpredictable and often cruel wiles. The storm had come with little warning, but that was nature's way on the mountain. In her anger, she had forced the men to pack lightly, perhaps promising to allow them to return for the rest of their gear when she decided to settle down. They stared back at the slender snowsuited man at the bottom of the hill who waved but made no move to join them; stared questioningly at the shovel in his hand, at his unsaddled horses in the corral, and then at him as though to ask "What are you waiting for? Get out while you can, you stupid fool! Rescue isn't cheap, you know."

Dan wasn't oblivious to the question he read in their faces; he had asked it of himself more than once.

"I know," he would have shouted if they could have heard him. "But I made a promise to myself. You wouldn't understand."

"We'll send someone to pick up your body in the spring," one of them would have answered matter of factly before turning his attention to the trail and hurrying on.

As he watched the struggling procession, riders bent in misery against the biting wind, anxiety mixed with anticipated loneliness began to fill his gut —

anxiety that told him to pack up and fall in at the end of the pack train before it was too late. But a louder voice held him to the snow-filled valley he had committed to be his winter home. It was a commitment, not only to himself, but to Billie (his partner of 10 years) and his buddies — a commitment a sense of duty told him he couldn't break, even though he realized he may not leave the mountain alive. He knew from the many stories he had heard how brutal Mother Nature could be in winter, knew that she could easily win in his inexperienced struggle against her for survival, and he hoped his instincts and what little knowledge he possessed wouldn't fail him when winter's wrath turned against him.

Leaning on his shovel, he watched the riders disappear into the cascading snow. Watched as their tracks disappeared with them, the falling snow erasing the reality that they, anyone else, or anything at all had been there. A chilly wind that had forced its way through the evergreens nipped at his shoulder, rippling a shiver through his body, and he recalled with longing the plethora of wildflowers that lay like a rainbow across the prairie in early summer when he and his two horses made several long trips up the five-mile steep and narrow Soldier Creek Trail hauling food and equipment to his hunting camp in preparation for whatever the following seasons had in mind.

At that time, Walker Prairie was an emerald grassland stretching near 10 miles north to south along the east edge of the Big Horn Mountains, the distance depending on what one considered its boundaries. Though from one end to the other it varies because there are few if any level places on the mountain, the average elevation is 7,600 feet. Big, Little, Walker, and She Bear mountains rise 500 to 1,000 feet above the prairie, lined up along its eastern edge, their formidable sheer rock sentinels abruptly meeting the grassland.

A thick lodge pole pine dominated forest surrounds the prairie on its three remaining sides, a refuge for the elk herd and other wild animals that cautiously emerge from its protective shadows to feast on succulent prairie grasses and sip from the lazy streams that drain snowmelt from the high country. In a normal water-abundant summer, Big Goose Creek flows furiously and vociferously into the prairie's southeast end, pushing, shoving, and tumbling, cutting a deep canyon into the rock before dropping dramatically off the mountain in a series of long picturesque waterfalls. Several smaller spring-fed creeks cut their own paths through the prairie, meeting and combining as they travel, breaking the monotony of an immense green ocean when the wildflowers begin to fade, as they seek the best route to level ground, their final resting place.

From the north, a winding trail stretches southward into the distance, visible only in snowless seasons as a long skinny rope snaking through the tall flower-speckled grass on the hill's edge. Several yards below the trail, Quartz Creek wanders lazily to its meeting with the Wolf, which hijacks the Quartz and speeds down the mountain in a roaring waterfall. A distance up the trail, Gloom

Creek emerges from a steep, thickly wooded canyon and it, too, dumps its load into the Quartz. As the trail approaches She Bear, Walker Creek, searching for its own route down the mountain, meets Buck Creek, and they journey together.

Along these waterways lie several hunting camps scattered along the opposite side of Quartz and Walker creeks, their lodge pole corrals (some of them obvious in their need for repair) barely visible through the tall timber, first-time riders or hikers passing through unaware of their existence. The last string of hunters escaping the mountain had packed quickly in deepening snow expecting the worst, though this time it was only a scare, a portent of things to come, leaving their tents to suffer Mother Nature's whims. These men had hunted the mountain often enough to know that danger, often disguised in the beauty that lures people to it, exists here in all seasons, but especially when winter snows hide it. They would be back to get the rest of their gear when the weather settled so the Forest Service wouldn't complain about litter betraying human presence that spoiled the wildness of the prairie or would think the hunters' intent was to homestead.

Though he had only been there in spring, summer, and fall, Dan, also, was not oblivious to the dangers winter on the prairie could deliver; especially the cruel, numbing wind as it drops temperatures and swirls falling snow into a blinding, biting curtain of misery one dares not wander into for fear of death. Dan knew a man who risked staying on the prairie in winter, but in the relative warmth of a log cabin with a soft easy chair, an efficient wood-burning stove, and a stack of good books, laughing at evil storms that pounded angrily on his windows and scratched at his door, determined to find a way in. But by the end of it, he decided one such winter had been enough.

"I learned a lot from him, especially about snow depth," Dan told the journal he had started in August. "But his cabin was five miles away where the snow is significantly less deep than it is in my camp. What I really wanted to know was where to keep my meat. He never did tell me. I had to figure it out for myself."

Not many of the sane, and certainly not that man, who considered himself brave living in a log cabin with comforts, would have considered spending winter on the prairie in a vulnerable canvas-walled shelter around which snow depths might reach 20 feet and the struggle to keep warm when a vicious wind roars through the prairie intending to tear down your shelter becomes a matter of life and death, Dan thought.

It wasn't only the mountain with its crevasses, canyons, steepness, severe weather, and wild animals that created risk; Dan, just by placing himself in the midst of it, created his own danger that, even if heeded, could lead to his demise - a careless moment, failure to recognize crucial details or potential danger, radio malfunctions when communication was crucial, runaway fire in his tent, wild animal attack . . . But dwelling on the dangers would be like spotting a mountain lion not far off and running from it rather than admiring it from a safe distance, careful not to annoy it.

With that thought, a sudden burst of biting wind brought him back to the reality that the calendar had just turned to November, winter had settled in for at least a five-month stretch, at which time it would challenge spring for territorial rights, and he must spend his energy preparing for the worst it was capable of delivering.

Suddenly coming down with a sense of urgency as the thinly blanketed sun dropped closer to the horizon, he wiped snowflake drops from his glasses, picked up his shovel, chuckled at his blue healers trying to romp in the deep snow, and set to work digging a large hole into which he would drop a 50-gallon barrel. That finished, he carefully piled his stash of frozen meat into the barrel and packed snow tightly around it. His meat would remain safely frozen throughout the long winter, he thought with satisfaction as he picked up his shovel and cleared a path to the creek, which was running thin and shallow in spite of the spring that fed it, dug a hole in the creek bottom and, using rocks gathered for that purpose, created a dam to hold back his water cache. By the time he had finished, it had quit snowing. He parked his shovel upright near the door and turned to admire a cloud-streaked sun that was beginning to redden as it sat briefly on the green tops of the tall timber.

Dan had put in a full day of work that his muscles hadn't yet become accustomed to. But he knew that, in time, his body would adjust to the hard physical labor he expected would be an almost daily necessity. He whistled to Misty and Spuds, who stopped wrestling in the snow and quickly came running, hungry and eager as their master to warm themselves. The dogs immediately curled up on an old rug Dan had prepared for them next to the stove, which by now, for lack of feeding, was nearly cold.

"That's your bed," he had told them firmly early on as, with possessive longing, they eyed the log bed he had made in August draped with three down sleeping bags that would keep him warm into subzero temperatures. Sometimes they ignored him, the temptation beyond resisting and, when his back was turned, jumped up and settled into its soft comfort stubbornly unmoving despite their master's protests. Depending on his mood, Dan either gave in or sternly demanded they evacuate. When the latter happened, the dogs moped for a long time until Dan affectionately scratched their ears and patted their heads, and they finally offered forgiveness.

Now he took off his boots and set them by the door where he could sit down and put them on in the morning and hung his snowmobile suit and cap on a hook fastened to a wood pole near the stove that supported the tent's roof. After adding wood to the disappearing fire, Dan filled a pot from a water jug and set it on the stove to boil. Then he dug into his food supply for a package of spaghetti and a jar of sauce. While he waited for the water to boil, he sat down and brought his journal up to date.

Well, today is November 2, and I haven't written anything in here lately. To get caught up, for the last 2.5 months, I didn't get up here much. Spent most of the time down below working - yuk! - but the times I did get up, I packed up three tables and then I packed up carpeting. Glad I did. I also made a bed out of logs, and it sure beats sleeping on a cot. It's getting dark in here, so I will take a break and try to get some lanterns lit.

His winter home was a 14- by 16-foot wall tent surrounded by a five-foot high lodge pole corral located on the west side of Walker Creek where She Bear Mountain cast its morning shadow when the sun decided to shine. Though the tent appeared large on the outside, his living quarters diminished significantly with each load of supplies he brought in, beginning with a layer of foam he set down on the floor then topped with a large piece of worn carpet so he wouldn't suffer the shock of setting his bare feet on ice when he climbed out of bed in the morning.

His kitchen was a long table holding his two-burner camp stove, utensils, and pots and pans, leaving a small piece of counter on which to work. Next

Photo courtesy of Danny Longwell

The kitchen was a long table holding a two-burner camp stove, utensils, and pots and pans, leaving a small piece of counter on which to work.

to that was the small wood-burning stove surrounded by a neatly stacked wood pile that lined the tent wall. An old table and a couple of folding chairs that defined his dining room and living room sat in a corner near the wood-burning stove. Several tubs filled with canned and packaged food, including a large box filled with eggs covered against the cold, were stacked in another corner. When the last load of supplies was emptied into the tent, Dan considered his living quarters comfortable and adequate enough to get him through a tough winter in spite of the lack of windows to let in natural light and slow the progression of cabin fever.

Now, he paused for a moment to examine the coziness of his new home. A sense of accomplishment was finally beginning to replace the frustration Dan had felt in August when, after spending several weeks in Sheridan preparing supplies, he arrived at camp to discover that undesirable visitors had broken into his tent and, thinking the place abandoned, or perhaps not caring whether it was or wasn't, moved in intending to claim ownership. In his tent, they found a perfect shelter from harsh elements and airborne enemies.

Though Dan discovered no sign of life when he walked in, evidence that they had been there was compelling. In one corner lay a roll of toilet paper that had been torn into small pieces and neatly woven into a winter home. Obvious leavings of small perpetrators decorated the tent floor surrounding their newly constructed home. Disposing of the mess that evening, Dan began thinking that keeping his tent to himself and his dogs all winter could be a continuing battle. Traps, and lots of them, became a priority on his supply list for the next load up the mountain.

Deeper into fall, discouragement had set in again when he rode into Walker Prairie after a long absence to find his camp in partial ruin, this time, the result of a destructive early winter storm. Examining the damage, he wondered whether Mother Nature was trying to tell him that he should climb on his horse, collect his dogs, and not return until winter's wrath had played out. That evening in the warmth of his tent, exhausted from a long afternoon of shoveling, cleaning, and repairing, he wrote in the journal he had begun in August to fuel his memory when off the prairie, especially in his declining years when he may have to content himself with looking up at the mountains rather than experiencing them from within.

This was my first trip back up after the big snow. I was worried that the tent would be down and buried, but I talked to several people, and they all said it was up, so I was happy, even though it took me four hours to get to camp, for the snow was really deep. My heart sank when I arrived and saw one whole side down and buried. I couldn't get to the door, for there was about four feet of snow blocking my way. Thank God I had packed a scoop shovel today. When I got inside, I discovered a mess (a much bigger one than the August intruders had left), the stove on the floor, and the stovepipe on the ground and buried. After shoveling snow for three hours by lantern light, I finally got the tent back up and a fire going. Don't know who was happier, the dogs or me. It's 13 below at 9 p.m., and time for bed.

Though it was early November, winter no longer considered melting its cloud-filled loads of frozen water to expose the green that lay sleeping beneath the white burial blanket they had created. Mother Nature's roller coaster temperatures (more downs now than ups), kept Dan busy the next several days cutting and stockpiling wood, for he had no idea how much it would take to keep his small, thin-walled abode at a bearable temperature. He guessed that 50 below zero with strong winds would soon become a formidable foe to be dealt with.

Since the first serious snowfall, snow on the mountain deepened daily, making navigation by foot impossible without a shovel in hand to clear the way or a pair of four-and-a-half-foot snowshoes designed to keep feet on top of deep drifts. Though he had no previous experience with them and didn't especially like them, Dan reluctantly decided that learning to manage them was a necessity if he were to walk farther than his tent door and down the cleared paths to his water and makeshift toilet. They would be most useful in his wanderings from camp to search for firewood, explore, or should he need to hike down the mountain. Without them, he could find himself over his head in a 15-foot snowdrift where it would take hours to dig himself out, an unpleasant, if not exhausting or even life threatening task.

November 3: It's 8 a.m., and the temperature is zero. I have lots of snow to shovel. It's 11:30, and I'm damned tired of shoveling. The rest can wait for another day. Finished lunch and went snowshoeing. What a joke if you've never been on a pair. It's not as easy as everyone says it is.

Dan stood outside his tent staring distastefully at the new snowshoes standing upright in the snow, Misty and Spuds standing beside him, wondering what he had planned for the day. "I know they're big, but they're the best for navigating in snow that's really deep," the clerk had told him when Dan explained why he needed them.

"I expected something quite a bit smaller — and less expensive. Are you sure I need them that big?" The clerk insisted he would be sorry for purchasing anything smaller, and Dan reluctantly gave in. "Can I return them if they don't work for me?"

He was assured he could, and as the clerk rang up Dan's purchase, he said, "Once you master these, you won't be sorry. Guaranteed."

"Yeah, once you master them; if you master them is what he really means," Dan told himself sarcastically.

Now as he removed them from the snow and placed them carefully on the cleared piece of level ground in front of him, his confidence in mastery of them was nil. "Gee, they're huge," he said, placing one foot into the snowshoe trappings. "How on earth will I learn to manage these things?" Misty and Spuds offered no answer, but instead set to chasing their tails, obviously disinterested in their master's problems.

The practice area was a stretch of snow-cleared ground next to the tent where Dan managed with only a little difficulty to get them fastened to his feet on the first attempt. Misty and Spuds, who moments ago were chasing an invisible foe in the deep snow, sprinted closer to their master and, sensing that trouble was ahead, lay down to watch. Dan stood up on his new feet and, with the adeptness of a peg-legged ballet dancer, tried to move forward, but his feet, heavy and clumsy, refused to cooperate. He tried hard to keep his balance, but lost the battle and landed hard on his backside uttering expletives that best expressed his frustration.

Considering their master's ineptitude a signal for play, the two tail-wagging canines pounced on his chest, painting his face with saliva as he lay on his back in a foot of snow, his boat-size feet hopelessly tangled. Dan struggled to rid himself of the dogs, wiped his face on the sleeve of his snowsuit, and sat up, yelling at them angrily. His next task was to release himself from the snowshoes, get to his feet, and start over - all, he hoped, without help from Misty and Spuds, who hadn't taken his anger seriously, rather seemed to be laughing at him.

"I'll never get used to these things," he said adamantly, as he tried to get up nerve to move his feet, knowing he'd be on the ground again if he did. He was right. "Damn! That's enough of this for today," he muttered, untangling himself for the second time, frustration obvious in his voice. "I hate these things."

In spite of it, the mountain gave him no choice but to persist. He knew he would need proficiency on snowshoes in the days to come, and there was no releasing him from it. That would be before the snow's deepness prohibited travel by horseback and as soon as Billie could come and get the horses he had borrowed from his friend, Kenny. But first, Dan needed the mounts to transport a few more supplies to camp before settling in for his five-month stint with Mother Nature.

The next day, his anger cooled, he tried again, with a little more success. "If I give up on these, I might as well give up staying here. I'll have been beaten from the beginning," he said to himself as he took a few steps, walking stick in hand to steady himself.

In the days to come, his progress mastering snowshoes was slow, often impeded by Spuds and Misty, who thought it fun to sneak up on him, put their front feet on the back of his snowshoes, and slide along with the movement of

Dan's feet. But when Dan discovered why his snowshoes had suddenly grown exceedingly heavy, he yelled at them angrily.

"Get off, you stupid canines. I have a hard enough time learning to make these damned things work without you two freeloaders along for the ride." Their feelings hurt, the dogs slinked away and hid for a while. Later on, when Dan had mastered the snowshoes and the snow became so deep Misty and Spuds, struggling to keep their chubby bodies and short legs on top of the deep snow, kept falling through and became exhausted with the effort, Dan softened and gave them permission to ride.

Though he was never comfortable with his cumbersome new feet, he practiced persistently, walking farther each time, his meetings with the ground gradually becoming fewer and navigation easier, his confidence growing with each outing. Soon, he was ready for the challenge of deeper snow, which he met with success.

November 4 dawned chilly with a blue and gray sky but no threat of precipitation, and Dan saw it as a good day to go after more supplies. After breakfast, he fed the horses - a white appaloosa that looked like someone had splashed dark brown paint all over it, and a handsome buckskin with a long black tail, mane, and forelock - then saddled and packed them for the long trip ahead, Misty and Spuds hanging close, determined not to be left behind.

The trip down the mountain was uneventful, the horses having little trouble negotiating the drifts, which had shrunk since the first snowfall that had sent the riders scrambling to get off the mountain. But the following day, gray, moisture-filled clouds floated lazily across their darkening highway, pushing and shoving one another, sometimes obscuring the mountain tops. Frowning ominously, they dropped occasional snowflakes, promising to deliver more, as Dan began the return trip up the narrow edge-of-cliff Soldier Creek Trail, his packhorse loaded with food supplies but not complaining under the weight. The horses had been ridden often and were well conditioned for hill climbing, which they did with little effort and few rest stops. But as they gained elevation, winter began to show spunk, making navigation difficult for the loaded-down horses, which slowed their pace, and for the dogs, struggling to keep up in the deepening drifts.

November 5: Got to camp at 3:30 p.m. with a load of groceries. I left soldier creek at 10 a.m., for the lane was snowed in. When I left, it was spitting snow, and by the time I got to the end of the lane, I was solid white, but not too cold. By the time I got to Whiskey Rock, there were three new inches, and the horses had a hard time of it. I stopped about every 50 feet to rest them, dismount, stomp some feeling into my feet, and have a smoke. But as soon as I got it lit, my moustache started to thaw and put out the fire. After 10 attempts, I gave it up.

When I finally reached the salt cabin, there were about eight inches of new snow on top of three feet of old. Walking, I tried to break trail, but kept falling. I was so cold and numb that I didn't think I could make the last 1.5 miles. When I topped out on Walker Prairie, it was snowing with the force of a blizzard, and fog had rolled in, hiding the trail and the dogs. So I just let the horse go and hoped he would get me to camp. When the fog finally broke, I was only about 300 yards from camp, and that was the farthest I have ever ridden in fog.

When fog attacks the mountain, it seems to appear suddenly from nowhere, poking ghost fingers across the landscape, hanging suspended and motionless a foot or two off the ground, or speeding busily across the prairie as though late for an appointment, often followed by a gang of companions that curtain the trail. To Dan, the fog's antics were fascinating. It seemed alive, teasing, purposely doing its best to confuse and disorient him. It was unpredictable, visible, but untouchable, not to be grasped, poked, or shoved aside. It was alive, yet dead, harmless, yet harmful. It was cold and damp, chilling to the bone, even on a summer day. Dan was glad when he had left it behind, leaving the trail ahead clear.

Once inside the tent, his numb fingers fumbled with the matches, trying to hold onto them long enough to light his cook stove. Finally, after several failed attempts, the stove sputtered into action and, holding his hands close to it for several minutes, he was soon able to get his fingers moving long enough to get a fire going in the wood stove. He placed his wet gloves near the heat, exchanged them for a pair of dry ones and went outside to unpack and feed the horses. That done, he put away the groceries and sat in front of the stove reading until 11 p.m. when warmth had chased the final chill from his body. Only then did he strip off his outer layers, leaving his long underwear to keep him warm through the night. The outdoor thermometer told him it was 16 below; time to huddle deep into a warm sleeping bag until morning.

That night, Misty and Spuds crept quietly through the tent flap and disappeared, unresponsive to Dan's whistles and calls. And when he awoke during the night to feed the stove, they remained absent, leaving his worried mind to conjure up stories of a wild animal, perhaps a mountain lion — for they were known to live on the prairie — using them for sport, or some other distant danger luring them to their deaths.

"How would I get through the winter without them?" he thought, as he lay awake listening for yips in the distance, or scratching at the tent flap. "They're the closest to human company I have up here. Without them, I don't know if I could survive the loneliness."

It was near morning when Misty and Spuds returned, and anticipation had kept Dan awake most of the night. The dogs repeated their excursions the next few nights, which aroused their master's curiosity. But he had been too busy restocking his wood and water supply to check on their nightly travels. Winter flexed its muscles the next several days as though to give Dan a small taste of what he was up against as the days shortened and the long nights grew progressively colder. The wind whistled and howled through the lodge pole pines, playing with the tent, keeping temperatures in the single digits at night and the horses in their corral on the mountain until the calendar turned to December.

During the day, Dan didn't have much time to be lonely; his struggle to keep up with winter's belligerence kept him busy from morning until bedtime, and he knew he would soon be seeing Billie. Until then, he had to cut wood daily to keep up with the wood burning stove's voracious appetite in the deep freeze of his winter camp. And he was finding that supplies he hadn't thought of when packing things up the mountain would have to be brought up before the horses were no longer available to haul them up. From then on, either snowshoes would have to suffice, or forgotten items he figured necessary gone without.

November 7: It's 7 a.m. Snowing and 10 above. Was going to go down today, but now I'm not sure. Have to get these horses down. It's 11 a.m., and it quit snowing, but the wind is blowing about 40 mph. Hell, it's a real blizzard out there. So I made up my mind I'm not leaving the tent until my bladder tells me to. 1:30 p.m., and I'm going to try and get down. Billie was expecting me yesterday, so I better at least try or she may send up a helicopter to check on me. I can't call her for my radio is broke down. So I'm gonna get off my wimpy butt and try it. Hopefully I'll be writing more later.

Brought the last of my supplies up. The trail was drifted in. I really had no right to bring horses up, but I made it fine. Well, all unpacked and stuff put away, and it's late, so think I will hit the old bed. It's 9 below at 9 p.m.

Went down early this morning to pick up Billie so she can bring the horses back down. The trail was drifted in a little and snowing. Was late when we reached camp; dark and cold.

Billie and Dan rode up the mountain in silence, too busy watching the trail to make conversation, darkness coming early and moonless, obscuring their surroundings. Near freezing, they unpacked and settled the horses, who seemed relieved to get rid of their loads and happy to be left alone with a pile of hay and a dish of grain, and set a fire to blazing in the wood-burning stove. Supper was fast, easy, and meager, as the hour was late, and all of them were near exhaustion. The dogs quickly settled into sleep, wishing for their master's bed but settling for the floor after being admonished by Dan, while he and Billie sat close to the stove sipping hot cocoa and talking about the days to come, Billie

Photo by Danny Longwell

Billie ready to ride out of camp, taking Dan's horse with her.

wanting to ask one more time if he was sure he wanted to do this. Thinking better of it, she turned the conversation to something more cheerful, something less likely to start an argument.

Her presence had brightened Dan's spirits that day and evening and into the next morning until they finished fastening the panniers on the appaloosa and saddling the buckskin, and Billie climbed on.

"You be careful," she said quietly, taking the reins. "It won't be easy going down the mountain on snowshoes that big."

"I know."

"Remember, you can always change your mind," she ventured, her voice betraying hope that he would give her the answer she wanted to hear.

"I'm not going to back out." His voice was firm. "What would everyone think?"

"To heck with what anyone else thinks," she said curtly. "You think too much about that."

Not wishing to argue, Dan set to fastening ropes to Misty and Spuds' collars and tied the dogs to the fence so they wouldn't follow her, for if they did, sanity during the endless stretch of short days and long nights that lay ahead would go with them. Then he turned to Billie, who sat watching, her horse waiting patiently for her signal to move out. That she was leaving was becoming

Photo by Danny Longwell

Billie riding away from camp.

reality, and he didn't know when he would see her again, or anyone else for that matter. The time had come for his severance from civilization. Once she and the horses were out of sight, his easy access to the world below would be gone.

Hesitant to turn her loose, but realizing he couldn't keep her there any longer, he handed her the lead rope attached to the appaloosa, hoping she wouldn't notice the moisture gathering in his eyes. She hesitated momentarily, as though she had something more to say and suddenly changed her mind, then waving goodbye, she tightened her grip on the reins, pushed her heel into the buckskin's side, turning the horses toward the trail, and didn't look back.

Though she had fair trust in his competence, and though she tried to keep it from her mind, the thought that he may never return from the mountain occasionally surfaced. And judging from his troubled mood of late, perhaps that was what he wanted and expected, for then he would be at one with the only world that understood his life's struggles. Billie was as uncertain of his reasons for being there as were others, and as uncertain of his chances of survival as were others. But talking him into coming home and forgetting about it would be as futile as asking the sun to rotate around the earth.

Dan's spirits began a long descent as he stood watching Billie and what could be his last human contact for several months, disappear into the prairie with the steady crunch of the horses' feet on the crisp snow. Stood and watched as the talk and comfort brought by her visit and the horses that had secured his link to the world below the mountain dissolved into a disturbing silence.

Cumbersome snowshoes and grueling navigation along the narrow, sometimes treacherous 10 to 15 mile trail were now his only escape from brutality to civilization should the need arise — or he should decide he had had enough of winter's punishment. Rescue wouldn't come fast if his life were at stake. Nor could he get himself off the mountain with any semblance of speed now that the horses were gone. Suddenly the word "alone" had turned from desirable and pleasant, something he had often longed for, to a pernicious beast he would have to do battle with as long as he was on the mountain.

"Perhaps I am a fool," he said to himself as he stared into the empty prairie.

Tears filled his eyes, blurring his vision, as he turned and walked into the tent to let his feelings flow until spent, leaving Misty and Spuds struggling against the ropes that held them back, yapping toward the end of the prairie where Billie had disappeared. Dan would turn them loose when enough time had passed for Billie to be well on her way down the mountain, at least an hour. In the meantime, he needed time to think, time to absorb the meaning of the aloneness he was facing. For he was as confused about it as were those who had watched him pack up and leave.

As he sat by the warm stove drying his tears, he suddenly he realized the dogs had turned quiet without even a half hour's passing. Stepping outside, he found two ropes lying next to the fence, limp and empty of all except two collars. He walked up the hill, scanning camp and the distant prairie, shouting their names, but no canines appeared from the woods or from over the hill, tails wagging, begging to be petted and fed.

He thought of going after them, but decided against it. Misty and Spuds were sometimes Billie's and sometimes his. Now, Dan figured Billie's going and his staying had them confused, unsure of to whom their loyalty belonged. "I'll give them a while," he thought. "Maybe they'll come back — I hope." If they had gone all the way down the mountain, he would face an even longer winter without company, without protection, without someone to talk to. Their absence and the thought of their not returning deepened his depression.

Billie left camp at 9 a.m., so I'm afoot now for five months. What a weird feeling it was when she left. I was about ready to cry when we said goodbye. I don't know if I cried because she was leaving or if it was because she took my horse, and I was stuck up here forever with those damned snowshoes. That's hard to believe the way we fight all the time. She's honest; she tells you what she thinks whether you like it or not, and I respect her for that.

Both dogs are with me. They're not sure what's going on. Billie's dog worked her way off her rope, and both of them left camp, returning after a half hour. The rest of the day, I didn't do much. I think it finally sank into my head what I was really doing, and it's scary. When she left, it struck me that this wasn't a game any more. This was going to be a fight for my life.

That night, as Dan lay in his warm sleeping bag listening to the wind tug at the tent walls trying to suck every bit of warmth out of it, his mind busied itself reliving his short time with Billie, savoring each minute, their conversations, their laughs, and their closeness, keeping sleep far off. Billie, his family, and his best friend were the only people Dan considered close. Or at least as close as Dan would allow them. In their presence, he could be himself, for he knew what to expect from them. Not so with others, those from whom he kept his distance, those who hadn't earned his trust. "I can get along without civilization," he had told Billie many times.

His mind shifted to pondering his situation, wondering about the wisdom of his decision to be here. "No one thinks I'll come out alive; they think I'm an incapable fool," he told himself. "They're the fools."

Nevertheless, it was a decision he wasn't about to abort; he had already gone to too much work for that. For the next five months, keeping warm would have to be his top priority. There was plenty of downed and standing dead wood on the mountain; he just had to make sure his chain saw didn't become belligerent.

Though untrained in winter survival, he seemed to know what he needed to be safe. He had armed himself with a stash of warm clothing, guns and ammunition, plenty of food, and made camp by a good spring-fed water source. And if he got lonely, there were the radios, one for listening to ball games, and the other for calling Billie or calling for help in an emergency.

As his eyes began to close in sleep, he wondered whether he had enough strength to win his five-month battle against the unpredictable winter that was just beginning to get serious. Its arctic breath had become an icy monster, paralyzing everything it touched, intent on Dan's death; he just needed to outwit it.

Now that he thought about it, there was a time when he didn't fear death. When it was your time, it would happen, and there was nothing a person could do about it. Dan was still young and, for him, death was far off. Besides, until now, it hadn't challenged him with serious intent. He could do for himself. Of that, he was confident, for his father had pounded self-sufficiency into him through days of forced hard labor on his parents' Wyoming ranch, labor that should have been beyond a 10-year-old's capability, a load grown ranch hands could and were expected to carry for a day's pay. But that load should have been lightened for a child to allow time to be a child. The way he figured it, he didn't ask to be brought into the world, so why should he have to earn his keep.

Hatred for his father for burdening him with sun-up to sundown ranch work balanced with school, leaving him no time for friends, grew steadily in him until he was grown, his father died, and Dan began to feel remorse and perhaps guilt for the hatred that had burned in him all those years and turned him into an angry man. It wasn't so much that he was dead, but that he and his father never had much of a relationship, had never mentioned the word "love" to each other. There had never been warmth or understanding between them. No words of encouragement or pride had ever come from his father's mouth.

It was only after his death that Dan forgave him, suddenly realizing how many valuable lessons had been embedded in his father's strictness. And he began to respect his father for them, perhaps realizing his father's ineptitude in expressing love and compassion for his family was something he couldn't help, something his father hadn't grown up with either. Now, Dan tightly grasped the value of self-sufficiency, a lesson lost on him growing up, but only put into remission the resentment and anger that had built up in him over the years.
As night temperatures plunged deeper into the thermometer, thoughts of the long unpredictable stretch of winter that lay ahead of him, seeming as long as the mountain was tall, began to work on Dan's mind. He had reached life's halfway point; he was at the top of the hill looking toward the bottom, wondering where the rest of his journey would take him and what lay waiting for him at the end, if it didn't come too soon. Now, perhaps death was something to fear. Not many people want to die before their time, nor do they want to die violent, long-suffering deaths; they would fight it viciously rather than succumb. That Dan, now in his 40s, wasn't ready for it would keep him in the battle, the only exception being a life-threatening emergency from which he would need rescue.

"I'll do everything I can to keep that from happening," he thought. "In the spring, I'm going to walk down this mountain on my own two feet knowing winter didn't get the best of me."

That was Dan's last thought as he dropped into sleep, warm in his long underwear, and settled deep into his sleeping bag.

The key to winter survival is making up your mind to do it. And, if you don't, you probably won't walk out of there (Walker Prairie).

Chapter 2

CRITTERS IN THE TENT

Dan awoke at five on the edge of shivering, climbed out of his sleeping bag to a rush of cold air that raised goose bumps on his thinly clad skin, grabbed the flashlight and stuck his head through the tent flap to check the thermometer. Fourteen below with a nippy slow-moving wind, and his body told him it was that cold in the tent as well. Hoping it hadn't lost its warmth, he got back into his sleeping bag and aimed his flashlight at the top of the chimney; two white globs clung to it just below the hole where it exited the roof. "Must have snowed last night," he mumbled to the huddled dogs who, without lifting their heads, looked up at him from their bed, thumping their tails as though to say, "Well, what are you going to do about it?"

"Okay, okay, I'm on it," Dan answered, grumbling something about just getting settled in and comfortable but still cold. Reluctantly, he got out of bed and brought a fire to life as quickly as his cold hands would let him. Misty and Spuds looked up at him questioningly as he settled back into his sleeping bag.

"What now? Oh all right. C'mon up." Before he had finished speaking, the dogs were on the bed in one unison jump and, after they had settled in close to him, Dan closed his eyes until he awoke again at 8:30 sweating. The tent had warmed enough for him to get out of bed and pull his jeans, a flannel shirt, and sweater over his long underwear. Misty and Spuds yawned, stretched, then jumped down and wiggled through the tent flap and into the bitter cold for their morning run, Dan following to check the weather. Partly cloudy, but crisp, he noticed. He quickly stepped back into the tent, the dogs rushing to get back in before he closed the flap, and started breakfast, beginning with his morning coffee.

"Think I'll make a couple of extra pancakes for the camp robbers," he said to Spuds and Misty who sat at the table as though waiting for him to take their order. "Don't look at me like that; you'll get yours, too."

It wasn't as though Misty or Spuds needed the pancakes. Their chubbiness betrayed that they had always been well fed, most likely rounding on more than just dog food. Both of them looked like potatoes, Misty being light brown, and Spuds a dirty white with specks, black ears, and a black patch over one eye stretching from forehead to nose.

By the time Dan had finished breakfast and the morning chores, the outside temperature had risen only slightly, and the wind had become a curmudgeon to be dealt with, a portend for the rest of the day, and he wanted more than anything to remain by the warm stove instead of working in the cold outdoors. But the need for keeping his wood supply replenished always nagged at him, for he knew much colder days and nights were coming, and his stove had as voracious an appetite as he did after a hard day's work. Besides, if he sat around in the tent all day, he'd be bored and vulnerable to loneliness. Staying occupied with purpose pushed time forward with greater speed. And now his thoughts, when he would allow them, sprang forward to Christmas, which he was hoping to spend with Billie and the rest of his family.

He grabbed a light jacket and his snowmobile suit off a hook by the door and pulled them on, Spuds and Misty flogging him energetically with their tails until he shoved them out the door and firmly told them to stay outside. Only then could he sit down and put on his overshoes without being knocked off his chair. He picked up a boot, looked at it suspiciously, muttered something inaudible, then turned it upside down over the dog dish and watched as Spuds and Misty's breakfast tumbled out of it.

Don't know if it was the dogs or a damn mouse that done it, but I will find out in time," he told his journal.

Checking the other boot and finding it empty, he put it on, pulled his cap snuggly over his ears and his collar up to meet his cap, and followed the dogs into what had become a biting wind that blew relentlessly at what he figured to be at least 20 miles an hour, stinging what little face was exposed, and freezing his gloved hands. Even the evergreens that surrounded his tent couldn't keep out the wind, which seemed to laugh at him in a bullying sort of way, as their branches danced sometimes wildly in an uneven rhythm.

"You think your father was hard on you?" he heard the wind say maliciously, as it tried to knock him down. "Winter has just begun to test you." Between trips to the tent to thaw his frozen fingers over the stove, Dan persisted in his cutting in spite of the wind until the sun disappeared behind the forested hills taking what little warmth it had offered during the day and leaving the mountain in frosty moonlit semi-darkness. By then, the wind, finished with its bullying, wandered off into the night. But the temperature continued to drop with the sun until it reached 17 below. By the time his chores were completed, the hour was late, and sleep came upon him like a heavy drug, pushing thoughts of loneliness into oblivion.

Early the next morning, Dan was awakened suddenly by a serious scuffle in the tent. "What the hell's going on," he yelled, grabbing a flashlight. "Can't a guy get any sleep around here?"

Spuds and Misty, who normally were sensitive to his anger, ignored him. They were focused on a serious chase that, when finished, left the tent looking like a battlefield with overturned tables, books, papers, and cans scattered in a very large mess that the dogs wouldn't be picking up. An intruder, invisible in the early morning darkness, had awakened them, and they weren't about to let him get away. They didn't need a trial to confirm the critter's guilt; their empty dish was evidence enough. Now it was time for serious justice - if they could only catch him. Soon Dan's flashlight caught the thief's tail streaking toward the woodpile. He was sure the dogs were going to tear the tent down in their tenacious efforts to catch the critter, but the chipmunk disappeared into the woodpile just in time, leaving the dogs sulking in defeat.

The party over, the dogs slinked off to their bed and Dan, offering them a few words of warning and grumbling something obscene about the mess he now had to clean up and his lack of sleep, slipped back into his no-longer-warm sleeping bag and fell asleep. Severe shivering woke him three hours later and, though he dreaded climbing out of bed, he knew bringing the stove to warmth was the necessary cure. Misty and Spuds, not waiting to be invited, decided to take advantage of the empty bed and their master's preoccupation to jump up and make themselves comfortable.

A few glowing red dots winked back at Dan from cold gray ashes when he opened the stove door. But, no matter how hard he blew on them, they were too weak to start a fire by themselves. His hands shaking, he quickly crumbled a piece of newspaper, threw it into the stove, added a handful of kindling, and touched a match to it. As the flames began to devour the kindling, he added as many larger pieces of wood as he dared, closed the door and, ignoring the dogs, jumped back into his sleeping bag. Soon the stove began to glow, his body heat kicked in to warm the sleeping bag, and his shivering abated.

Late that afternoon, Misty and Spuds disappeared down the prairie and into the woods as they had done many times before. But this time, Dan decided to follow. "There's something down there that's luring them away from camp," he said to himself. "Time to find out what it is."

Several hunting camps sat vacant on the prairie, an occasional camp littered with junk and salvageable equipment, which made the Forest Service unhappy because sometimes hunters intended to abandon their camps, never returning to empty them. As Dan approached the last in the string, he found the dogs, oblivious to his approach, occupied with something lying in the snow. As he knelt to get a closer look, Spuds placed a protective paw over a large bone she was chewing on, and lifted her lip in a low warning growl.

"So that's why you've been coming down here," he said, backing off.

"Don't worry. I'm not going to take it. Must be that some of the last hunters to leave in the fall left a quarter of elk hanging in the tree and never came back for it.

"A coyote or mountain lion got some of it before you did. You're lucky they didn't catch you at it. This is one for the game warden," he said, heading for the hill.

"I know whose camp it is, and they're not going to like that I reported it."

"Yeah, that's against regulations. I'll contact them and come up as soon as I can to get what's left of it," the game warden told him. "They'll get a ticket, and it won't be cheap. Thanks for reporting it. I won't tell who called it in, but I'm sure they'll guess."

It was approaching mid-December, the days were growing shorter, and Dan knew even colder weather lay ahead, possibly lasting for long stretches. So he worked daily to keep his tent supplied with wood stacked floor to ceiling along three walls. But it seemed no matter how much his woodpile grew, it was never enough to keep the tent as warm as he'd like it, for the stove was small and could only handle a few pieces at a time. Much of the wood he cut was dry and burned quickly and completely, though hot, leaving little for coals because the tree had been dead for years.

Many times Dan awoke after a long arctic night to a gaping hole in his wood supply that he felt an urgent need to fill. Fearful of falling behind in his cutting and chopping, he felt he had no choice but to bundle up each day and face the relentless biting wind, which often reminded him of his father's harshness when he was growing up.

"Seems I burn as much wood at night as I can cut during the day," he would grumble to himself, as he climbed out of bed and glanced at his woodpile, which seemed to have diminished greatly overnight. "Wish it would warm up. But not too much," he quickly added. "Don't want my meat to thaw."

That day, he put on his snowshoes and climbed the hill above camp where he found two dead trees whose height he estimated at 70 feet. Misty and Spuds wanted to follow, but their short legs sank into deep snow, leaving them struggling to free themselves. Days ago, when Dan was walking through the forest looking for wood, he had noticed a tall dead pine that would supply him with enough wood to last several days. It rose at least 50 feet above him, but its trunk was divided several feet above the ground creating a woodcutter's enigma, for an unpredictable danger lay in the cutting of it. He had examined it closely, taking in the possibilities for direction of fall, and trying to determine the danger it posed. Perhaps he would be brave enough to challenge its unpredictability after he had had more practice felling trees, he thought, and walked away.

He knew cutting down trees of any size was risky, especially when using a chainsaw. Knew that the unexpected could happen when he was least aware, for its cooperation depended on the tree's size, its surroundings, whether it leans in the crotch of another tree (a widow maker), and how accurately he could determine whether the cut was likely to pinch or kick back a saw blade. Dan often wondered if he would he be able to get out on the radio if something did happen. He wondered about it especially during the times he couldn't get it to work when he tried to call Billie. Alone in the woods, his life would be at stake.

He thought of these things as he carefully examined the first tree he would cut that day for lean and estimated direction of fall. Satisfied the spot he expected it to fall was clear, he yelled at the dogs to get out of the way, revved up his chainsaw and, looking up one more time to be sure, set to slicing a chunk out of the trunk. That day, the trees complied with Dan's expectations, falling where he had directed them to fall. And he was relieved. It took most of the day to strip the trunks of their branches and cut them into five-foot lengths, and by that time, his body was beginning to complain.

Dan put down his saw and watched Misty and Spuds pull each other's ears and bite each other's noses without hurt behind the bites or the ear-pulling.

"Well, you two may not be tired. All you've done is play all day. But I'm beat. The dragging, cutting, and stacking will keep until tomorrow. And if I get all that done and feel up to it, I'll split some wood as well. But now, I'm gonna go in and rest my weary body."

Satisfied that he had met his goal for the day, he picked up his chainsaw and, followed by his two companions, who nearly dropped out of sight as they tumbled playfully in the deep snow, causing Dan a hearty laugh, headed down the hill to the warmth of his winter abode and the supper his nagging stomach was yearning for.

Though physically wearied by the time supper was over and the dishes done, and even with the lateness of the hour, Dan couldn't sleep; thoughts of home, the people he cared about, and loneliness that even the thought of Christmas couldn't make disappear, were playing with his mind, and an endless stretch of winter lay ahead. It was the radio's fault, he thought. It had worked when he climbed the hill that evening to get reception.

Called Billie and Brandy and then started feeling lonely. Think I need to throw this phone away. As I was sitting here, I spotted a mouse, but he got away, so I moved my trap and just about the time I went to bed, I got him, so I was happy. That was 12:30. I went outside and it was about 24 degrees; I couldn't believe it.

That night, Mother Nature mischievously granted Dan's wish for warmer weather, seeming to know something he didn't. The next three days temperatures rose enough to sticky the snow, hindering navigation and tree-hauling. Each time he took a step, his snowshoes grew twice as large, and his efforts at scraping them clean were futile and time consuming. It was like walking on glue.

"What I need is a four-legged mule instead of a two-legged one," he quipped, as he struggled down the hill with a single log that gradually grew in circumference as he tried to roll it in the moisture-laden snow. Giving that up, he wrapped a rope around it and pulled. But the log lodged stubbornly in the wet snow. Lifting, pushing, and pulling, Dan was, with much effort, able to get the log to camp. When he got it there, it looked like a huge hotdog wrapped in a white bun. By the end of the day he had only 12 pieces dragged down, far from his goal. His muscles were sore, and his body ached. Though it was only 4 p.m., he couldn't muster enough energy to do more.

"I'm still too far out of shape, but I'm getting better all the time," he admitted to no one. He was about to go in, when he heard men's voices and the crunch of trotting hoofs breaking trail in the snow. He looked eagerly toward the top of the hill as Misty and Spuds began barking, their warnings gobbled by a vociferous wind. Perhaps they would stop and talk a while, bring him news from town, he thought. But they merely glanced at the barking dogs, seeming either to miss Dan or to ignore him, and traveled on without hesitating.

It was about 4 p.m. when I saw riders coming. It was Vernon coming up to pack out his camp. They had seven pack horses, and they need every one of them, for they have a lot of junk.

"Didn't even wave," Dan said. "Oh well; that's Vernon."

Disappointed, he put his tools away and went in to relax before starting supper. "Think I'll turn on the radio and listen to the football game," he thought later, as he finished wiping the supper dishes. He let the rambunctious dogs out for a short run, fiddled with the radio for several minutes, cussed at it, then gave up trying to get a signal. "Wrong idea; can't get a damn radio station, so I'm going to bed."

Fuming, he let the dogs in and, before climbing into his sleeping bag, checked the temperature. It had dropped to 12 degrees. "Hope it stays cold; otherwise my meat will be spoiled, and I don't need that," he told the dogs. Misty looked up at him questioningly before closing her eyes in contented sleep. That night, the wind pushed and pulled at the tent, picking up corners of the tarp and slapping them down annoyingly and repeatedly, waking Dan several times to crawl from his warm bed and into the night to repair the consequences of its mischievous antics.

December 13: It's 7:30 and 10 below. One side of the tent fell three times tonight, and I'm not a happy camper.

The next day, Dan made sure he was visible from the trail, occasionally stopping work to watch and listen, hoping to see Vernon and his helpers ride by with horses loaded with camp supplies. Perhaps if Vernon and his companions saw him, they would stop to share the latest news from town, perhaps sit and enjoy a cup of hot coffee or cocoa with him.

Sheridan, with its population of approximately 15,000, was considered a small town by big-city people because people were very likely to encounter friends and acquaintances on the street, or in Wal-Mart or K Mart, or the local hardware or grocery store. Or recognize someone on a sparsely traveled back-road, pull side by side, and roll down windows for long visits until someone happened along and broke up the conversation. But now for Dan, being on the mountain, the content of the conversation wasn't as important as his hunger for human contact.

As he worked and watched, the day wore on with no sign or sounds of human life. "Had Vernon left quietly during the night? Or early in the morning?" Dan wondered. "Or is he just avoiding me?"

As he fed his chainsaw for the last time, he noticed his gas can was nearing empty and that what little was in it wouldn't last much longer considering the amount of wood he was burning each day and night - something he had seriously underestimated. When he ran out of gas, there was only the ax and handsaw, which would be near impossible to use on larger trees. And, though it would be possible for smaller ones, the slowness of his progress would never allow him to keep supply equal to or ahead of demand. The problem was what to do about it now that he was on foot.

Called Connie (Billie's daughter) tonight, but I couldn't hear her. I need to have the radio worked on. Might come down the end of the month. It all depends on the weather. Plus, when I was packing things up, I forgot to bring more gas, so that has to be replenished. So, I don't know what I will do at this time.

One option was to hike the Soldier Creek Trail down to Sheridan, an all-day trip on snowshoes he dreaded and wouldn't take if he could find another way. Perhaps he could hold out until December 20 when he thought he might to go down the mountain to spend Christmas with Billie and the kids — that is, if the weather would allow him release from the mountain. Or maybe he could get someone to bring the gas up by snowmobile in the next few days, he thought. That would depend on whether he could rouse someone on his two-way radio and, that accomplished, find a friend or family member willing to deliver. On the mountain, the radio's signal, sometimes weak, noisy, or non-existent, couldn't be depended on, and that caused him uneasiness, for it was Dan's only link to civilization, a security that, early on, he was assured he could depend on for help in case of an emergency. But he soon found it wasn't working out that way.

An operator was supposed to make the call, which they didn't do very often. Not like they're supposed to. Because of my situation, they had me at the top of their list, and they knew my exact location at the beginning of winter and assured me they could get help if I needed it. It sounded like a sure thing.

Since the radio system had failed several times, he no longer trusted the dependability of the signal or its operators to save his life. If his chainsaw bit him, or a tree fell on him, or he got caught in a blizzard and froze, only Spuds and Misty would know it. And all they could do is slowly plow their way down the mountain and report to Billie, who would have to guess why they were there - if they made it down. By the time help arrived on the prairie and someone found him, it would be too late.

"People can't be depended on to do what they say," Dan told Misty and Spuds one evening. "The only one you can trust is yourself. My father was right to teach me self-reliance. That's the only way we can survive up here."

The nearest navigable road was 15 miles away, and there was only one way down the mountain in winter when all other trails and roads were blocked by deep snow. Though Soldier Creek Trail hugged the mountains edge (the creek visible as a thin ribbon hundreds of feet below wedged between two mountains), it was barely wide enough for a team of horses hauling a wagon to navigate, which it did in the early 1900s when mail needed to be delivered to the other side of the mountain.

Winter snows, especially as they melted and froze, added treachery to the trail, now only cautiously navigable on snowmobile, snowshoe, or perhaps by foot if a person had the stamina to handle its steepness and three to ten-foot snowdrifts. One serious slip could quickly send a person over the edge and into the canyon. Once a person reached PK Lane, where the land leveled to rolling hills and ranches spread over distances, there was no guarantee it would be navigable by vehicle.

In the next few days, temperatures dropped further, and Dan continued with limited cutting to stretch his gas supply into another week, focusing more on dragging, chopping, and stacking wood, a never-ending project alternated with shoveling snow that insisted on closing the paths to his bathroom and water and food supplies and piling snow on his makeshift toilet as fast as he could clear them. Added to all that was the steady flow of critters that interrupted his life and sleep by insisting on sharing his quarters.

At the end of a particularly exhausting day when all he longed for was recuperating sleep, Dan climbed into his sleeping bag, turned out the light, and began drifting into dreamland. Soon the quiet and his sleep were disrupted by the snap, snap, snap of traps going off like a series of hand grenades, causing him to sit up with a start and turn on the lantern, momentarily wondering if the tent were under attack — again.

"These damned mice are all over," he exclaimed in disgust as he watched mice crawl in and out of the dog dish, along the wood pile, and over Misty and Spuds, who lay in their bed resigned and unconcerned. "No use fighting it; too many of them to win," they seemed to say. Unable to go back to sleep, Dan disposed of the bodies and reset all the traps. "These things are driving me crazy."

Though he went back to bed and pulled the sleeping bag over his head, the unpleasant thought of large numbers of mice he knew were still out there using his bed for a freeway during the night kept him from sleeping until unconsciousness overtook him.

For several evenings, invading critters continued to noisily consume and pack away dog food, some of them cleverly escaping traps after devouring the peanut butter, their antics frustrating Dan and Misty and Spuds, adding to his chores, and interrupting his sleep. At times, he was outnumbered and outsmarted, making it a battle it seemed he'd never win. It was wildlife he and the dogs could do without.

"Damned, dirty rotten germ-infested critters. The battle's not over yet," he threatened with unmatchable determination.

December 14: Was up most of the night. A damn mouse was in the dog food again. I set traps all around the dish, and that didn't work. So I set a trap right in the bowl. I heard him in it, but I fell asleep. This morning, every crumb of food was gone, and no mouse. Battle bowl two is coming up tonight. Was real cold; minus 28 the last time I looked. I was victorious in battle bowl two, but I had to be really tough on him. Had to dig out the peanut butter, and that did him in. That's number five, and I hope he's the last.

December 15: Sat in the tent drinking coffee and saw another mouse run across a log on the outside of the tent, then come in at the end of the tent. I caught number six just a minute ago. There's another one out there running back and forth looking for his buddy. Hope he comes in.

It's been spitting snow all day, but hasn't amounted to much. But the wind blew hard. At 9:30, it's lightly snowing and 12 degrees. Checked my mouse traps. The peanut butter was gone and no mouse, so I set the traps again. Hope this doesn't go on all winter. If it does, I'm gonna be mouse crazy.

Mother Nature's mood deteriorated to belligerent the morning of December 16 when a dismal, snow-laden sky dropped its load into a mischievous wind that tossed it around and dropped it in random piles, swirling it decoratively as though frosting a cake for a special occasion. Visibility diminished, and temperatures quickly sank below the thermometer's zero mark. By the time

Dan stepped outside into his work area, where he kept the snow cleared nearly to grass, the snow was over the tops of his calf-high overshoes, and the tarp covering the tent sagged with the weight of it.

The roof of the tent is really weighted down. Need to get it off, but I'm trying to get the tent warm first. I put 10 pieces of wood through the stove already, and it's just beginning to get warm in here. So I'm gonna drink my coffee and eat breakfast before I venture outside for very long.

When he finished clearing snow and came in at noon, it was 17 below with a destructive wind that Dan estimated was traveling at 25 miles per hour. "It's a cold SOB," he told Misty and Spuds as he herded them into the tent after a few minutes of shoveling. "With that wind, a person can only stay out 10 minutes at a time. I'll warm up for a while, then go down and see if I can get some water," he said, rubbing his cold fingers to get the circulation going. There was urgency in his voice. "I hate to go out there, but I need to store all I can for today and tomorrow."

He reached the creek an hour later to find his water supply locked beneath eight inches of ice. Releasing it and filling his containers would keep him out in the cold much longer than he had anticipated. Followed by his canine companions, who were nearly lost in the deepening snow, he trudged to the tent, picked up his chainsaw, headed to the creek, and carved a large square hole in the ice.

"That should do it," he thought, as he turned off the chainsaw and set it on the snow. He grabbed one of his containers and bent down to fill it when something caught his eye. He peered into the hole, examining the water closely. Something thick and black was floating on its surface. He dipped a finger into it and pulled it out, the black stuff dripping onto clean snow.

"Oh no," he said to his finger. "Oil. Who knows how long it will take to clean up this mess."

I thought I was pretty smart, but I ended up spilling chainsaw oil in the water. It took me four hours with a coffee cup to dip all the oil out of the water. That's a mistake I'll never make again.

It was late afternoon and growing dark by the time the creek water ran clear. His fingers nearly numb with cold, moustache and beard frozen, Dan quickly filled his water containers and transported them to the tent, where he set them near the stove to keep them from freezing. The last one filled and in place, he went back outside to clear the roof of snow, then back inside where he removed his gloves and snowsuit, added wood to the fire with barely working fingers, and stood by the stove for a very long time, relieved that his day's work was finally finished.

 Have every container full. The coldest thermometer reading that I saw was 18 below and that's what it is at 4:30 and snowing. I didn't think it snowed hard when it's this cold, but it is right now. Went up on the hill and tried to call Billie, but couldn't get out. Don't know if it's the weather or if the tower went down. Maybe I'll try later on. Had dinner and waiting for dishwater to get hot. Trip over dogs every time I walk over to the stove. I think they're colder than I am.

 7 p.m. It's not snowing now, but the damn wind has really picked up. It's 21 below right now, and with the wind, it's probably 70 below. If you let the stove get down to just coals, you can see your breath in here in just a few minutes. So I'm gonna stay up all night and keep the fire going. Well, it's 11:30 and the temperature hasn't changed.

 While sitting here playing solitaire, I been thinking about what the hell I'm doing up here. I don't know how to put it in words; it's just real scary, especially when it's this cold, for it don't take very long to freeze in this shit. If something should happen and you can't get out on this damn radio, you're screwed. Maybe this sounds screwy to everyone else, but talking about it (spending the winter on the prairie) and doing it is two very different things. Even the dogs are wondering what the hell we're doing up here.

 Dan loaded the stove as full as he dared and, without stripping down to his long underwear, sought the warmth of his down sleeping bag and picked up a deck of cards, intending to play Solitaire until he tired of it. Misty and Spuds sat near the bed staring at him with longing in their deep brown eyes, yipping just loudly enough to get their master's attention.

 "Oh, all right," he said, patting an empty space beside him. "C'mon up. We can all keep each other warm." At his first words, the dogs, in unison, leaped onto the bed, searched for the softest spot, arranged it to their liking, and lay down.

 There was no quiet on the prairie that night. The raging wind tugging noisily at the tent as though trying to pull it down tortured his mind, and he knew snow was piling heavily on the tarp he had placed strategically over it in October. He dreaded the possibility of having to deal with a collapsed tent in the middle of a black subzero night - a disaster he wasn't prepared to deal with. Even if the wind and snow were merciful, the thought that he would never wake up if he fell asleep and the fire died, kept him struggling to stay awake.

 Finally bored with playing solitaire, he gathered the cards and put them on the table beside his bed. Then he settled deeper into his sleeping bag, reached over and turned off the lantern, and lay in the blackness trying to work logic into his being there. It was the fault of all the exciting adventure and survival television shows he loved to watch, he reasoned. They made the challenge of struggling for survival against nature's belligerence in the wilderness appear glamorous and even easy - so easy that he knew he could do it, too, for he was no stranger to difficult times.

In his younger days, he had ridden the rodeo circuit, had been married for three years, served his country in the armed forces, worked in the oil fields, and put in long days of hard labor on his parents' ranch. Over the years, the mountain had become his friend, welcoming him as summer neared, sending him home when hunting season ended. Each fall, thinking about the boring colorless winter that stretched endlessly ahead increased his reluctance to leave. He wearied of spending mundane winters trapped in a mundane job he didn't like, staring longingly at the mountain from his picture window, wondering what was going on up there, longing for an escape into solitude but knowing spring was a long way off.

"To pack up and leave before winter set in is for your own good," the mountain seemed to tell him as he closed up camp and headed for the trail down to civilization. "Winter is much worse up here, and you would regret it if you stayed." But what if he did stay, he had always wondered, and the wonder wouldn't let him go, wouldn't release him until he satisfied it.

All he needed was the right equipment, a thorough knowledge of the mountain, especially the prairie, and determination. And he already had all that. He wouldn't be challenging a place he'd never been before, he reasoned. This mountain was no stranger to him or to Billie. Each summer, they had spent as much time camping in different parts of it as work would allow, and they were both aware of the dangers hidden within its folds or over the next rise.

Earlier in the summer of 1995, he had stood looking out the picture window of his rural home in Sheridan, as he often did when bored, admiring the mountain as its majestic top disappeared into playful low-lying clouds. It was a different world within its folds that drew him to it, a world where wild animals (which Dan felt displayed more wisdom than did people) ruled, a world devoid of cities, billboard signs, signal lights, fast food restaurants, traffic noise, ringing telephones, and people demanding his time and money. It was a place of solitude, an escape from nosy people who tried his patience with their lies and prying questions, people who continually harassed him, and those he knew inwardly made fun of him because of his differing viewpoints and lack of trust.

To strangers, Dan seemed aloof, unfriendly, hardly ever smiling, possibly carrying a chip that had nothing to do with him or anyone else. They sensed a wall around him, an unbreachable barrier, and his solemn moods offered the impression he had a dark side they dared not rouse. But those who failed to persist in chipping away the barrier missed discovery of Dan's inner self in which dwelled a sense of humor and an honesty and sensitivity he found lacking in most humans.

Now he longed for a deeper relationship with the mountain's quiescence and the wild life that called it home and for a challenge his mundane life couldn't deliver. And perhaps to discover and prove his self worth, something that had been missing in his growing up because his parents had been too occupied with mountains of ranch work to assure him he had it. Then there was Billie. Dan admitted they did a lot of fighting, and he had sometimes wondered if their relationship would weather the storms. Perhaps a winter apart would heal any wounds resulting from their many disagreements and strengthen the ties that bound them to each other.

He had thought about it for years. Now there was no more thinking. Confident he was up to it, he cautiously approached Billie with the thought. She had long ago sensed his restlessness, known about his love affair with the mountain and his yearning for adventure, and now knew he couldn't let it rest even if she had protested. The matter settled, he nonchalantly, and perhaps without intention, mentioned his plans to a couple of guys who stopped him on his way up the mountain one summer day with his loaded pack horse. A load one normally wouldn't need to survive the short hunting season when everyone wisely got out before the snow deepened and settled in to stay.

Stopped and talked to a couple of guys on the way up. They asked why I was packing so much, and I told them I thought about spending the winter on the mountain. So the next time I came downtown, the only thing I heard was "Oh, you're going to spend the winter up on Walker Prairie." And I kind of joked and said "yah." Well, I just kept packing stuff up, and before you knew it, it was too late to back out. Everybody says you can back out, but I didn't know what kind of person I'd be if I did.

That summer, almost without realizing it, he had his horse loaded with gear and was riding up the mountain toward camp, never questioning the reality of his actions. But those who knew him wondered, perhaps questioning his sanity, guessing what he was up to and passing along stories about it. For he was packing much more than the usual hunting season gear, and for his actions, Dan felt he owed an explanation to no one except Billie. So he answered questions without really answering and continued on his way, leaving them to wonder what he had just said.

Toward morning, Dan awoke, realizing he had slipped into sleep unintentionally, happy he had survived in spite of it. It was 24 below, and for that, he wasn't happy.

After lunch, I kicked the dogs out. Otherwise, they would never go out. I'm gonna put on my snowshoes and walk around a little. I'm damn tired of sitting in this tent. Don't know if I will be able to see anything, but I will take the camera with me. The wind let up for maybe 10 minutes, and when it came up, it about blew me over. And before I got back to camp, my face was numb.

The snow had eased, but the wind had pulled a curtain of fog over the prairie and mischievously bitten the back of his snowshoe into brittleness so it would fall off when he tried to put it on. It was a fixable prank, though a chore he hadn't counted on. Staying outdoors for any length of time that day was futile, the wind often forcing Dan to seek shelter against the cold that numbed his fingers into uselessness. That night, he intended to stay up again and keep the fire going, but sleep tugged on his eyelids, pulling them irresistibly into deep unconsciousness, Misty and Spuds happily snuggled close to him on the bed.

December 18 dawned crisp, windless, and yellow, the first peek at the sun Dan had experienced in many days. "Looks like it might be a beautiful day," he told the dogs cheerfully as he let them out for a run, then stepped outside the door where he deeply inhaled the air's cool freshness and admired the sparkling whiteness of sun glistening on prairie where color lay under a white sepulcher, and the evergreens bowing as though in prayer under their white loads. No dirty city streets to mar the snow's purity or to fill the air with its obnoxious polluting odors, he thought.

Walker Prairie is almost as beautiful in winter as it is in its other three seasons: spring when prairie flowers rise from their dark beds, pushed into colorful bloom by the warming sun; and fall, when shorter days turn green aspen leaves to yellow, contrasting spectacularly with the green-needled lodge poles and the red-tinted willows. In winter, the prairie sleeps in black and white beauty under a gray sky, its white quilt-covered hills and snow-laden evergreen branches only splashed in sparkling color when the wind pushed the clouds aside to reveal a yellow ball fired up against a deep blue background.

The morning had begun that way, but the day's niceness was gone by mid-afternoon when the shadows disappeared into the gray gloominess of ominous clouds that appeared from behind the hills and pushed their way across the sky, dropping an occasional snowflake. By the time Dan was finished with supper, the temperature had risen to zero and the clouds had begun to drop their snow loads with serious intent. Snow continued to fall during the night, tapering off late the following morning while Dan chopped wood, refurbished his water supply, cleared snow from around the tent and down his paths, and tidied the tent in preparation for his trip down to Sheridan for the holidays.

December 19: Called Billie tonight and told her I was coming down Saturday the 20th. I need a few things right away: batteries for the radio, chain for the saw, and some gas. Billie was gonna send it up with a snowmobiler, but that's been a week ago. So I will do it myself and have it. Also, it will be nice to spend Christmas with her and the kids. I had not planned on coming down, but after being up here, I discovered there are a lot of things that you need and never thought about when packing. It's 9 p.m. and just about bedtime and it's only zero out tonight, and to me that's warm. If it would stay like this all winter, I would be happy, but I know it won't. Had four hot toddies, and it's about done me in, so I better go to bed.

December 20: I'm going get things put away so they won't freeze. Now I'm worried about my eggs and potatoes, but will stash them in my bedrolls so they should survive while I'm gone. Got everything packed and ready to go down. Tried to call Billie, and the radio went dead, but did leave a message earlier, so hope she was able to hear it, for I really don't want to walk all the way.

Listened to the weather report tonight and they are putting out a winter storm warning for tomorrow, so hope I beat it down. Think I'll leave earlier than I was going to. I would like to leave tonight while it's good out, but I would have no way of calling and don't know how long it would take me to get down. I think right around 3 hours. Guess I'll find out tomorrow. The dogs know something is going on; every time I move they're right on my heels. Maybe they think I'm going to leave them behind. Going to eat, do dishes, and go to bed. It's 3 above and snowing again.

Dan awoke early the next morning not daring to look outside, fearing that shoveling the very deep snow he was sure had fallen during the night would be an overwhelming task. Rather than peeking outside to check it out, he turned on the radio, sat down with a cup of hot coffee, and savored it for a long while as it slowly warmed his insides.

"Two to four inches are expected today," said a voice over the radio. "That, combined with blowing and drifting snow will make travel difficult. No travel is advised unless absolutely necessary."

I hate to inform them I'm not driving, so I'm ready to take off, me and my girls. For we smell turkey and ham down there somewhere, and that in itself is enough to keep us going. Hope to hell someone is down at PK Lane to pick us up. (It was at least three miles from PK Lane to the road, an added distance he was hoping not to have to walk.) *Hope Billie didn't think we done the smart thing and sit tight, for she should know by now that I have never done anything smart in my life, and I'm not changing now.*

Misty and Spuds had hung close that morning, sensing something was going to happen and determined they would be part of it. His decision made, Dan put on a pair of wool stockings, pulled on his snowsuit and overshoes, and stepped into lightly falling snow, Misty and Spuds at his heels. A dusting of snow had fallen overnight, hardly enough to merit shoveling, he decided. Besides, he was eager to get down the mountain before serious weather closed in.

Low-lying clouds that hid the top of She Bear glowered down at him ominously as though warning him to return to the safety of his tent if he didn't want to chance becoming trapped in winter's escalating wrath that threatened to come down on him. But he merely laughed at them, stubbornly determined as he fastened the snowshoes to his feet, secured the tent, whistled at the wrestling dogs, and lifted his feet toward the long journey down the mountain over deep snow, keeping the thought of a warm vehicle waiting for him at PK Lane, Billie's cooking, and a warm bed in his thoughts.

Chapter 3

HOME FOR CHRISTMAS

The winter solstice had arrived, and with it, slowly lengthening days until summer. That, seeing Billie, and the promise of ham and turkey with all the trimmings lifted Dan's spirits. But for now, daylight was short-lived, as he expected it would be until Daylight Saving Time arrived again in the spring, and especially when thick clouds allowed little of the sun's light to sift through, as was often the case, darkening the sky into night long before sunset.

Now that he was on his way down to civilization, his feet, clumsy with snowshoes, a sense of urgency crept into his being; he knew he had to get down the mountain before darkness obscured the trail. Knew by this time that three hours wasn't going to do it. Perhaps not even four or five. But he mustn't push himself, for that would surely lead to an accident. And he didn't want Billie to find his body at the bottom of the canyon.

Soldier Creek was always steep and narrow, the canyon dropping sharply on one side, and a wall of hill rising from the trails edge on the other side, a portion of trail twisted, narrow, and filled with rock. Except for the narrow part that twisted around a curve, the mountain's edge much too close, it wasn't as treacherous in summer when it was a popular hiking and horseback trail, though only well-trained, sure-footed horses unlikely to spook were trusted on it. Because it was only a five-mile climb from the mountain's foot to its top, Soldier Creek was a short trip compared to other routes for hunters hauling several hundred pounds of elk meat from the prairie down the mountain. That and the likelihood of a successful kill made Soldier Creek Trail the favored route for guides taking hunters up the mountain each fall.

Now, winter snows covered the trail with an uneven wind-strewn blanket that made navigation difficult and slow, especially when Misty and Spuds shared his snowshoes on deep drifts. With effort, and the help of a walking stick, Dan managed to keep his snowshoes on the uphill side of the trail, hoping to keep them from slipping toward the mountain's edge, especially at its narrowest section. His concentrated efforts to keep his feet in obedience to his wishes temporarily kept his mind off the windless cold and gently falling snow. Now, especially, he was thankful he had mastered the art of navigating in snowshoes. Half way down the trail, he stopped to rest and noticed that a determined breeze that had silently tiptoed in was attempting to pick up the snow ahead of him and rearrange it. Growing in strength from a caress to a slap, it picked at his reddening face with icy fingers and tried to pry its way into his gloves, under his hat, and down his neck, intent on making him miserable. The worst section of trail behind him, Dan tried to pick up the pace, for he knew it was afternoon, and darkness would come soon. But his legs were tiring from the difficulty of maneuvering his heavy snowshoes, putting a strain on his muscles.

Hungry from the exertion and cold that rapidly burned his inner fuel, he stopped, pulled a peanut butter and jelly sandwich from his pocket, and quickly devoured it, satisfying the growing pain in his stomach. Misty and Spuds hung close, eyes glued to the disappearing sandwich. When he had finished, he threw the crusts and a handful of dog biscuits to the dogs, adjusted his collar to cover his neck, shoved the long dark hair the wind had pulled loose back under his cap, picked up his walking stick, and continued on, Misty and Spuds attempting to stay on top of the snow by following in his tracks.

Billie and the kids occupied Dan's thoughts as he trudged down the trail. It had been three weeks since he had last seen Billie, and longer since he had seen his son-in-law, Joe, and Billie's daughter, Connie. He imagined the house festively decorated for Christmas, the company that would gather around the table on Christmas Day, and the traditional present opening that would follow. It would be a good time — a respite from the cruel winter that awaited his return, and he had lots to talk about and lots to learn from them about family life in civilization.

The sky was beginning to darken as Dan neared the bottom of the mountain, only a couple of miles to go before arriving at the Lane and warmth. That is, if Billie had received his message and remembered to pick him up. If she hadn't, the trip would be several miles longer. Misty and Spuds, walking a short distance behind him and realizing they were on the last stretch, the trail packed down by snowmobile tracks and a little less deep, broke into a trot for home, most likely thinking the old man was moving much too slow.

Dan heard them trotting behind him and quickly turned to avoid being run over. As he moved, he felt something pull inside his leg and then a sharp pain. "Damn dogs," he yelled after them. It was pain speaking words he didn't mean. But they kept going, deaf to his admonishing shouts, never turning back. He stood still for a moment hoping the pain would subside, and after a while it did. But each time he lifted a snowshoe, a sharp pain originating from his groin shot down his leg, stopping him. He had come all this way; he had nearly made it. But the pain that screamed in his groin with every move made the remaining distance seem like a hundred miles, and at the end of it, the possibility of no rescue.

With great effort, Dan struggled on, stopping in spurts when the pain was at its worst, until he met the fence line at the edge of the lane. Though it was beginning to grow dark, he could tell it was covered in snow, but thought a vehicle, especially one with four-wheel drive, could make it through. Desperately cold, yet not able to take another step, he collapsed against a fence post, hoping to hear the sound of an approaching vehicle, knowing he wouldn't make it the rest of the way on his own.

Minutes seemed like hours as the snow kept falling. There was no sign of life in the empty fields or on the road, just darkness and the sound of the wind whispering across the snow. Something inside told him she wasn't coming. She had missed his message. Maybe this was it, he thought. The end of his winter on the mountain, the end of life for that matter; and he had only begun. All that work: sawing, chopping, hauling, shoveling. And for what? To die at the mountain's foot?

The hunters' words came back to him. "You're a crazy, stubborn fool, Longwell. You have no business on the Prairie in winter. We're the ones who will have to pay to rescue you. Go home while you still can."

He imagined the wind that had grown stronger laughing in victory as it began to drop the temperature for the night and the sky attempting to cover him with a white burial blanket. The mountain had won. It only allowed animals on the prairie in winter because they were an important part of it. It resented human presence, Dan concluded. But there were animals that didn't make it either, their sleeping bodies discovered in spring as the warm sun slowly uncovered them. Unless coyotes, mountain lions, or bears discovered them in winter and used them for their own survival, leaving only the bones to bleach in the hot summer sun, the only evidence the animal had been there.

It seemed endless time had passed, Dan sitting in the snow, legs outstretched, head drooping, struggling to keep his brain working against sleep, for if he succumbed to it, it would be all over. As he sat there, he no longer felt the cold. He was too numb to feel anything and growing too sleepy to care. He was tired of fighting, and though winter had only begun, he wasn't sure he wanted to face three more months of its brutality. He was ready to face humiliation and admit defeat. But he wouldn't have to face it if he . . . Suddenly, through half-closed eyelids, he thought he saw vehicle lights approach and stop a short distance away. Was he hallucinating, or was it real, he wondered, as he forced his eyes open.

"Billie, I hope it's you," he muttered weakly to the darkness. "Because if it isn't . . ." With numb fingers, he grabbed the fence post and struggled against it to pull himself to his feet, his intent to make himself bigger, more likely to be seen. But he couldn't move, couldn't stand, for his legs were gone, his snowshoes holding him down. He could only sit there, hoping desperately that Billie, or whoever it was, would find him. He tried to keep his sleep-heavy eyes on the vehicle as it drove closer, turned on its high beams, and aimed them in his direction, bathing the cascading snow in a yellow light that made him think he had gone to heaven. He imagined the light beam stopping several yards away; someone getting out of the vehicle; now walking toward him slowly, as in a dream. Someone was with her, helping her unfasten his snowshoes, pulling him to his feet, half dragging him to the vehicle, his frozen legs buckling under him, Billie's concerned voice floating through a dark tunnel inside his head.

Suddenly his head began to clear. He was in Billie's car, safely on his way home, and she had opened all the windows so he wouldn't overheat. The ride seemed to take forever, but when it ended, he was home at last, being pulled into the house, plopped into a chair, his boots, cap, and outer clothing removed, and a cup of hot chocolate shoved into his icy hands. His body still shook with cold, but not as violently as it had before. Knowing how to treat someone who was near freezing and the dangers of thawing too fast, Billie helped him into a cool tub of water, gradually adding warm water until a rosy color began to appear on his face and hands and he could move his fingers and feel his toes and answer questions coherently.

Later, when Dan was closer to being himself, Billie's voice betraying concern asked, "Do you feel like eating something?" Dan nodded, and Billie left for the kitchen to warm up leftovers from that evening's supper. After eating, he picked up his walking stick and saying he needed sleep, he hobbled to the bedroom, helped by Billie.

The next morning, though he felt better and there was no permanent damage from the cold, the pain in his groin wouldn't go away. The next several days, he would be warm, looking up at the white mountain with its arctic breath, knowing he would soon return to resume the battle against the deadly cold of winter. But should he, and did he want to? Right now he wasn't sure. Perhaps. But not until he had been fully warmed down to the bone, well-fed and rested, and could walk again. Then he would decide.

Christmas Day arrived with all the festivity and house-filled aromas of the holidays including a roasting turkey and all that it was custom to go with it. Dan, by this time recovered from the cold, ate heartily, savoring home cooking and the variety of it prepared by experienced cooks. He considered it a treat after a month's diet of packaged food prepared by a novice on a small camp stove. After dinner, he hobbled to his easy chair where he sat, legs and feet extended, eyes half closed, listening to the chatter of conversation that permeated the room, knowing it would soon be replaced by a silence broken only by a mischievous wind, Misty and Spuds his only companions.

"Dan, are you all right?" Billie asked, breaking into his thoughts. "You're so quiet."

"Just listening," he said without offering more.

When his leg would allow, he indulged himself in a haircut, a beard trimming, and the pleasure of several long warm showers. And he savored it all, wishing to make each moment last, for all too soon, it would be a memory that he would pull out to relive on lonely evenings. Most of all, he was thankful to be alive to enjoy the camaraderie of family and friends, his weak moment of considering conceding banished as though the thought had never occurred.

Time passed all too quickly, as it seems to do every holiday season when festive get-togethers with family and friends drown worries and lift spirits. Those times were over now. A new year had begun, six days of it already dissolved into history. Dan was on his feet, strong enough to return to the prairie. He awoke the morning of his departure to sunshine and relative warmth, though the air was crisp - a perfect day for a long walk. After breakfast, he stood in front of the picture window, his hands wrapped comfortably around a hot cup of coffee, enjoying the warmth while staring at the mountain looking slyly peaceful and benign, its top fully visible in a cloudless sky, and wondering if it were ready for his return. Or, if he was ready for the mountain, for that matter.

"Are you sure you want to go back?" Billie asked, breaking his deep contemplation.

"Yup," was his only reply as he turned and walked into the kitchen where he put down his coffee cup, picked up his snowmobile suit and began putting it on.

"Are you sure your leg is ready for the long uphill walk?"

"I'm sure."

But the expression on her face told him she wasn't sure. "Call me when you get there."

Billie put on her jacket and helped him pack his things into the truck when he was ready. Misty and Spuds, always determined not to miss a ride, jumped into the back seat with haste, climbing over each other in competition for the best spot and, with little conversation, Billie drove to the end of PK Lane where Dan had collapsed two weeks ago. She put the dogs on leashes, reminded him to call her, and stayed until his snowshoes were fastened, his backpack on his back, goodbyes said, and with Misty and Spuds in the lead, he had taken his first steps up the trail. Stood and watched as he and the dogs slowly gained altitude and faded into the mountain, never looking back.

As he traveled, Misty and Spuds straining on their leashes, Dan began to relive Christmas, the warmth of it, the aroma of turkey with all the trimmings, every word of conversations that took place, the laughter, and the overall pleasantness of it all. His time with family had flown much to fast, his return to loneliness come to soon. He had thought of staying; he had had enough of winter's hardships; but decided against it. If he had, he would have been giving up, and giving up wasn't in him. He had learned better when growing up. Besides, he could hear people's taunting if he had stayed.

"Couldn't handle it, eh, Longwell? I thought as much."

"What were you thinking — living in a wall tent in who knows what kind of weather?"

"So you finally came to your senses."

Though they may have thought it, even said it to his friends, no one in his family had tried to talk him into staying, and he was thankful for that. He had never felt imprisoned by Billie or the rest of the family. They always encouraged him to do what he wanted, and he respected them for that. Perhaps Billie, knowing Dan was a stubborn man, wisely realized it wouldn't do much good to fight his determination. Better to let him live his dream and get it out of his system.

She, too, loved the prairie and knew it well, having grown up near the mountain and explored it on horseback with her father since she was a child. In the 11 years they had been together, she and Dan spent time there together as well, riding new areas, discovering more of the mountain's hidden beauty each summer. It was always a pleasant escape from the 90- to 100-degree heat and the busyness of life below. And she knew he had more common sense than others might have thought.

"She's a neat lady," Dan had said about her. "I have a lot of respect for her, and I hope to be with her for the rest of our lives." Billie didn't believe in tiptoeing around the truth, dressing it in political correctness to soften the sting that its telling might cause. For those to whom she spoke, there was no guessing at meaning, for it lay naked and unashamed in her words. And that was what Dan liked best about her.

When he reached Whiskey Rock where, far below, PK Lane lay stretched out like a gray ribbon on the landscape, he stopped and turned around, searching the Lane for a sign of Billie, hoping for a last glimpse of her before the Lane disappeared for the rest of the winter. But the Lane was empty, and loneliness began tugging at him as he turned and continued on.

Whiskey Rock was a popular stopping spot for hunters climbing the mountain to allow loaded-down overheated horses to rest as they labored up the trail's steepness. Recreational horseback riders and hikers as well liked to eat lunch and have a drink or two while admiring the panoramic view of towns, ranch buildings, and cattle spread out decoratively on rolling foothills below the mountain. Because some of them occasionally deposited their empty bottles and cans at the base of the rock, where Dan picked them up and carried them off the mountain to be properly disposed of, he began to call it whiskey rock — a name that stuck.

"Don't know what's the matter with people," he would say angrily. "If they can pack full bottles and cans up the hill with them, why can't they pack empty ones back down? They're not as heavy as when they're full, but maybe they don't realize that. They have no respect for the mountain, and I have no respect for them. They spoil the national forest for everyone."

When he first set out that morning, the trail had offered no resistance, rather welcomed him as a friend, and he made good time, though he was careful not to rouse the pain in his leg that may be lying dormant, waiting for a wrong move to set it off. A quarter of the way up, the snow began to deepen and turn to powder that made navigation on foot or even snowshoe difficult, especially when travel was uphill. "It's like plowing sugar with your feet," he thought to himself.

"Looks like it snowed while we were gone," he told Misty and Spuds as he turned them loose. Then looking up at the curmudgeonly grim sky with its lowering dark clouds, "And it looks like it could snow again — soon." It was as though the mountain were saying gruffly, "If you want to come up again, you'll have to earn your way. I'm not going to make life easy for you."

Dan understood the warning but, with no other choice, continued anyway, stopping often to rest. The mountain's peaceful appearance that morning had been deceiving. Looking at it from below didn't always reveal the unsettled weather within it. Blue sky and sunshine could reign at its foot, while turmoil plagued its higher elevations. That the mountain was moody and unpredictable in any season would have been known by anyone who had spent serious time in it. Dan knew to be caught unprepared, as many inexperienced people he had heard about had been, would be foolish, and now he had had enough taste of winter in it to know he was as prepared as he would ever be.

Though his progress seemed slow to him, Dan was making good time in spite of the trail's difficulty. He was finally past the halfway mark by early afternoon. In his absence, the wind had rearranged the snow into deep drifts, and he had nowhere to go to avoid the trail's edge but to step into one of them. The unevenness of it caused his leg to slide and twist, and a familiar pain suddenly shot through it. With a loud gasp, he stopped abruptly to lean on his walking stick. "Damn it, not again," he shouted. His only answer was the squeaking of a widow maker rubbing against its neighbor as a burst of wind set it in motion. After several minutes had passed, Spuds and Misty, who had scampered up the trail nearly out of sight, noticed he wasn't following and ran back, parking themselves in front of him, tails wagging, as though to ask their master why he wasn't moving.

"Just be patient," he told them in pain-filled anger. "We'll make it." Misty and Spuds lay watching him as he rested his leg a bit longer, then wincing, tried to push on through the powdery snow. The best he could do was 50 feet before the pain forced him to rest again. He wouldn't reach camp before dark at this pace, but he had no choice but to continue up the trail, stopping when the pain was at its worst. As he stood there, thoughts of death surfaced from a small corner of his mind, refusing to let go. Another choice was to sit down in the snow and let winter take him, as it nearly had on his way down the mountain. Dan did his best to shove those thoughts back into oblivion. That would be a coward's choice, he muttered to himself. If he could make it a little farther to the Salt Cabin, he would be okay.

They would continue their journey in the morning after a comfortable night's rest and the darkness had passed. Perhaps by then, his leg wouldn't object to continuing on to camp, a shorter, less difficult journey. The Salt Cabin's purpose in days past had been to store salt blocks for cattle that grazed the mountain in summer when pasture grass on ranchland became dry and sparse. Billie remembered accompanying her father up the mountain on horseback many times as a child when he needed to drop off salt blocks for ranchers below. Now it lay empty, its useful days over, slowly succumbing to the harsh elements that would some day bring it down, unless someone recognized a gleam of value in it and decided to save it.

Dan leaned heavily on his walking stick, mind set firmly on the Salt Cabin and a warm fire, as daylight began to wane. "I'll make it in spite of the pain, even if I have to crawl," he persisted. "It's not much farther now."

It was full darkness and the sky was silently weeping gently falling snow when he and the dogs arrived a couple of hours later. Snow had drifted half way up the side window, but the front door was fairly clear, and Dan had no trouble shoving the snow aside and opening it just enough for the dogs and

Photo by Danny Longwell

The Buck Cabin, shown above, is also on Walker Prairie. It is a small structure much like the Salt Cabin, and can provide lifesaving emergency shelter.

his slender body to squeeze through after he had shed his snowshoes and stood them upright in the snow.

The pungent odor of bare earth greeted them and, though there was no fireplace, a small pile of wood leaning against the back wall was sufficient to start a fire, which Dan tended to first. In spite of the broken windows that sucked out the smoke, the cabin was soon glowing with greater warmth than he had been able to achieve inside his tent, and he reveled in it. That done, he dug in his backpack for the can of soup he had carried up the mountain, opened it, and set it on the fire. After sharing it and what few crackers were in his pack with Misty and Spuds, he spread out the tarp he always carried with him when he left camp, climbed into his heat blanket, and settled into sleep, the dogs curled up on the floor close beside him. Coyotes howled off and on during the night trying to strike up a conversation, but even the dogs were too tired to respond.

I finally made it to the buck camp around 5:30. That old cabin looked like a room at the Holiday Inn. The dogs and I had vegetable soup for dinner, and were bedded down by 6:30. Left there around 9 a.m. and still snowing. Over a foot had come down during the night. We had not gone 200 yards when the dogs spotted nine coyotes, and they were gone in a flash.

Breakfast the next morning was a couple of granola bars Dan shared with Misty and Spuds. It wasn't enough to satisfy their hunger, but it was all he had left in his pack to provide them with renewed energy. Finding it picturesque in its alpine setting Dan stood in the growing morning sunshine admiring the log cabin resting on a white blanket set against a mixed forest of lodge pole pine and spruce. He set down his backpack, pulled out his camera, and snapped a few pictures.

The cabin's back side, settled nearly to the roof in snow, touched the edge of the thick pine forest. A set of very tall bleached elk antlers, an obvious hunter's trophy, decorated its front near the door, and most of the wire fence that lined its south end to keep the cattle out in summer, was buried in five feet of snow, only the top of an occasional post peeking through. Dan tucked his camera into a pocket in his pack, slung it over his back, picked up his rifle, and turned his snowshoes toward camp.

The pack of coyotes that had called to them during the night showed up near the trail teasing for a chase, as Dan and the dogs left the cabin. Deluded into thinking they could catch up with them, Spuds and Misty accepted their invitation, but quickly returned outwitted, resigned to chasing each other in circles and tumbling head over heals in the deep snow instead. They were no match for their well-conditioned opponents, which was probably a good thing, Dan thought. He was nervous each time the dogs took after them, wondering if they would return uninjured — or not return at all. Coyotes were known to lure dogs into their pack where, outnumbered, they would easily succumb to a deadly attack.

Dan's leg had recovered enough overnight to allow him a safe arrival at camp an hour after leaving the Salt Cabin. Apparently the heat blanket had done it some good. All the way, he worried that the tent would be down and buried, meaning hard labor for him and his bum leg before he could get inside and fire up the wood stove. But, to his surprise and relief, though the roof sagged some from the new snow, the tent was still standing, everything inside appearing as he had left it.

He set down his pack, brought a fire to a full blaze, paused to bask in its warmth, then took off his snowsuit and sat down to rest and enjoy a cup of coffee before going out to clear the roof and shovel the two feet of snow that had fallen since his departure from the mountain. He had only a space cleared in front of the tent when the pain in his leg returned, telling him to quit and spend the rest of the day off his feet, a command he had no desire to challenge.

January 9: Called Billie and let her know that I had made it ok, for she was worried. In all, it took me nine hours to walk up, and it took six and a half hours to walk down. I guess it was worth going down. I had a very enjoyable Christmas and New Years, and I enjoyed seeing Charlie and the gang down at the Legion. I also got a new pair of glasses so I can actually see again. 9 p.m. Been in bed reading. Got up and stocked the stove. It's about 5 below and still snowing.

Dan was disturbed as he walked slowly down the hill to camp reflecting on his conversation with Billie. Something she had said, something in her tone of voice, though she wouldn't say it directly, told him she thought Dan had decided to spend winter on the mountain to fulfill a wish expressed many times that upon his death his ashes rest on the prairie for eternity. Deviating from her usual directness was rare, but Dan thought perhaps his demise was a subject she wasn't ready to deal with. And neither was he. But convincing her she was wrong wouldn't be easy.

The next morning, Dan's leg was no better. And though he could barely stand on it, he had to get the fire going, coffee made, and water that had frozen in his absence thawed so he could make oatmeal for breakfast. Between rests, he cleared paths just enough to make them navigable and stocked up on wood, for there was still a good chunk of winter left and, with it, the certainty of sub-zero weather's return, and an increase in the stove's appetite.

Temperatures rose and fell during the next few days, mostly falling, as the mountain settled into the depths of winter, the coldest being January 11 when the mercury in Dan's thermometer dropped to 50 degrees below zero, the lowest temperature it was designed to measure. That evening, the wind decided to enter the fray, its icy breath roaring in gusts as it slammed into the tent, pushing deadly tentacles into tiny cracks, pulling the coldness to well below arctic.

January 11: Don't know what time it is, but it's damn cold. My watch and alarm clock are froze and my radio batteries are dead, and I haven't got them changed yet. Just ran out and looked at the thermometer, and it's 48 below. This damn thing only goes to 50 and I can only see one little line left on it. But it looks so damn peaceful and beautiful out. The sky is clear and the sun is shining through the snow-covered trees. It looks like it should be plus 50 degrees and not 50 below. It's so cold I can't even keep this tent warm. I filled my dishpans with water. Put one on the stove and when it got hot, I went to get the other, and it had started to freeze a thin layer of ice on it. And it's only 1 p.m., and I have gone through more than 80 pieces of wood. I'm gonna have to go out and chop enough to get by until tomorrow, for I'm not letting the fire go out tonight.

It's at least 50 below at 7 p.m. Wish my thermometer would register to lower than minus 50 so I could tell just how cold it really is. Stayed up all night and read and kept the fire going. Finally went to bed at 6 this morning.

The night had been long and cold, the little wood stove working hard against the gusting wind and falling temperatures to throw warmth but not succeeding in raising the inside temperature to anywhere near comforting. Shivering in their short-hair coats, Misty and Spuds sat looking up at Dan appearing warm in a light jacket over his long underwear, buried in layers of sleeping bag, and with a pathetic unison whine, begged to join him.

"Okay, c'mon up and I'll tell you a story," he told them, patting the bed in invitation. "It'll help keep me awake so I can keep the fire going." Misty and Spuds were on the bed in their usual simultaneous leap, landing on their master's lap. He motioned them to the foot of the bed and said admonishingly, "I didn't invite you to lie on my lap. Now settle down or you'll be back in your own bed, cold or no cold."

Misty began pawing at the sleeping bag, trying to find an opening. "No, you can't sleep inside my sleeping bag with me," Dan said firmly, pushing her toward the end of the bed. "What did I just tell you?" Misty looked at him with hurt feelings, then realizing he had given in as much as could be expected, she obediently joined Spuds at the end of the bed.

Their new sleeping quarters arranged to their liking, the dogs lay down close to each other and looked up at Dan as though anticipating the story he had promised. "My life has been a mess. Seems I never stuck at anything for long," he began pensively. "Was in the Service when I was young. Might've been wise financially to stick it out a few more years but unwisely, I didn't. Got married instead. That was a big mistake. But it was my fault. I jumped into it too fast. Didn't last but three years. During that time, I rode the rodeo circuit as a bronc rider. That didn't last long, either. Don't look at me like that. You can only get bucked off a horse so many times before it starts taking a toll on your body. And all that traveling takes a toll on married life, too. Never kept a job for long, either. I had to keep going where the work was. It was all hard physical work. That's all I've done since I was a child growing up on the family ranch near Thermopolis. But that's a story for another time, when I feel like going into the pain of it. You two have had it easy, so I don't want to hear any complaints. And now, this is hard endless work, too, keeping enough wood chopped, paths shoveled, water hauled, and keeping you two fed and warm and happy. But I opened my big mouth bragging about it to everyone, and it's my fault we're doing it."

By the time Dan had run out of life to talk about, or perhaps was tired of talking, Misty and Spuds were sound asleep. Careful not to disturb them, he quietly left the warmth of his sleeping bag, fed the stove, and picked a book off the stack on his night table. He opened it to the first chapter but sat staring at the words, reading the same paragraph many times without comprehending. The mention of his childhood had stirred up memories that commandeered his mind, making him relive the anger and the pain. And it was only with a great deal of effort that he was able to shove them back into the darkness from which they had come and focus on the story in his hands until morning's early hours when he piled more wood into the stove and settled into sleep.

It was noon when Dan awoke, and as he slipped out of bed expecting a stab of pain in his leg, he noticed a lack of it. No need to rest it any longer. It had improved significantly since yesterday even with all the ups and downs to keep the fire going all night. Now hunger gnawed at his stomach, but he wasn't sure whether he wanted breakfast or lunch. Misty and Spuds, who had already been outside to tend to their duties, sniffed their empty dog dish, pawed at the tub of dog food sitting in the corner, then sat at Dan's feet, looking up at him as though to say "In case you haven't noticed, we're hungry, too. How about it?"

"Okay. You can have your dog food, but I'm going to have lunch for breakfast."

Two hamburger patties were beginning to sizzle in the frying pan he had placed on the stove, and he was buttering the buns when he stopped and listened to the distant drone of an engine growing louder. Soon it was a roar that told him it was an airplane that would soon clip the top of his tent. He quickly put down the pancake turner and raced outside in time to see a red and white light plane diving toward the tent like a hawk to its prey, then disappear, only to return again with a buzz. Misty and Spuds were barking incessantly, though silently, their voices drowned in the roar of the plane's engine. Dan's lunch, sizzling on the hot stove, was forgotten in the commotion as he and the dogs turned their eyes upward to watch the plane bank, circle, then gain altitude.

Dan thought he had seen someone wave as the plane banked, but he couldn't recognize the pilot. "Could that be . . .? I don't think so. But maybe." Dan couldn't make up his mind, only speculated as the plane flew low over the prairie, seeming to drop a speck of something in the distance, then barely skimming the tree tops, disappeared over the timber, leaving him baffled. "I wonder what he dropped. Guess we'll find out after lunch. I'm more hungry than curious right now." That was the last he saw of the red and white airplane.

"It must have been someone I know," he said, as he and the dogs ran into the tent to see smoke rising from the frying pan. "Otherwise, why would he . . . Oh, no! My lunch!" he exclaimed. "Well I guess that's the end of that."

January 13: I don't know who the hell has a red and white plane, but it flew over and then circled the camp three times. I went out and looked and waved at whoever it was, and when I got back inside, my hamburger was burnt all to hell. So I ate the bread and said to hell with it. The dogs liked it, though.

Misty and Spuds expressed no remorse or sympathy for their master over the burned hamburgers, just eagerly and quickly gobbled them as though they hadn't eaten in days. They were seldom fussy about what they ate, and Dan would confess to anyone that he didn't know much about cooking. At home, that was Billie's' job. Packaged was normally the best it got when he was in charge, which was seldom if Billie had anything to say about it. But now, he sometimes longed for something that didn't come from a package or jar, and he had plenty of ingredients with which to experiment when he was in the mood for it.

Sometimes I didn't want just a can of soup or hamburger, so I started experimenting with putting different stuff together. I'd always let the dogs taste it first. There were several times they would stick up their noses and wouldn't even take a bite of it. So I got rid of that stuff real quick and went back to something simple. That was the reason I had those two little girls up there, to help me with my experiments. They kind of told me what to eat and what not to eat.

Testing food for palatability was the least of Dan's reasons for having Misty and Spuds spend the winter with him. Companionship took the top of the list with protection and entertainment following closely. Their clumsy efforts at navigating deep snow with their short legs and round bodies, plus their playful antics as they tackled each other and wrestled and rolled playfully in the snow, were often good for a laugh, especially when the seriousness of winter didn't leave him much to laugh about.

That afternoon, Dan put on his snowshoes and trekked across the prairie to see if he could find whatever it was that fell from the plane. "If it was something he meant to drop in my camp, I can't say much for his eyesight, because he missed it by at least a mile," he said as he dug a tightly wrapped package from the snow. He carried it back to camp and set it on his outdoor table, carving through the string and heavy wrapper with his Leatherman.

"Well I'll be damned. It's some of the supplies I had asked Billie for. I wonder how he knew . . ." Dan thought for a while, then he remembered a recent radio conversation with Billie. "That was it. Someone heard me on the radio when I told Billie that I had lost a bunch of food from spoilage. And she said there was nothing she could do about it. That person must have gotten hold of the game warden, or someone else. Gotta watch what I say on the radio. Some things are none of anyone else's business. Well, guess we'll have pork chops for supper tonight." Misty looked up at him and woofed in agreement, as though she knew what he had offered.

That night, Dan was awakened off and on by howling coyotes he guessed were above the hill near camp calling for Misty and Spuds to come out and give chase. When Misty and Spuds weren't chasing chipmunks and mice, they took after their canine cousins, oblivious to the possibility of being torn apart should they catch up with a sizable pack. Spuds would only give chase during the day when they were spotted but weren't howling. Possibly knowing something Misty didn't, Spuds ran for the closest hiding place (her favorite being under the bed) when they howled during a dark ominous night when scary creatures roamed the prairie searching for little dogs to eat.

Coyotes were nearly as abundant on the prairie as the mice that kept invading Dan's tent all winter. Like mice, there didn't need to be a season or a license for them to be hunted; they were legal sport for him and the dogs when warm weather and the desire for play won out over cutting wood. Though Dan hunted them off and on during the winter, he never was able to shoot one, nor did he care; it was merely sport. Misty and Spuds never caught up with them. And Dan never thought the dogs, with their short legs and over-weight bodies, ever would.

January 14: The dogs and I got up early this morning and went up on the prairie to see if we could get a coyote. We saw nine of them, but they were too far away to get a shot, so I put the dogs on them and they chased them all over until they tired of the sport.

The fun is over for the day. Going to eat breakfast, then go out and finish cutting and chopping wood and get it hauled in. Then all I have to do is cut my trees down and start all over, but I'm going to take a couple days off and try to get a couple of coyotes. Nine p.m. and ready for bed. It's 4 below.

For the most part, weather dictated Dan's activities. Though he liked to hike the prairie, sometimes hunting coyotes, sometimes heading to the bridge to fish, most of his days were occupied with life-preserving work: clearing snow, hauling water, and cutting, splitting, stacking, and loading wood into the tent. Fortunately for someone depending on wood to survive the winter, dead trees were abundant in the forest due to drought weakening or pine bark beetle infestation.

Though Dan knew using a chainsaw when alone in the woods wasn't recommended, he didn't worry about it, couldn't worry about it. But even so, he couldn't help but think about it every time he revved the machine into action. It was something he needed to do if he were to keep himself supplied, for he would never keep up using a handsaw or ax. And he couldn't let his wood pile dwindle to dangerously low levels in case a paralyzing storm moved in and kept him prisoner in his tent for several days. He considered himself as good a sawyer as most men, which he reasoned increased his odds for safety. But he also knew that even the best could succumb to an unforeseen situation such as a hidden flaw or weakness in the tree or its manner of standing, or the unpredictability of its surroundings.

The greatest danger cutting wood lay in felling tall dead pines, especially those leaning in the crotch of another tree (called widow makers) that could pinch a saw or kick it back at the sawyer. He had heard many stories of gruesome accidental deaths caused by chainsaws hungry for an arm, a leg, or even a head. Should an accident happen, though he took every precaution to avoid one, and he lived through it, the radio was his only hope for rescue, though it might be a long time coming. Meanwhile, with no one to give him first aid, his survival would be in question.

As he rode up the mountain carrying supplies to his camp in the fall, he had thought about his safety using a chainsaw alone, even worried about it some. Safety was one thing, but if his saw broke down and needed replacement parts, or if he ran out of gas, he would be in trouble. In the planning, he could only guess how much gas he would need to keep his saw going through the winter, for he had no idea how much wood his stove would have to burn to keep the tent at a comfortable temperature. And most likely, his inexperience would have him figuring wrong. He had gone through more than he expected during the past couple of days and nights, and winter promised many more like them before turning its reign over to spring.

"What other choice do I have?" he asked Misty and Spuds as though they could offer an answer. "I can't call and have someone deliver gas when I need it, or come up and keep me company every time I need to cut wood. As long as I keep in mind everything that could go wrong, I should be safe."

Chapter 4

THE ACCIDENT

Sunshine tried to warm the prairie the day of the accident. But try as it may, the temperature, which had dropped to 25 below overnight, keeping Dan out of his sleeping bag more than in it feeding a dwindling fire, it could only climb to 10 above before beginning its descent again that evening. All the sun could do that day was bounce its decorative spectrum off the snow-laden evergreens, dressing the prairie in irresistible beauty, which it did quite nicely. Later in the day, it tried its best to make the branches weep, but didn't succeed at that, either. As long as the wind stayed at kissing speed, anything above zero, Dan considered relatively warm, relative to the subzero temperatures to which his body had become acclimated.

That morning, Dan decided he had better leave the coyotes alone and work at restocking the rapidly diminishing woodpile that, until recently, had lined two adjacent tent walls near the stove, touching the ceiling, and that had taken up space under his bed. He had had his two days of play, and in just one sub-zero night, the hard-working stove had gobbled 80 pieces of wood, leaving a large hole in the middle of the pile, every piece fed counted and carefully recorded in his journal. On those frigid nights, no matter how diligent Dan was in keeping the fire going, it was all the little stove could do to raise the inside temperature to zero. It was even more difficult when a strong wind picked its way through the walls and down through the chimney hole, stealing heat with its arctic breath.

"I had no idea I'd burn the amount of wood I did," Dan told his unbelieving friends when winter was over. "I was very much surprised at how much wood I had to cut. And glad there was enough dead wood around."

Dan didn't linger over breakfast. The days hadn't grown much since late December, the hours of light still short, and working into the evening by lantern, which caused gigantic dark shadows to fall on his work area, wasn't nearly as productive as work done in full daylight. Still chewing a mouthful of food, he stacked his dirty dishes on the table, leaving cleanup for after supper, and dressed in layers for a day of outdoor labor so he could strip down as his body heat cranked higher with physical effort.

Misty and Spuds wiggled out the door first followed closely by their master, who stepped slowly out of the dim tent into the sunshine, the glare of it off the snow's unbroken whiteness nearly blinding him. "Oops. Forgot my sunglasses," he said as he quickly stepped back inside to pick them up off the night table and put them on over his glasses. His eyes adjusted, he stood outside the door for several minutes, unable to begin the day's work without pause to admire the prairie's stunning diamond-studded blanket where the sun's rays bounced off snow crystals, and the forest's lodge pole branches bent low under the weight of its winter attire. Days like this were rare in winter.

He reached down to give Spuds and Misty a pat, then sent them off to play their wrestling game somewhere else. Dan's ambitious plan for the day was to begin cutting and stacking the five-foot lengths he had dragged to his work area a few days ago. That would make room for the new logs he would cut and drag down today, perhaps leaving time to cut them to size and stack them as well.

Morning passed quickly, and by early afternoon, Dan was ready to take down another tree. But first, he whistled at the dogs who followed him into the tent for a lunch break while he thought about which trees to tackle. The temperature had climbed to above zero with a tolerable wind, and he didn't mind walking a distance to gather in the pieces. If he couldn't finish it today, he could do it over several days if he had to. But if he could find a tree closer to camp, that would make him less work, he thought. He shoved the rest of his sandwich into his mouth, giving part of it to Misty and Spuds, then shooed them out of the tent, telling them, "You're not going to lie inside sleeping all day. If I have to work, you're going to work."

Though he had cut many of them already, there were still plenty of dead trees in the vast forest that surrounded the prairie. Lodge pole pines clutched the ground with shallow roots and a comparatively gentle hold, forced to let go by the hundreds when powerful wind storms ravaged the mountain, leaving forest trails in a tangled ruin of piled-high logs that some day would become serious fuel for a lightning-caused fire. Hikers or horseback riders using those trails would thank him for the clearing. And possibly the Forest Service would as well.

Because Dan had cut trees close to camp first, thinking they would provide enough wood to last the winter, or because it had been too cold to drag the pieces far, they were becoming scarce. Of the few that were left standing, one was a widow maker that stood a few yards from camp — a tree he had been avoiding — a tree with a possible attitude. Its trunk divided into identical twins a few feet above ground, then rose approximately 40 more feet into the sky. It appeared to have been dead a long time, its bare branches brittle and brown, its insides most likely infested and drained of sap. There was a chance it would burn hot and fast, providing instant warmth and then longer lasting warmth when combined with slow burning logs.

When he first saw it, he thought better of attempting it because its weight, balance, and lean made its fall difficult to predict. But every time he passed, it seemed to taunt him to the challenge, daring him to take it on. "C'mon Dan. It's not as difficult as it looks. Just do it. I'm tired of standing here - dead," the tree seemed to coax. "One day I'll fall with a huge crash anyway, scattering my limbs over the forest floor, vulnerable to ignition by a swift, stabbing light from the sky."

"There are lots of trees I could cut," Dan mused. "However, this one's big, and it's close. Lots of wood, and only a short distance to haul it."
He stood looking up its trunk to its topmost branches noting direction of bend as a gentle wind played in them, pushing them one way and then another. Its thick trunks, gradually tapering to a point at their tops would supply him with an ample amount of wood for many days, leaving him time to explore the prairie with Spuds and Misty and perhaps to even get in a little fishing when the weather permitted. He had been cutting trees most of his life, and though he knew this tree was different than any other he had ever felled, he knew that if he was careful he could do it. He would just have to take his time.

It was settled. He had talked himself into it, and nothing would change his mind. He set the chainsaw on a log and walked around the tree several times, carefully examining the crotch where the tree split. Misty and Spuds sat and watched, listening as he muttered to himself, wondering what he was up to and why he was taking so long. Finally, he stepped back, shouted at the dogs to get out of the way, revved the chainsaw into action, and began the first cut, making a small notch in the trunk. Satisfied that it was going well, he stopped, turned off the chainsaw, and examined the tree one more time, taking note of the topmost branches and their gentle sway.

He wiped his forehead, pulled out his handkerchief, and blew his nose, something inside holding him back. Though he considered it, he couldn't walk away now. The chip that was missing left the tree vulnerable and weak. It couldn't be left. A knot was beginning to tighten in his stomach, and he tried, with little success, to calm himself.

"There's no reason it shouldn't fall where I planned it to fall," he assured himself. "Just do it."

The chainsaw's roar echoed through the prairie as he revved it. Hesitating, he took a deep breath and sank the saw's revolving teeth into the tree, chips and sawdust flying in all directions. Partway into the tree, he paused to check his work, looking up at the highest branches to determine lean. It was leaning the right way, begging for the final cut, the one that would send it crashing down. He looked it over one more time, then sank teeth into it again, quickly pulling the saw out when the huge trunk began to crack and groan in agony as gravity ripped it from its stump. The last thing he remembered was the tree breaking loose from its foundation, twisting as it separated, the chainsaw dropping from his hands, a deafening crash, and sudden pressure against his head.

Dan opened his eyes to a splitting headache and a green canopy spinning wildly above him in a gray dimming sky as though it were engaged in some sort of ritual dance for the dead. For awhile, he thought he might be dead. He couldn't feel his body - he only knew it was somewhere in the deep snow, arms spread out, desperately clutching the lifting, turning ground to keep from falling as it rolled - falling forever into nowhere. Misty and Spuds lay next to him, breathing a warm, foul odor into his face, their sporadic yips that seemed to come from far away insistently urging him to be alive and on his feet, heading for the tent, warmth, and supper.

As he lay there, eyes closed to slow the earth's spinning, he became aware of a cool breeze nipping at his head and ears and realized his cap had left him in the fall. Slowly, he raised an arm and placed his fingers on the mountain of throbbing pain in his head and wondered how long he had been unconscious. By now, his brain had cleared enough to tell him why he was lying flat in the snow, that all was not well with it, and that he needed to call for medical advice - and more likely, rescue. Feeling sick and crawling slowly on his hands and knees, he made it a short distance to the top of the hill. Keeping his eyes closed, he fumbled for his pocket, reached in, and pulled out the radio (which he always kept with him when he left the tent), turned it on, and held it close to his mouth.

"Hello! Hello anyone!" he shouted as loud as his pounding head would allow.

"This is Dan on Walker Prairie. It's an emergency! I'm hurt, and I need a helicopter."

The radio responded with a "beep, beep, beep," that said "I'm busy; you'll have to try later. You're not important right now." Then it went silent. He waited a few moments, then tried again, desperate, listening anxiously for a response, but the radio was as stubbornly quiescent as the mountain. "Damn radio! It's worthless." Disappointment had turned to frustrated anger. He knew his injury needed medical attention, knew he had had enough and was ready to quit the mountain. But someone else was in charge and wasn't listening.

"For somebody who is supposed to be on red alert, this radio sure doesn't work." With an impulsive kill-the-messenger attitude, he lifted his arm to throw the radio as far as he was weakly able, hoping it would smash into a tree, its irreparable pieces falling deep into the snow. Seconds before common sense was beaten by impulse, he turned it off and shoved it back in his pocket and lay down in the snow again.

"Worthless piece of junk. Where is help when you need it." Misty and

Photo by Danny Longwell

The mischievous tree he had felled lay in pieces, remorseless and still.

Spuds backed off at the tone of his voice, tails between their legs, wondering what they had done to incur his anger, anger that only made his head pound harder.

"Now, along with my other occupations up here, I'll have to add doctor. Take two aspirins and call myself in the morning," he mumbled sarcastically. The dogs turned and gave him a strange look, as though they wondered where his sanity had gone. That is, if he had any to begin with. With painful effort, Dan rolled onto his side and opened his eyes. The world was still spinning, but not as fast as at first, and a sick feeling had grown in his stomach. He pushed himself to sitting, vomited, and gently brushed the snow off his head. Slowly getting to his knees, he crawled to the nearest tree, hoping it would stand still long enough for him to pull himself to his feet.

The mischievous tree he had felled lay in pieces, remorseless and still, a short distance from him, his chainsaw nearly buried in the snow next to it. His cap was nowhere visible. He'd find it tomorrow — if he lived until then, he thought. But now, he needed to get to the tent, take something to ease the pain, and put something cold on his head for the swelling. He closed his eyes again for a moment, paused to be sick again, then let go of the tree, staggered a short distance, and fell, unable to keep in step with the earth's moving.

The walk, perhaps a half block but seeming like miles, was in spurts, stumbling alternated with falling, falling more than walking, his stomach occasionally protesting the earth's instability. By the time he reached the tent, Misty and Spuds arriving long before him, it was nearly dark. With difficult, agonizing slowness, he brought the stove to warmth, fed the dogs and, skipping supper, gratefully climbed into the warm comfort of bed where he could close his eyes in temporary relief from the tent's spinning and engage the healing power of sleep or perhaps to meet death if his injury was serious enough.

But his sleep was fitful, the cold waking him often as the fire threatened to die. Each time he arose to feed the stove, the head pounding and dizziness were still with him, and he wondered whether it would ever go away. If it were still with him in the morning, he'd have to find a way off the mountain, though he had no idea how.

Sleep didn't come easy that night, but after taking something for the pain, the pounding eased, allowing him rest. And in the morning, though the lump on his head was still there, he felt well enough to return to the accident site and look for his hat and pick up his chainsaw, which he thought might be damaged by the falling tree. But he found it in one piece and operable.

The tree hit me pretty hard, so I came in and stayed in bed for the rest of the day, for I was real dizzy every time I got up.

January 17: I feel a lot better this morning. Went out and found my hat; it was buried under the tree, so I feel damn lucky that it wasn't me under that tree. Called and talked to Brandy this morning. Was glad to talk with him. A guy doesn't realize how lonely he gets until he calls someone. It's like don't you dare hang up on me. That's when I have to hide the radio or I would be calling everyone.

I'd better go tackle my tree - get some of it dragged into camp so I can get it cut and chopped up. Later in the day: I cut 12 pieces into five-foot lengths and got them dragged to camp along with a big pile of branches for fire starter. So I had a busy day. It's 20 above at 6:30 p.m.

Called Billie and found out I have a meeting that I must attend Tuesday. I tried a week ago to get out of it and thought I had succeeded but, as usual, I was wrong. So now I have to walk down the mountain at 2 or 3 in the morning when the snow is frozen, for it's getting too warm during the day. You keep falling through, and that's too hard on me.

January 18: Woke up at 7 a.m. sweating, and went out and checked the temperature. It's 28 above. I knew it was warm, for I didn't zip up my sleeping bag until 3:30 this morning. This is the damnedest winter I have ever seen. God only knows what's going to happen next.

Though Dan felt recovered enough from the blow to face the long trip down the mountain, occasional dizziness and recurring headaches plagued him the next several days. He and his companions left camp at 3:30 the morning of January 19, traveling slowly in the cold darkness and stopping often, guided by sparkling starlight, a waning crescent moon that had risen late and promised to stay with him well into the next day, and a flashlight full of new batteries. Three hours and only halfway into his journey, daylight began to creep over the horizon, slowly absorbing the stars and fading the moon's light into a cloudless sky. Stopping briefly when he reached Whiskey Rock, he took out his binoculars and focused them on PK Lane. As he suspected, the wind had pushed snow into the road in long, deep piles along its length, making it impassable by even by four-wheel drive vehicles.

"The wind knew I was coming down," he said, tucking his binoculars into his backpack. "Did it on purpose just to make me walk an extra three miles. I guess we'll rest here for a bit before tackling the rest of it. I'm too tired to go on right now."

Misty and Spuds, seeming as tired of the trip as he was, lay at his feet as he took off his pack, set down his rifle, and sat on a rock. He pulled a candy bar from his pocket, shared it with his friends, and closed his eyes for a few minutes before picking up his pack and continuing on. It was 2:30 in the afternoon when he dragged himself to his doorstep, removed his snowshoes, walked in, and plopped himself in the nearest chair.

Billie greeted him with a somber expression when she returned home from work. But he was too exhausted to notice the darkness in Billie's eyes and mood that would have told him something unpleasant was bothering her, something she would hold off from telling him until his body was rested and his mind cleared of the business he had come down the mountain to tend to, for what she had to tell him would fill his whole being with despair.

Despite that the business that had forced him off the mountain had been taken care of in a few hours, when it was finished, Dan decided to stay off the mountain a few days catching up on family news and spending time with Billie. But his plans took a turn when come evening and supper was finished, Billie, hesitant about telling it but knowing it was necessary, for he was growing curious about the somber mood she couldn't hide, sat down with him in the living room and, with sympathy in her voice, gave him news that would shatter his spirits for a very long time. There was no way of telling it softly. No way to avoid the stab in his heart she knew telling it would cause. It had happened; there was no way of undoing it and no sense in talking around hurtful words that needed saying.

Dan's reaction was worse than Billie had expected, his mood growing dark as the night creeping in, and she knew there were no words of comfort she could offer when the hurt caused him to withdraw into himself. Her words kept going around in his head, his mind now emptied of all else.

"Unexpected. Came as a shock to all of us."

"A sudden heart attack you said?" Dan was puzzled. People don't have heart attacks when they're only in their 40s, he thought. "He was so young."

"I heard heart problems ran in the family. Who would have guessed?"

"Why didn't you tell me earlier? When it happened?"

"Didn't want to tell you over the radio. That would have been worse. You might have killed yourself trying to hurry down the mountain to attend the funeral. And if for some reason you couldn't make it down, like a blizzard for instance, you would have beaten yourself up for a very long time for not being there for him. This way, it wasn't your fault you didn't get there."

There being nothing more to say, Dan fell silent. He knew Billie was right, as she almost always was. Now he felt a desperate need to be alone with his thoughts, alone to deal with the shock of it and life's unfairness, alone to shed tears he was holding in. It was a different kind of grief than he had felt when his father died, a more intense grief made unbearable by the suddenness with which the news had been delivered. It was like a lion had grown within him and was trying to tear him apart. It had to be dealt with in his own way, and until his grief was resolved, he wouldn't be a fit companion for anyone. His emotions told him to pack and leave right away, but since the hour was late, he had no choice but to stay the night and begin the long trek back to camp in the morning.

Only the mountain could help him now, could wrap him in its folds, quietly offer the comfort he so badly needed without offering advice, without saying it was sorry for his loss, or that it was time to deal with it and move on. The mountain would never ask someone else how he was taking it, as though denial, at least in front of others, should be the route taken. In the mountain's quiescence, he could scream, cry, throw angry curses at the sky, and the mountain would simply be there, unjudging, silently absorbing his anguish, the gray sky weeping gently falling snow in sympathy. It would listen as his painful cries rent the prairie. It had no rules or expectations about grieving. It understood the resolving of his grief was only within himself, not in the words of others he didn't wish to hear, regardless of their intent to comfort.

Having known his friend most of his life, Dan considered him one of few to whom he could open his heart without fear of reprisal; someone with whom he could trust his private thoughts; someone with whom he could be himself; with whom he didn't have to mimic the political correctness of the world just to fit in; someone with whom he could disagree knowing their friendship was secure for a lifetime; someone who had many times pulled him out of despair when his life had gone awry. And now that life was over — much too soon. Now he must deal with that loss, with death, and with the meaning of the rest of his life, which had now become lost, insignificant, perhaps closer to that end than he realized.

That evening, he was eager to sink into the depths of sleep, his only escape from pain, hoping in the morning he would find his friend's death had only been a bad dream, a cruel joke, eaten by a good night's sleep after which the sun would climb back into his spirits. But his sleep was fitful. His mind wouldn't allow it, and he kept awakening to a nightmare reality he desperately wished had never happened. He arose the next morning looking and feeling like he hadn't slept for days.

"I'm not fit to be around people right now," he told Billie dismally. Her concern was obvious in her voice and demeanor, and she understood when he said, "I need to work this out by myself." Assuring her he would be all right, he kissed her goodbye and, accompanied by Misty and Spuds, disappeared down the snow-covered PK Lane.

The agonizing return trip up the mountain had taken him more than 10 hours, a small part of it spent resting at Whiskey Rock where, at last far from civilization, he sat, took off his glasses, and released some of his grief to the wind playing softly through needled branches. Though it was still cold, the clouds that decorated the sky were fluffy cotton balls that occasionally allowed the sun passage and carried no threat. It was as though Mother Nature understood his grief and had graciously decided not to add to it. A half hour had passed as he sat staring at the hills below the mountain searching for answers that wouldn't come. Sadly, he picked up his pack and continued up the hill.

When he stumbled into camp at 8:30 that evening, all energy spent, his mood unsettled, he found it untouched, except for a dog dish that had been knocked over. He examined the scene curiously, but could find no revealing evidence pinning the guilt on anything or anyone specific. He also discovered he was missing his new glasses and remembered taking them off on the way up the mountain when he stopped at Whiskey Rock to rest, his thoughts in a turmoil. He would have to get along without them until he went down again or until someone coming up could find and bring them to him. After cleaning up the dog-food mess, he climbed into bed, too tired and deep in grief to care what animal had made it or about his glasses. He would tend to both later.

Misty and Spuds, sensing their master's sadness and his mind's preoccupation, quietly pushed their way through the tent door and, careful not to disturb him, settled on the floor beside his bed, wanting closeness and assurance that he would be his old self in the morning.

Regardless of Mother Nature's mercy the previous day, his body's lack of recuperation time between trips had none of it. Sleeping until 9, Dan awoke to a body rebelling against winter's hardships and his long strenuous walks up and down the mountain. Those would have to quit; they were too hard on him, he thought. His head seemed back to normal, the pain and dizziness gone, but now one knee was significantly out of order and full of pain.

When I got up, I found out my right knee was two times bigger than it should be. Can hardly stand on it. Didn't get my first cup of coffee until 11, for I had to go out and get water, and that took awhile. It's been snowing off and on all day. Have about 2.5 inches at 4 p.m., and I'm staying in all day. Maybe tomorrow I'll go out and shovel everything out if I feel better. Time to eat and then kick back and read until bedtime.

The walking stick Dan used to steady himself when walking about the prairie on snowshoes stood upright in the snow outside the tent door, ready for the next trip. He reached out and grabbed it, thinking it would be his companion until his knee was normal size again, and hobbled down to the stream, chopped a hole in the ice, and filled enough containers to last at least another day or two. That night he stepped into the darkness, lifted his head to the stars that winked down at him, cold and unfeeling, and shouted at them as though they were to blame. "Why? Why? Why?" But his words were gobbled by the night's empty darkness, perhaps heard by awakening owls or other animals that prowled the night, but never answered.

Other than the mundane chores that needed doing to survive winter, Dan spent two weeks within himself, his tasks meaningless, wrestling with his grief and the meaning of life and loss and hardships that were always trying to take him down, wandering the prairie as though on a hunt for answers lying somewhere in the whispering forest, the silent creeks, the white mountains that looked down on him, majestic, stately, and unsympathetic. But it seemed there were no answers. At least, not where he was searching.

During that time, his pen was silent, his grief plugging the flow of ink to paper. But all the while, his mind was busy examining his life, mistakes he had made in living it, how he had come to those mistakes, his reasons for being on the mountain, reasons for continuing his life when all seemed dark and lacking merit and meaning. Meanwhile, Misty and Spuds moped around camp, staying close, hoping the master they once knew would soon return.

Temperatures gradually sank over the next couple of days during which Dan's knee shrank back to its normal size and allowed him painless mobility once more. His return to normalcy was accompanied by Mother Nature's calling him to activity, as though she were thinking he had slacked off much too long. Giant snowflakes came down fast and thick the morning of February 3, as though from a huge invisible dump truck above the clouds, reducing visibility to less than 10 feet. Despite Mother Nature's intent, the storm kept Dan inside for a greater part of the day.

Called Billie to see if she caught a ride up to the end of the lane so she could walk up to Whiskey rock and get my glasses that I left behind the other day when I stopped to rest and eat lunch. It would take her two hours to go up and back, and for me, it would take about nine hours. But she couldn't find anyone with a four-wheel pickup to take her up. Maybe I'll be healed up enough by next week sometime to go get them, for they're sure not going anyplace.

While he was waiting for the storm to subside, he busied himself preparing a lumberjack breakfast of pancakes and eggs, making a few extra cakes, which he placed on the fence posts for the camp robbers, and in the dog dishes for Misty and Spuds, who deserved a treat now and then. Her appetite unsatisfied by the pancakes she had just finished, Spuds sniffed around her dish, searching for any crumbs that may have escaped her. Finding none, her nose lured her to a peanut butter aroma not far from her dish, an additional sumptuous treat waiting for the taking, and she was the only one who noticed it. Though it wasn't meant for her, she would get it before Misty discovered it and a fight ensued.

Oblivious to the dogs, or anything else for that matter, Dan, his mind lost in planning the day's activities, hands occupied with kitchen chores, was roused from the depths of thought by a sudden yelp. It wasn't the usual attention-getting or begging yelp, or one of warning. It was an unmistakable scream of fright and sudden intense pain. Dan immediately turned to discover the source and found Spuds' nose had turned into a mousetrap. He hurried over to her and, quickly and as gently as he could, lifted the trap off her nose, which grew a little larger once it was released, but remained intact. After that, Spuds stayed close to her master most of the morning, whining occasionally in pain, seeking comfort, trying to show her appreciation for releasing her from the nastiness that had caused her so much agony, but becoming a nuisance as well.

By 11:30, it was still snowing heavily with no sign of letting up, and Dan was becoming desperate to get outside and clear the snow from around the tent and to haul in some much-needed wood. Finally at 1 p.m., a great distance began to grow between flakes. The white curtain that had hidden the prairie was parting, revealing an uninterrupted blanket, a new sheet of paper ready for a story to unfold on it. There wasn't much daylight left, but he needed to clear paths to his water supply and to his bathroom. He would make up for the lost daylight by working into the evening hauling wood into the tent.

Surrounded by a tarp earlier in the winter, the wood platform that was his bathroom now sat exposed to the elements. The wind, weeks ago, decided he didn't need privacy and pulled off the tarp and threw it into the woods. Dan, agreeing there was no one around to see him anyway, never replaced it. Now, sitting out in the open, his toilet was often buried in a couple of feet of snow caused by a storm or the antics of a mischievous wind.

I'm the only human being that has to sweep the snow off my toilet before sitting down. I guarantee that you wait as long as you can, then make a mad dash for it, because you damned sure won't sit there very long. It would be real embarrassing to survive up here and end up with a frostbitten butt. Wouldn't that be a joke.

That night, the temperature began a slow descent into the depths of his thermometer, stopping at 26 below in the early morning, his stove devouring a good portion of wood he had hauled in the day before. But he had another woodpile outside, which only took an hour or so to stack inside the tent, after which he would spend the remainder of the morning and perhaps into the afternoon cutting more so there would always be wood nearby to stack indoors.

Dan hadn't planned on putting in a full day of work. He figured he had earned some leisure time, a respite from working in the bitter cold, perhaps lying around reading, playing Solitaire, or just relaxing with the dogs and enjoying the warmth brought by the fruits of his labor. But his chainsaw, perhaps thinking it had worked hard enough and deserved a rest as well, snapped, bringing his woodcutting plans to a halt. That didn't worry Dan. He had an extra chain, so it was a fixable setback. But it wouldn't get done today.

Though the temperature had risen a few degrees, it was still too cold to fumble with replacing the chain, his bare fingers freezing against icy metal, he thought. There was work other than cutting wood that he could be doing, of most importance, replenishing his water supply, which he knew by this time would be trapped beneath ice again. What he didn't know was how thick the ice had become.

I went down to the creek and chopped a hole two feet by two feet, then put some wood around it and covered it with a tarp. The damned ice was 20 inches thick. Maybe this will keep it from freezing so hard.

His water supply opened once more, Dan turned his attention to making supper and listening intently to the news on the radio, his source of evening entertainment, a connection with civilization that, when his batteries weren't frozen, brought him the excitement of football and basketball games and kept him apprised of local and world happenings. And, it kept him from turning back into the grief that, as long as he could keep his mind from it, was beginning to heal. Dan, in turn, discussed all of it with Misty and Spuds, who lay on the bed or sat at the table looking disinterested, except when he cheered loudly every time the right team scored or made a touchdown. Then they would look up at him as though wondering what was happening that sent their master over the edge, wondering what merited his disturbing their sleep.

That evening, Dan listened expectantly for the news anchor who was about to announce a guilty verdict for O. J. Simpson, a former football star of questionable character now on trial for killing his wife, most of the world voting for guilty, but many who idolized him defending his innocence.

This time it will be guilty, I think. Had to wait until 9:30 to find out something I already figured out. It's already 17 below, so it will be damned cold in the morning.

That night, the temperature only fell one more degree and didn't rise much during the day. It seemed the mountain would be stuck in subzero weather for a very long time. The next day, Dan awoke hungry for egg sandwiches. When he opened the sleeping bag in which the eggs were wrapped to prevent freezing and pulled out the box of eggs, a foul odor attacked his senses. He had noticed a hint of it the last few days when he approached the sleeping bag but thought it might be a dead mouse he hadn't discovered and couldn't find, most likely buried in the wood pile. Now Misty and Spuds, normally beside him eager for a breakfast treat, backed off and hid behind the stove. Searching for the offender, Dan reached for an egg and cracked it into a bowl. Wincing, he held his nose and backed off.

"Sure can tell a bad egg from a good one," he said, holding his nose. "Never smelled anything like it in my life. I wonder if all my eggs are spoiled." After breaking nine eggs that had frozen and thawed, he found four good ones that were edible and set them aside for breakfast. He quickly disposed of the bad eggs, then came inside and began scrambling the good ones.

"I'll have to go through my whole supply after breakfast and cull out the bad ones," he told the dogs as they emerged from hiding. "We can't live with the smell of rotten eggs. It's hardly appetizing." Later, after culling the eggs, Dan counted the good ones finding that of the 72 eggs he began the winter with, less than half remained unspoiled. Winter was far from over, and Dan wondered how soon the good would follow the bad.

After breakfast and chores, Dan spent considerable time tearing his chainsaw apart, cleaning it, installing another chain, and sharpening it. When he was through, he pulled on his jacket and boots, carried the chainsaw outdoors and grabbed a log off his pile. The chainsaw started on the second pull and purred happily. But when he sank its teeth into a three-inch diameter log, it took eons for the saw to cut through it, and Dan couldn't figure out why a newly sharpened chain wouldn't slice through effortlessly as expected. There's only one explanation; the chain must be defective, he thought.

Called Billie and told her I needed another chain. (And some cigarettes.) Hope to hell someone will bring them up to me. Then I spent the afternoon working on the saw. Don't have any idea what I did to it, but it's working for now. So maybe I can get some wood cut tomorrow, for I want to go fishing down on Big Goose Creek on Sunday. But for now, I'm going to lay down and listen to the ball game and then off to dreamland and thoughts of a cigarette and a beer.

That evening, Dan recorded that he had caught four mice in the tent, some of them babies, since the end of January, and 13 mice altogether.

"Where there are little ones, there are big ones, but I'm bound to run out of the little rascals sooner or later."

In the meantime, they were robbing food from Misty and Spuds, carrying it off to hidden nests no one would find. Early one morning, Dan was awakened by a noise and directed the flashlight at Misty and Spuds to find them once more covered with mice that had been stealing the dogs' body warmth as they slept. Now their beady little eyes blinded by the light, the mice quickly scampered off into the woodpile, avoiding the traps, the dogs looking up at Dan unconcerned.

"They were only keeping us warm," they seemed to say.

"This is getting damned ridiculous and disgusting," Dan said. "The damned dirty little varmints. Where did they live before I got here? Do they think this is some sort of mouse motel? Guess I'll have to get more aggressive in setting my traps. Got to get rid of these obnoxious critters before they start sleeping with me, too. The dogs might like their new blanket, but they had better stay away from me."

He turned off the flashlight, turned over in bed, pulling the sleeping bag over most of his head, as he had done the last time the tent was infested, and closed his eyes. Thousands of mice swarmed behind his eyelids, some of them growing into rats with sharp teeth, gnawing everything in the tent, and no matter how hard he tried to replace them with pleasant thoughts, they wouldn't go away. Though the night's blackness was only beginning to turn to into gray dawn, it being too early to start the day, the thought of his winter home taken over by rodents forced him from his bed. He lit the lantern, brought the fire to blazing, and began setting traps. Then a thought occurred to him.

"I wonder where these little creeps are nesting?" he said to Misty and Spuds as though they ought to know something. He lifted the sleeping bag hanging over the side of the bed, got down on his knees, and shined his flashlight into the gaping darkness under it where an old spare sleeping bag he had forgotten about was stored in case it was needed for the dogs or some other purpose.

"Yuk," he exclaimed, carefully pulling it out into the light. Much of it had been gnawed into uselessness, mouse leavings and urine decorating it in scattered blotches. Wincing at the odor, he carefully rolled it up and threw it outdoors to be burned later. Then he continued searching the tent to see what else they might have gotten into and destroyed. "At least they haven't gotten into my food. Thank goodness for plastic tubs."

    Later, as he stuck his knife into the peanut butter jar, he noticed there wasn't much left. It seemed the mice were taking all of it. But he could live without it if it came to that. Eradication, with which he was now obsessed, had suddenly become more important than peanut butter and jelly sandwiches, which he would gladly sacrifice for peace of mind.

Chapter 5

THE GAME WARDEN

Over the past few weeks, time, physical labor, and the mountain had worked their magic on Dan, slowly pulling his mood out of the grim darkness of despair and lifting his spirits. While a chunk of grief remained stuck deep within him and he sometimes still wrestled with the lion of self-criticism that occasionally tried to tear him apart, it no longer dominated his every thought, no longer immobilized him. He was beginning to take control, his upward climb growing easier, and though he had a distance yet to conquer, it didn't seem as formidable as it was weeks ago.

It would have been better if the weather had also made an upward climb but, though the worst of winter should have been over with January's departure, the thermometer's mercury seemed stuck near 20 below, perhaps moving a half inch or so in either direction. Because of it, the stove gobbled wood as fast as Dan could cut it and haul it in. It seemed he would never win his race to get ahead or to even keep up with his diminishing wood supply, for the cold would give him no respite.

All that was positive about the weather lately was that the wind had taken a vacation, and the little clouds that hardly moved in their sea of blue were, for the time being, white as snow and unproductive. The sun occasionally squeezed between the clouds just enough to brighten and prolong daylight a bit and let Dan know it was still there, though it appeared a cold yellow fire in the sky refusing to part with its warmth.

Significant snow was predicted to arrive soon, according to the radio's meteorologists, though sometimes their predictions became truth and other times mistakes. But Dan knew that the mountain, more so than the land below it, was susceptible to heavy spring storms that toppled trees like match sticks, and he wasn't going to chance being caught with even a mediocre wood supply.

A few inches of snow dropped on low elevations usually meant at least twice as much dropped at higher elevations, and it was usually accompanied by strong winds that liked to play with it, speed its coming down, and limit visibility. Not to speak of biting exposed skin and generally making life miserable for anyone or anything caught hiking or attempting to work in it. His instinct for survival told him to use as many tolerable days as possible to cut and stack enough wood inside the tent and even more outside to last several days if a storm decided to immobilize him.

Though his tent stood below the hill encircled by a fortress of tall, thick-trunked, low-branched spruce and lodge pole pines huddled close together, arms overlapping as though to protect his living quarters, the clouds always found the hole above their circle where they dumped large quantities of snow on the tarp that covered his roof, causing it to sag threateningly. And the clever wind, joining forces, gathered speed, pushing its way through gaps in the fortress or climbing over the top, tortuously pushing and pulling at Dan's small habitat like a grizzly bear pulling skin off its catch. Many times, when the snow deepened and the wind picked up, Dan spent a worrisome night envisioning himself and the dogs buried under a fallen roof weighed down by three feet of heavy snow unable to move, his breathing waning, and no one to dig them out.

It was 24 below February 9 when Dan got up early longing for warmth, stoked the fire to roaring dangerously, put on the coffee pot, and climbed back into his sleeping bag where he lay contemplating the day's activities. It was Sunday, and days ago, he had promised himself a day of fishing now that he was ahead with his wood cutting. But in his mind, a sense of duty played a tug of war with his desire for a day off from cutting wood.

Don't know what I'm going to do today. I want to go fishing, but on the other hand, I should get a couple of trees dragged in, for it might snow hard.

He discussed both plans with Misty and Spuds, offering convincing arguments for each plan. "We always need wood," he explained, trying to work logic into his argument. "And it would be good to get further ahead in case a wicked blizzard decides to pile snow so deep around the tent we can't get out. Then we'd be in a terrible fix." Spuds and Misty cocked their heads to the side as though trying to figure out what he was saying.

"But then, we already have a lot of wood," he said, glancing around him. "Think it's enough?" Everywhere he looked, there was wood, piled along every wall, even under his bed. And he wanted more stacked outside his door. It was as though he were obsessed. However, there was his body's need for a respite from woodcutting. And he really would like fish for supper — a welcome change from the packaged food his taste buds now considered mundane.

"How about fish for supper?" he asked Misty and Spuds, who stared at him questioningly. Hearing no argument against it, Dan's mind was made up. It was a meal he promised to share with his canine friends, a promise he didn't wish to break. His body was crying for a break from hard labor and a change in menu, and that was the winning argument for going fishing.

By the time he had finished breakfast and chores and stood in his snowsuit with fishing pole in hand, his gun slung over his shoulder, it was 10:30. He secured the tent door, fastened his snowshoes, and climbed the hill from camp to the trail, Misty and Spuds happily racing back and forth ahead of him, seeming to know where they were going. Though the day was crisp and partly cloudy, the calmness of it made it feel tolerably warm for someone dressed against sub-zero temperatures. As he went, his body warmed even more from the exertion of his snowshoe walk, causing him to lift the flaps on his hat and unzip his snowmobile suit nearly to his waist.

The footbridge crossing the Big Goose River marked the most productive and popular fishing spot on the prairie where, nearing the end of its journey, the river flowed deep and slow in spots. Harbored in its many rock nooks and crannies were good size rainbows and cutthroats resting in the shadows, easily lured into the open by a skilled fly fisherman to grab a quick meal, the unwary ones becoming a meal. Dan knew how to cook them in beer batter to best bring out the flavor.

It was the meal he was thinking about when a half-mile from the bridge, Misty and Spuds stopped and listened, turned to face an invisible enemy, and began to bark loudly and incessantly. Dan stopped as well. Shushing the dogs, he listened, glancing up and down the prairie for the source of something droning softly in the distance, droning that was fast growing into a roar as the source drew closer.

Dan's face lit up like someone who had been stranded in the wilderness for months, facing death, and for whom now the hope of rescue loomed strong. "Snowmobiles," he shouted excitedly to the dogs, as two specks became riders in black suits, unrecognizable in matching helmets that protected their heads and shielded their eyes from the cold and the bright sun bouncing off the snow.

"Hmmm. Must be the game warden. I hope they stop and talk a while," he said as they drew close enough to reveal the emblem on their snow machines and suits. "Sure enough, Game and Fish."

The riders slowed as they approached, looked toward Dan and the barking dogs, then stopped their machines, leaving the engines idling. Dan stood watching, wondering what they were going to do. Suddenly the riders, seeming to recognize him, waved, shut down their machines, and walked toward him.

I'll be damned if it wasn't the game warden and one of his friends. They had come up to check on some moose, and there I was standing with my fishing pole, looking innocent as hell.

The game warden lifted the front of his helmet and stared at Dan. He wouldn't have recognized him if he had met him on the streets of Sheridan, but here on the prairie, the disheveled man staring at them could only be Dan Longwell, changed over time by the rawness of winter. His nearly black, unkempt hair met his shoulders, hanging in strands from his knit cap, some of it meeting his eyebrows. His moustache and untamed beard covered much of the rest of his face. Coffee stains and patches of chainsaw oil decorated his worn snowmobile suit. Three months of hard physical labor and exposure to the cold were reflected in his coal black eyes and in what little face was exposed.

The game warden spoke as though he and Dan had been friends for years. "Hi Dan. How's it going up here? Had enough of winter yet?"

Pulling a cigarette and lighter from his pocket and lighting it, Dan took a deep draw and returned his greeting. After a few minutes of small talk and a pause in the conversation, he waited for the obvious inevitable question that his fishing pole standing like a sentinel beside him was begging someone to ask.

"You heading to the bridge to fish?"

"Yes I was," Dan admitted, taking another draw off his cigarette and blowing the smoke into the wind.

"I don't suppose you have a license."

"Nope." Matter of factly to the ground.

The game warden started to say something, then paused, Dan wondering how much this was going to cost him, but he made no move toward his ticket book. "Well, uh, we're just doing a wild life count today. Nice day for it. Bit nippy, though."

"It is," Dan cautiously agreed.

"You haven't seen any moose hanging around lately or spotted tracks meandering through the prairie, have you?"

"Earlier in the season but not lately. I saw some elk tracks headed toward She Bear a few days ago."

"When you're out and about would you keep track of what you see and mark down locations for me? We've put collars on some of the moose, so if you see a moose that's wearing one, let us know that, too. And the color."

"No, I don't mind keeping a record. In fact, I've already started one. Gives me something to do when I'm not cutting wood or shoveling snow."

"Appreciate that. Good to see you're surviving the winter so well Dan."

Then reaching in his pocket for what Dan was sure would be the ticket book, "By the way, I found your glasses. Thought you might need them."

The game warden handed them to Dan, and he and his friend turned, got on their machines, revved the engines, and drove off, quickly becoming specks in the distance, leaving Dan staring into the prairie, puzzled.

He took a long draw on his cigarette, stomped on the stub, then picked it up and put it in his pocket. "It's not over yet," he told Misty and Spuds, as he turned his snowshoes toward camp. "Need bare fingers to fill out a ticket, so he'll do that in the comfort and warmth of his office." The dogs stared at him. "Don't look at me like that. He knows where I live. In the meantime, I don't want to complicate things. It's back to cutting wood, and sorry, no fish for supper tonight, girls."

When they left, I stashed my fishing gear and came on back to camp the long way around. I was just about there when they were headed back. So they stopped and had coffee and shot the breeze for a while.

Since they had little distance left to go before reaching the bridge, Dan decided to continue to their destination and stash his fishing gear under the bridge in case he wanted to try his luck another day. By the time they had turned around and were nearly at camp, the Game and Fish snowmobiles were again headed toward him.

"Can I get you a cup of coffee?" Dan asked hospitably as they turned off their machines above his camp. This time he wondered if the game warden was going to ask where he put the fishing pole he had been carrying, but the warden seemed not to notice.

"I guess we can stop for a few minutes." The men followed Dan down the hill to the tent where they politely stomped the snow off their boots before walking in, removed their helmets, and sat down at the table, closely followed by their host.

Dan took out his handkerchief, blew his nose, wiped the melting snow from his moustache and beard, and threw a couple of logs on the still-burning coals. "The coffee will be ready in a minute. It's the instant kind. Just have to heat the water. I'd have it ready sooner, but my microwave isn't working right now," he quipped.

When it was ready, the game warden sat with his hands around a hot cup of coffee, sipping occasionally, his eyes surveying the tent as though trying to memorize every detail. He seemed to have forgotten about the ticket and was now engrossed in examining the stack of wood lining two walls from floor to ceiling. "Judging from the amount of wood you have here and piled up outside, you won't have to worry about freezing this winter."

Dan laughed. It wasn't a hearty laugh, for laughter and even smiles didn't come easy for a man who carefully guarded his emotions for fear someone may discover what he was thinking. It seemed the seriousness of his childhood and his developing mistrust of people in his youth had stolen that ability from him, though not his sense of humor. Now his expression became serious.

"Staying supplied is a never-ending job. There have been some damned cold nights up here when I've stayed awake to keep the fire from going out. Eighty pieces of wood in one 50-below night, and I could still see my breath.

But, as you can see, I'm still alive."

The game warden turned serious as well. "How about food? Do you have enough to finish the winter?"

"I'll be taking food home in the spring. Most of it is in those tubs there,

Dan said, pointing to a corner near the bed. A lot of it is packaged food that won't spoil. But I also have eggs, bread, and potatoes. And there's plenty of meat in a barrel outside under the snow. Hell, I could last two winters up here."

"Is that the best place for keeping meat frozen?" The game warden seemed skeptical.

Dan looked at him as though wondering why he would ask. "It's been okay so far."

Satisfied Dan wasn't about to starve and had plenty of warm clothing and other necessary supplies as well, the game warden thought for a moment, then asked, "Have you seen much human activity up here this winter - snow machines, hikers?"

"A snowmobile or two earlier in the winter. Other than that . . " Dan paused, looking suspiciously at the game warden. "A red and white airplane buzzed my camp about a month ago. You wouldn't know anything about that would you?"

The game warden shifted in his chair and laughed. "That was me. Just checking to see if you were okay. You know, you really shouldn't be doing this. The Forest Service kinda frowns on it. Normally no one would be checking. But since we were in the area on a mission anyway . . ."

"I know; I know," Dan interrupted. But he made no excuse for himself.

"Judging from the smoke rising from your tent, the tracks, and evidence of recent activity, I concluded that you were okay. So it was just a hello buzz. The real purpose of our flight was to take an elk count east of here to see how they're surviving the winter. Just made a short detour is all."

"I kinda suspected it was you, but wasn't sure. It about scared the crap out of me. Thought the plane was going to end up on my roof. Burned up my lunch trying to figure out who it was."

Laughing, the game warden put down his coffee cup, stood up, put on his helmet and, thanking his host for the coffee, pulled on his gloves. His friend did the same. "Well, we'd better get going before it gets dark. Thanks again for the coffee; we enjoyed talking with you. Maybe we'll see you again if we get back this way before winter's over."

Dan stood up and offered his hand to both of them. "I'm sure you will."

"And remember to keep track of animal presence for me. Doing that will sort of justify your being here. Sort of like you're working for us."

Dan nodded and followed the men out of the tent, his spirits sinking as he watched them mount their machines, pull down their helmets, wave a final goodbye, and ride slowly into the prairie. Even when they had disappeared, he stood as though savoring the sound of their machines until it faded into the distance. Somehow, he couldn't let go. The game warden's visit had been much too short to satisfy someone who so desperately hungered for human camaraderie. Though his spirits had begun a slow descent as the machines disappeared into the hills, that evening he admitted to his journal that he had had a good day, the best in a long time, and that human visitors had greatly lifted his spirits — at least for a little while. It was as though someone had given him a sumptuous meal, allowing him one bite, and then taken the rest away, leaving him with unsatisfied hunger.

When the game warden and his friend had reached the end of the prairie, far out of Dan's sight, the game warden signaled his companion to pull alongside and stop. Engines idling, they lifted their helmets for a moment of conversation.

"Strange man, that Dan," the game warden said. "I still don't understand what's driving him to do this. He's taking a huge risk. Especially using a chainsaw with no one else around."

"Seems like a loner," his friend responded.

"Yeah, but on the other hand, he seems to like company. I guess months of solitude will do that to a person even if he is a loner. I sure wouldn't want to be up here in the winter. It's a tough life. It's hard for the wild life, and they're used to fighting for survival in extreme conditions."

"Do you think he'll make it? What if he gets caught in blizzard and dies up here?"

"I worry about all that wood, cardboard, paper, and other things piled so close to the stove. Those aren't the best stoves in the world, either. They weren't designed for winter survival."

"No, and that one appears weakened by hard use."

"Nothing much we can do, though, except make periodic welfare checks. Preferably without his knowing it. He's a determined fellow."

The game warden flipped the front of his helmet over his face, a signal to his companion to drive on and continue their task.

It seemed the temperature couldn't please Dan. It was either too cold or too warm, and the condition of his frozen food supply was a constant worry. But when the temperature rose during the day, then plunged to below freezing at night, he reveled in the beauty of a frosty lace-covered prairie and forest, every needle of every tree painted white by an invisible artist who worked quickly in the early morning hours well before the rising sun appeared to destroy his work. However, the beauty of warm temperatures came with a price; the creek began to thaw in the warming sun, threatening his water supply.

The damn creek is starting to thaw, and that's raising hell with my water hole. The pressure of it is building up, and my water is full of melted stuff. It's stale and dirty and doesn't taste good at all, not even in coffee. So I dug that down some today and got it so it runs really good. Now maybe I can get some decent water. Quit early today for the fog really set in, and that stuff is cold. Going to have hot beef sandwiches for supper because it comes in a can. After I ate, I ended up going out and cutting down another tree right by camp that I hadn't noticed. I had to have ridden by it a thousand times. Got most of it brought in, so I'll get it chopped up tomorrow.

    Supper and chores over, Dan stepped into the night to let Misty and Spuds have one last run before bedtime. As he stared into the inky blackness of the universe, it seemed to him the cloudless sky had dropped closer to earth. Sparkling like diamonds embedded in black velvet, a myriad of stars and galaxies so close he felt he could almost touch them winked at him. He stood frozen, awed by their vast number, their brightness, and their closeness. The big dipper balanced on its handle, ready to scoop him into the black abyss. And toward the south, there was the hunter with his diamond-studded belt, a friend looking down at Dan, so near they could almost shake hands. Suddenly Dan was a miniscule speck smaller than a grain of sand in the ocean of solar systems and galaxies that blinked down at him, and he marveled that he was part of it, insignificant as he was.

    The wonder of the universe sparkling with busyness could have kept him there until the stars disappeared into the rising sun if it hadn't been for the biting wind forcing him toward warmth and the comfort of bed. But first, he strained to listen over the faint scratching of the dogs wrestling in the snow, hoping to hear sounds of life in the distance. But the coyotes were silent. All he could hear was the vast, lifeless universe and the stirrings of the wind telling him how alone he was with an enemy that wanted him dead.

    As he stood listening, he could hear his father's voice whispering from the void. "I know how much you hated me. I stole your childhood, and I'm sorry for that. But don't ever forget, I made you strong. Self-reliant. Loneliness can be as unbearable as the harshness of the winter winds and snows if you let it. But if you survive it, it will be because of me. You could never have done it without the lessons I held you to in your youth. Some day you'll thank me for being so hard on you; you'll see."

    Dan stood silent for a moment, wondering if his father had anything else to say, then whistled at Misty and Spuds, who emerged from the dark woods, and disappeared into the warmth of his tent. His father hadn't been convincing. "I don't need them," he had often thought to himself when people around him had been particularly annoying. "They don't know what respect is. I can get along just fine without them."

    Though he was confident he would survive the winter and loneliness on his own, a hunger for human companionship would haunt him until he eagerly filled his backpack and headed down the mountain at the first sign of spring's arrival. Without Misty and Spuds, he may not have survived this long, he told himself.

    "Heck. They know my whole life story by now. But it isn't the same.

All they can do when I talk to them is acknowledge with a blank stare, a wag of their tails, and an occasional woof. And most of the time, they just fall asleep. Some listeners they are."

The next morning, he called Billie to tell her he had spent his last drop of chainsaw gas cutting down a tree the day before and needed someone to bring him another supply. Afterward, he wished he hadn't called. Billie responded unsympathetically to his request, telling him what he knew but didn't want to hear, that the purpose of his adventure on the mountain was to survive the winter alone through self-sufficiency, depending on no one, cutting all ties to civilization. And especially to shopping centers.

I got the riot act. "Why didn't you take up enough when you were packing everything up this summer?" With trying to get everything up here, I just flat out forgot it. Now that I have been up here for a while, there are over 100 things I could use but I will make out one way or the other without. That's the reason I'm up here is to do things on my own instead of running to the store every day. It's just that you have to set your mind to it and stay off the damn radio asking for everyone to bring you something. Well, time to forget all this crap and go for a walk. Can't cut wood the easy way and since I have plenty of wood for now I'm going to go for a walk.

More disgusted with himself than he was with Billie, Dan fed the stove, picked up his camera and rifle, and with several hours of daylight remaining, caught the trail to the Big Goose River intending to pick up his fishing pole and drop his line in from the bridge, unconcerned about his not having a license, for it wasn't likely that anyone would be there to report him anyway.

By the time he arrived at the bridge, his temper had cooled and, though he had picked it up, he decided to leave his fishing pole under the bridge, just in case. He stood momentarily staring down at the mesmerizing swirling water, noting the peacefulness of it, placed the pole back in its hiding place, and began hiking toward She Bear intending to see how close to the top he could get before he'd have to turn back toward camp to avoid traveling in the dark. It was his day off and, if he couldn't go fishing, he intended to enjoy it by exploring.

He knew there was a cave somewhere toward the top inviting him to visit, some unusual rock formations waiting to be examined, and perhaps some elk or coyotes to photograph. What he didn't realize was that the snow was deeper toward the top than on the trail below the mountain and that the hiking wasn't going to be easy for any of them.

Well, I went to the top, but getting there was a bitch, for it's straight up, and with all the snow, it's hip deep. I thought that was bad, but it was twice that deep on top. Could only walk 10 feet at a time; then it was rest time. I didn't walk all the way down the other side, for I wasn't sure where I would come out. So I just stayed on top and looked around. It was pretty neat. I got lots of pictures, but didn't see one coyote or even a track of one. Don't know where they disappeared to. Did see one moose, though.

From the top of She Bear, Dan could see a great distance across the forested rolling hills and white meadows to high snow-covered peaks 15 to 20 miles distant. It was an awesome sight looking down on hawks effortlessly soaring the thermals high above the tree tops, yet below him, searching for a meal or just being lazy or showing off their magnificent flight skills. As he approached the mountain's face, he could see small trees poking through the snow in the distance, but he was wise enough to know that danger lurked there, for these were no small trees. A few steps closer and he could sink deep into the snow near the submerged tree bottoms 40 feet below him, never able to free himself.

Instead of continuing in that direction, Dan turned and scanned the distant hills, delighting in recognizing familiar landscapes that marked places he had camped in his motor home during the summer. He stood mesmerized for a while, admiring the magnificent beauty and the power and vastness of the mountain. Until spring arrived, these endless acres as far as he could see were all his, for there was no human with whom to share them, only occasional snowmobiles passing through. And when they traveled too close to his tent, Dan considered them trespassing. He was especially critical of people who littered — a gum wrapper here, a pop or beer bottle there — or who chased deer, elk, or moose with their snow machines or ATV's. They had no business on the mountain, and if Dan had his way, they would be prohibited from setting foot in the national forest, for they showed no respect for it.

"Sure looks different in the winter, doesn't it?" he said to the dogs, pointing out how the mountain's white attire disguised familiar rocks, buried trails and frozen streams, and shortened full-grown trees. But Dan wasn't fooled. He knew where the rivers ran, knew the location of most of the rock formations, had memorized every draw, and had familiarized himself with many of the open meadows Wyoming people call parks.

"After you study it for a while, you recognize things," he told Misty and Spuds. "See that over there? About seven miles distant behind that hill is where the ranger station is." Misty and Spuds looked up at him unimpressed. "We'll hike down a little ways and then go back," he said. "Don't go too far, and watch where you step."

During the afternoon, the wind crept in on tennis shoes, pushing the white clouds that had decorated the sky earlier off the mountain to allow room for an army of large gray, ominous clouds that quickly blended into one another to move in, covering what little blue there was with a low, moisture-filled blanket. But Dan's attention was on navigating deep snow and admiring rocks and the caves imbedded in the mountain wall that were invisible from a distance, and the panoramic view as they neared the top of She Bear.

Somewhere on the back side of She Bear, Dan stooped to examine tracks leading toward the east that had become blurred in the snow. "Are those dog tracks?" he asked himself doubtfully. "They're awfully big. Bigger than dog tracks." For a moment, he thought of following them, but they were heading away from camp, and he thought better of it. That would be a trip for another day.

He had been so absorbed in examining tracks and admiring the view that he barely noticed the sun slipping away, the sky turning ominous. Nor did he feel the dampness creeping in. By the time he thought of turning around, daylight was waning, the wind had picked up, and large wet snowflakes were dropping from what seemed a slow-leaking faucet. He zipped his snowsuit to his neck, pulled his collar up against the wind, and covered his ears.

"C'mon girls," he called to the dogs. "I lost track of time. We'd better get back before it really opens up." The deep snow made it difficult for him to turn his snowshoes around, and though he stumbled, he managed it without falling. Every step tightened the muscles in his legs and put more effort into his breathing. Concern for their safety was beginning to dominate his mind.

Misty and Spuds had nearly as difficult a time as their master negotiating the deep heavy snow and could only make a few feet before stopping to rest, panting with the effort. By now, the sky had lowered the clouds to ground level and was dropping and blowing snow hard and fast. Dan couldn't see beyond the extension of his walking stick. To make things worse, the thick cloud cover and resulting storm had begun to darken the mountain early, and they were still far from camp. Unless the storm quickly played out its wrath and hurried on, there would be no returning to a warm tent and the comfort of a soft bed that night. "We'll never make it back to camp in this," he told Misty and Spuds, trying not to show his concern. "Now where's that cave I spotted earlier? We'll head for that — if we can find it."

He stood for a moment, trying to get his bearings, trying to remember landmarks. But rapidly diminishing visibility made it increasingly difficult to know where anything was. He would have to go by instinct. Snow machines had made a packed, worn path to the cave, but it would soon be unrecognizable under several inches of new snow.

"It can't be much farther. We'll just have to watch for it. If we miss it, we're in big trouble." A large rock marked the cave's entrance. Of that, Dan was certain. If he could only find it, they would have it made. Providing the cave was unoccupied, they would be safe there until the storm let up, if it were going to let up.

A strong wind gust pushed hard against Dan's back, nearly sending him face down into the deepening snow, but with the help of his walking stick, he managed to stay on his feet. He knew that, if he went down with his snowshoes on, it would be a difficult, lengthy struggle to get to his feet again, and the wind biting his bearded face and gloved hands, trying to push icy fingers through his snowmobile suit, was beginning to sap his strength.

"The temperature is dropping, too," he thought. "If I don't find that cave soon . . ." He stopped to catch his breath and wipe the snow from his eyes. But he must. If wasn't an option. "You can do it if you put your mind to it," he told himself as he trudged on, his snowshoes sinking into the new snow. Though travel was difficult for them, Misty and Spuds led the way, seeming to know where they were going, an occasional yip floating faintly through the fog of swirling snow, telling Dan they were fairly close and weren't going to leave him.

With the repeated effort of lifting his feet out of the deep snow and setting them down again and the increasing heaviness of his snowshoes, he was growing more fatigued. "Mustn't give up," he kept telling himself. A few weeks ago, he would have gladly sat down and allowed the storm to turn him into an ice statue so he could join his friend where ever he was in the great beyond.

But, several serious discussions with himself and his canine companions about leaving this world, just allowing winter to take him, brought him to a different mind.

"I'm right behind you," he yelled to Misty and Spuds, hoping their yips would keep floating back to him, telling him where they were so he could follow.

He trudged on, trying not to think of the outcome should they miss the cave and spend the night in the open at the storm's mercy. Winter will have won. The dogs may find a place to hunker down, but someone would find his body in the spring when the snow melted and wonder if that had been his purpose. At his funeral his friends would say to one another, "I told him his idea was foolish, that he'd never make it. Staying the winter in a tent? What was he thinking? I always thought he was a little . . ., you know, off balance."

"Stop it!" he scolded himself. "Just stop thinking that way. We're going to make it. I made a mistake and let down my guard. I'll never do that again. But I'll live to tell them I wasn't as foolish as they thought. I'll live to tell them I'm a stronger person than they are for having won this battle. I doubt they could have done the same. Misty and Spuds will find that cave."

His anger at himself giving him renewed energy, he tenaciously bent into the raging wind and pushed on, thinking he knew his feet were somewhere in his boots, though he could no longer feel them, or his fingers for that matter.

Chapter 6

SCREAM IN THE NIGHT

Dan could barely see Misty and Spuds' tracks a foot or two ahead of him as he bent low and turned into the wind with renewed energy and determination, the fast-falling snow erasing them as quickly as he spotted them. As far as he could tell, they were leading him in the right direction, but keeping their tracks in sight before they vanished took all the energy he could muster. That and the effort spent keeping his snowshoes near the top of the deepening snow. Though relentlessly bitter, the wind took an occasional break, offering flashes of visibility, during which Dan studied what surroundings he could see in an eye blink in an effort to get his bearings.

Years of experience and an occasional mistake had made him wise to the mountain's antics. He knew not to be caught in a canyon or to test the snow in an area he had never explored in summer, or to wander too deep into an unfamiliar forest. Seasons and weather were known to play tricks on unwary human minds, disguising familiar places, hiding them in fog. And, in winter, hiding familiar summer landmarks and frozen streams in ever-deepening snow. It seemed the mountain enjoyed playing with one's sense of direction, rendering inexperienced travelers hopelessly lost and at its mercy, its laughing streams and whispering wind seeming to repeat mockingly, "ignorant flatlander."

After what seemed like miles of fighting the deep snow and merciless wind, the tip of his snowshoe slammed against something hard, nearly throwing him off balance. "Damn! Where did that come from? Could've broken my snowshoe," Dan exclaimed.

As he started to go around it, he suddenly realized it could be the rock he was looking for. "That would be too good to be true," he said to himself as he stopped and brushed the snow off one side to examine it closely. "It seems to be the right size and the right shape. It's gotta be the one."

If it were, the cave would be to his right, he guessed, turning his snowshoes toward the rising hill. He whistled to the dogs, hoping they hadn't gone so far ahead they wouldn't hear him over the whining wind. To his relief, they were beside him in seconds, wagging their tails as though they were as relieved as he was. He could tell that they, too, were tired and cold, snow-covered, and eager to seek shelter.

"We're going this way," he yelled at them as he started the climb. "It's only a few yards to shelter now, girls. Soon we'll be toasty warm, but the sad thing is, we'll miss supper. If I could only find that trail to the cave." But Misty and Spuds weren't listening. As if they understood what their master was saying and where they were going, they had gone ahead, leaving Dan to struggle on his own, eager to get out of the wet snow and biting wind.

"I think I missed it," Dan said. "Maybe that wasn't the right rock. I should have found it by now." He stopped and poked his walking stick into the snow. After several tries, it hit an area of packed snow a few inches down. "The snowmobile trail," he exclaimed. "That's why I couldn't find it; it was buried just like everything else. Why didn't I know that?"

Just then, he saw two dark eyes peering through a curtain of white, and for a frightening moment, he thought it was a wolf or a coyote. But it was only Misty staring at him from her snow blanket, who had come to lead him the last few feet to the cave. Once inside, she shook off as much snow as she could and stood looking up at Dan as though he were a stranger, himself draped in white, his once-black hair turned gray, his moustache and beard turned to ice. But the sound of his voice assured her it was Dan and not a stranger intending harm.

His first impulse was to search the cave to make sure it wasn't already occupied, something he figured the dogs had already done, but that he decided to do anyway, just to be certain. Satisfied they were the cave's sole occupants, he took off his snowshoes, glad to be rid of them, leaned them and his rifle against the wall, and brushed the snow from his snowmobile suit.

The cave was well used — a popular campsite in summer, a shelter from heavy rain storms for hikers and horseback riders, and a winter shelter as well. When Dan first discovered it, he was surprised to see a stack of wood and a small pile of kindling leaning against one wall, and charred remnants of a campfire scattered on the stone floor. Whoever had used the cave last had restocked it in anticipation of using it for shelter another time, or kindly considering someone else may need it. It was a shallow cave that faced away from the wind, narrow and deep enough to keep a fire's warmth from escaping through the entrance, and high enough that Dan could stand without hitting his head on its ceiling.

There should be enough wood here to last the night, Dan thought, picking up the kindling. With stiff fingers, he pulled his emergency fire-starting kit from the inside pocket of his snowmobile suit, arranged a small amount of kindling in the center of the ring, and held a match to it. Soon the fire was blazing, ready for larger logs that would keep it going. Kneeling, he held his hands over the fire to thaw his fingers. Misty and Spuds lay as close to it as they could, contentedly absorbing its warmth as their eyes closed in temporary sleep. Snow

Photo by Dan Longwell

The cave on She Bear mountain provided welcome overnight shelter.

that had clung to their coats gradually turned to water that dripped onto the cave floor and quickly disappeared.

Dan sat by the fire contemplating the situation. "Doesn't look like it's going to let up any time soon," he said to no one, aiming his flashlight into the storm. The snow seemed to be coming down heavier with each minute that passed and the late afternoon had come to evening's full darkness. "Guess we'll be here for the night." He had no problem with that; his emergency equipment was always with him whenever he left camp, and now he pulled it from his pack and readied it for the night's stay.

"We decided to spend the night. Didn't have much choice because, when you're wearing five-foot snowshoes, you don't want to come down off She Bear when you can't see, because your snowshoes get stuck underneath trees, and the only thing you're going to do is fall on your butt, and that's just a good way to get hurt.

After sharing some water and part of a sandwich left over from lunch with Misty and Spuds, who at the rattling of its wrapper had become alert, Dan lay down his tarp, picked up his rifle, found as comfortable a spot by the fire as the cave with its hard uneven floor offered, and set the rifle within reach in case a wild four-footed intruder should appear seeking refuge from the storm. The thought of coyotes approaching wasn't a concern. Misty could handle them. It was the mountain lions he feared. They roamed the prairie in summer and, though he hadn't seen tracks so far this winter, he knew they were around. But perhaps he had seen tracks, he thought, pursuing a flicker of memory.

"Those tracks we saw earlier this afternoon, the ones I couldn't identify," he said to Misty and Spuds, who were half asleep by this time. "Could have been cat tracks." Their sleeping quarters might not be far from this cave, he thought. Bears should be snug in their dens, sound asleep for the winter, but wild animals were unpredictable.

At their master's invitation, Misty and Spuds huddled close to him, as he covered himself with the heat blanket he carried in his backpack and lay on the tarp as close to the fire as he dared. The dogs were soon snoring, but for him, sleep would come in spurts that night, a chill from the dying fire, which begged to be fed, waking him occasionally for that purpose. Each time he awoke, he searched the cave with his flashlight and lay listening for an intruder that may be wandering in, his free hand gripping his rifle. Satisfied they didn't have company, he turned off the flashlight and allowed his eyes to close.

As he lay dozing, his father's words surfaced in his mind as they often did when he was lonely or ran out of things to think about or let his mind have free rein to wander where it would. Sometimes it seemed his father's ghost wouldn't leave him alone. It was here, on the mountain, following him where ever he went. Though Dan had forgiven his father long ago, anger caused by his father's disciplines and lack of love remained dormant in a dark corner of his subconscious, summoned when he was least aware by some distasteful event or aggravating person in his life. Try as he may to get rid of the anger and leave the past to quietly disintegrate, he couldn't, for it clung to him like a predator to its prey. It seemed he needed his father's memory to justify his actions - needed his father's approval, even in the after-life. But nothing had ever been resolved. No discussions had taken place, no acceptable reasons and no apologies given for his father's actions.

"If my father were still alive, what would he think of me now," he asked himself bitterly. "The same as other people? That I'm foolish for doing this?   That everything I do is a mistake? That I'm incapable of making wise choices? He destroyed my childhood. For that, I forgave him. But try as I may, I can't forget."

Toward morning, Dan awoke in the blackness of an absentee sun, shivering. The fire had burned down to little red coals that seemed to have trouble enough keeping themselves warm. The dogs, curled nose to tail next to him, stirred but didn't awaken as he got up, coaxed the fire to full blaze, and lay down again. By the time daylight peeked into the cave and poked his eyelids into waking, the fire had burned down to coals and ashes again. The cave had remained tolerably warm overnight, its narrow walls trapping the heat, and for that, Dan was satisfied. Hearing their master stir, Misty and Spuds opened their eyes, stretched, got up, and licked his face, their tails wagging. They were hungry and eager to get back to camp where they knew their food, and perhaps a bite or two of their master's as well was waiting.

Understanding it was food they were craving and that he was craving it as well, Dan walked over to his pack sitting against the cave wall. The dogs followed, their tails sweeping the cave floor, their eyes fastened to their master's hands. "I have two candy bars left," he said, pulling them out of his pack. As he unwrapped the candy, Misty and Spuds sat at his feet eagerly begging for a morsel. Dan divided one candy bar, gave half to each dog, which they gobbled in one bite, nearly taking his hand with it, and ate the other one himself. The dogs stared at him as though to ask, "Where's the rest of it? Is that all we get? How selfish of you to take it all."

"That's as good as it gets for now, you gluttons. See? No more," he said, showing them his empty hands. Still hungry, the dogs sniffed the floor searching for crumbs that may have been dropped. "Okay. Let's get going," Dan told them as he piled snow on the remaining coals, picked up his gear and plunged his walking stick into three feet of new snow. "This could be a long, difficult hike. I just hope my legs hold up."

The wind was nearly nil in the bright sunshine of morning, and the temperature had risen comfortably overnight. "Going to be a nice day today," Dan said, putting on his sunglasses and examining the sky. "I hope it doesn't get too warm, though." Partway down the trail, he stood for a moment amused by the antics of three small clouds that broke the plainness of the intense indigo sea overhead.

It was really quite amusing, for there was only three little white fluffy clouds in the sky, and everything else was clear and blue and sunny. But these three clouds were just going around and around pouring snow. Yet, when you looked straight up, there wasn't a cloud to be seen. Just clear blue sky and sunshine, and that snow looked like diamonds falling from the sky. Then all of a sudden, you would see this little bitty white cloud coming over. It was really neat to watch.

Misty and Spuds wisely followed in Dan's tracks where negotiating the deep snow was easier for them, sometimes placing their front feet on his snowshoes to keep from falling in. Drifts that had been deep the day before had grown significantly deeper overnight making going down She Bear more troublesome than the climb the day before, even with snowshoes. But once they were on the main trail that connected all the hunting camps below the hill, they made better time, arriving at camp by early afternoon, hungry, tired, and need of warmth. Dan's plan was to get a good fire going first so they could fill their stomachs by the comfort of a warm stove while regaining some lost energy.

As they approached camp from the top of the hill, his priorities suddenly changed, though not of his choosing. His eyes grew wide, and his spirits sank as he stared down at his storm-devastated camp. Snow buried a portion of the tent, its roof sagging hopelessly on one side where a five-foot drift reached over the roof's top, leaning heavily on the tarp. The door was barely visible behind a wind-arranged snow pile he estimated to be more than three-feet deep.

It was as though Mother Nature were admonishing him for allowing himself to be caught in a storm that forced him to spend the night away from camp. "You were negligent, and now you expected no consequences? Fooled you, didn't I?"

Judging from the thick gathering of new snow on She Bear, he had suspected the storm had done the same in camp over night and was prepared for it, but was disappointed when he saw that the storm's eagerness to destroy the tent had nearly succeeded. Much of his energy spent from the difficult trek home and badly in need of rest, Dan set down his gear, picked up his shovel, and began clearing the roof and doorway while Misty and Spuds, eager to be fed, dug at the snow in an effort to speed his progress.

Dan shoved them aside impatiently. "You're in my way," he yelled at them. "Lunch will have to wait until we can get in and get a fire going, and I can do it much faster without your help." Misty and Spuds knew his tone of voice as a warning to be taken seriously and contented themselves with sitting a distance back, watching, but with little patience.

The wall that encircled camp with less than a foot of snow in early winter had grown steadily with each snowstorm. When Dan had left camp the day before, it was six feet high and, by the time he had finished shoveling from this last storm, the wall had grown to 10 feet because there was no place else to put it. Though concerned about spring melting, which he saw as an unavoidable problem, he would deal with it when the time came, he thought. At the moment, he was too tired and hungry to think about it.

That evening, he treated himself to pork chops and stuffing, sharing with Misty and Spuds who had worked hard to keep him safe during the storm and had kept him company while he cleared snow. Afterward, he sat on the bed, legs stretched in front of him, the dogs by his side, reflecting on the previous day's adventure and the post-storm cleanup that had depleted his energy and caused his legs to begin knotting. In spite of all that had gone wrong, the day hadn't all been bad, he thought.

Saw one moose above camp on the way back today. She stopped right here above camp, then trotted off. Called Billie to find out if Lloyd and them were going to make it up today. I guess he can't get a day off, but he would try to get up sometime this week.

While he was on the hill, he called Billie, who perhaps sensing Dan's desperate loneliness and concerned about his well-being, promised to come up with the rest of the family for a visit the first Sunday in March, and Dan was happy about that. Though two weeks off, it gave him something to think about and look forward to when his spirits began to drop. He hadn't seen another human in several weeks and the family since Christmas. That was two months too long, he thought pensively. It was family he missed the most, and being away from them so long fueled his loneliness.

Normally, he considered people in general a pain that he was better off without, for he found them curious about things that weren't their business and often dishonest. Dropped into situations where human activity forced him into a closeness he found stifling, he longed for escape. But on the prairie in the deep quiet of winter when there were no humans around or even signs that they exist, loneliness was like being dropped into a black-as-ink hole where, if you fell too far, you would never escape. In the summer, Dan could crawl into a secluded spot with his camper and enjoy as many days of mountain solitude as he desired. Loneliness didn't bother him then, for proof of human existence, if he desired it, wasn't far from him.

Bored and lonely after concluding his conversation with Billie, he picked a book off the stack on his night table and jumped into its pages, soon absorbed by the story that unfolded within them, until his head began to nod, and sleep became inevitable. Misty and Spuds hadn't moved since supper. They lay beside him on the bed, their soft occasional snores, soon joined by Dan's louder ones, the only sounds breaking the night silence.

Dan awoke early the next morning feeling refreshed. A calendar hung on a support pole next to his bed, each day that had passed marked with a huge X. Not only did it keep him apprised of remaining days of winter, but should he die here, the calendar would reveal his last day on earth to anyone who cared. Today was February 17. Not long before spring, he thought, as he turned the radio to Swap Shop, a buy, sell, and give-away program much like a garage sale, broadcast daily from Sheridan. If something offered aroused his interest and was cheap enough, he would call Billie and ask her to buy it for him — if he dared. He laughed at the thought. That might be pushing it with Billie. So that wasn't likely to happen, nor was it his intent; the radio merely connected him with local and world happenings, and assured him he wasn't alone in the world, just on the prairie. And it kept him in touch with time, especially when his watch batteries froze.

Outdoor temperatures were beginning to moderate toward spring, though they were still capable of arctic nastiness, rolling up and down and keeping him guessing. This morning, it was 18 degrees and climbing, the tent warming nicely for dressing and undressing. A perfect day for a shower and clean clothes, Dan thought. But only Dan, whose body had acclimated to constant cold, would think that way. This would be his second shower since winter began and likely to be his last until he was home with running water as steamy as he wanted to make it. But now, with visitors coming soon, he thought it a good idea not to smell like something rotting in the closet.

"Taking a shower isn't something you do every day, or even every week up here," he told Misty and Spuds, who looked at him as though asking why not. "The water would be frozen to my blue body before I could grab a towel." In no hurry to get to it, he took his time with breakfast, sitting at the table reading and sipping coffee while the stove heated a couple of gallons of water and the tent enough to allow him to strip down without freezing. When finished with breakfast, he dug in his clothes tub for clean underwear, a shirt and a pair of jeans for quick dressing and set them near the stove. A second tub was filled with clothes that had been part of his skin for several weeks. These he sorted for washing.

Well, it started getting real warm out, so I set up my shower and scrubbed myself good, then got more water and washed clothes. I had to heat 30 gallons of water for that ordeal, but I'm glad it's done for a while. Have clothes hanging everywhere. Wish they would dry so I could get back in the tent without knocking something down. The high today was 34. Wish it would cool off just a little, or I won't have any meat left worth eating.

Dan's shower was a large plastic tub near the stove, and a shower bag with a spigot filled with hot water that hung from a rope above the tub. Stripping down, he stepped into the tub and released the water a little at a time as he soaped his body and long scraggly hair. By the time he was ready for rinsing, the water had edged toward cold, and he was in a hurry to get it over with. It was a messy process, water splashing everywhere, Dan uttering an occasional "Damn, it's cold!"

As the water began to flow and splash onto the floor, Misty and Spuds, wondering if they would be next, scrambled under the bed, nearly colliding with each other in the effort. When he was finished, he turned off the water and, grabbing a towel, wrapped it around himself and stepped out of the tub, shivering. "There's more water on the floor than there is in the tub," he commented to Misty and Spuds. Then looking around, he realized they were no longer in sight. "Hmmm, must have gone outside." When he had dressed, dumped the dirty water, and put the shower away, the dogs, feeling safe, crawled out from under the bed.

"You sissies. Did you think you two were next in the tub? I know you could use a bath, but I'm not going to subject you to it. Too cold, and I'd have a hard time getting you dry. Now I have a mess to clean up, and fighting to give you two baths would have made it a bigger one," he told them. "Seems my work is never done as it is."

Later in the day, his clean clothes hung up inside and outside the tent to dry, Dan went outside and pulled a roast from the barrel that stored his frozen food. It was partially thawed and dark spots were beginning to grow on it. He took it inside and cut off the chunks that were spoiled, wondering how much of the remaining meat in the barrel was turning bad. Recalling how much he had spent on food for the winter, Dan decided to throw as little of it as necessary. "It's too expensive to waste," he told Misty and Spuds.

Meat would have to be his main course from now until he left the mountain or until it became too spoiled to eat. He would continue to throw away the spoiled parts and eat the rest, hoping to avoid getting sick. That night, he made hot roast beef sandwiches with green beans, sharing the scraps with his canine friends.

February 19: It's after 11, and I'm going for a walk after I get water and wood hauled in. I'm expecting Lloyd to come up some time this week with some much-needed supplies, so I want to stay close. Later in the day: No one showed up, so I walked behind camp to see if I could find any moose tracks, but I didn't. The wind was blowing about 40 miles per hour. Couldn't even stand up. The temperature is 28 degrees, but it doesn't feel like it with this wind. Several times during the evening, I thought the tent was going to come right up. And if it does, it's going to find me in bed, for that's where I'm headed for now.

When he awoke the next morning, the tent hadn't fallen. Gray clouds blanketed the sky, dropping snow in spurts, behavior that would continue through the day. "Wish it would just snow like hell for a while and get it over with. Then I would be happy," Dan told Misty and Spuds as he worked to keep the snow cleared from in front of the tent.

The wind that had blown incessantly the previous day continued its tenacious attack on the tent as though to test Dan's patience, repeatedly pulling and pushing it and blowing snow back into areas he had just cleared. Its persistent battering bent the stovepipe, laying it horizontal. Now all else would have to wait until the stovepipe was restored to its former condition and fully operable. The wind worked hard at making the task a miserable one, throwing snow pellets in his face, pulling at the tent, and working hard to grab the pipe from him and throw him off balance.

"Haven't you had enough of this?" the wind seemed to be taunting. "Why don't you just pack up and leave the mountain. Can't you tell by now it doesn't want you here? I'll make your life so miserable you won't ever come back. Winter isn't over yet, Dan. Worse is coming. You wait and see. Spring won't come without a fight."

Dan stubbornly stood and faced the wind as it tried to knock him down. He braced himself against it, ignoring its taunts. He had been through too much to give in now, and spring wasn't far off. The stove could be fixed, the snow kept clear, and the tent put back up if it should fall. He wouldn't be beaten. Especially now, so close to spring, so close to beating the odds. There was too much to lose.

I straightened that and the top of the stove and cleaned it out good and put it back together, and it still works. Going to attempt to make popcorn and get ready for the Wyoming basketball game. Well, got it made, but I ate it before the game came on.

Dealing with continuing snow the past few days was occupying so much of his time he had little left for cutting wood. In spite of it, he had to maintain his chainsaw, for there was a good chunk of winter's nastiness and sub-zero temperatures left, and his wood supply was dwindling. What tools he needed for the job, but was missing, he compensated for through ingenuity he didn't realize he had.

Worked on the chainsaw, and I finally got it fixed. Had to put on a new starter rope but didn't have an Allen wrench to tear it apart. So I made one out of a nail. I really didn't think it would work, but it did. So I did get one tree cut down and two pieces dragged in. The damned thing fell the wrong way. The snow is about four feet deep, and I can't get close enough to it with my snowshoes to tramp it down because of the branches. So, I was waist deep in snow trying to cut it up and cut the branches off. It was not fun at all. Plus that it was still snowing. What a pain. Hopefully, I will get parts to fix it next Sunday, for that's when Billie is supposed to come up. Need to call Billie and finish putting in my order.

That evening, Dan dug into his meat supply again, finding a couple of packages of steak that would satisfy a lumberjack's appetite. He took out one package and set it near the stove to thaw, then continued to stack wood inside the tent. Unwrapping it later, he was surprised to find it was spoiled. Not even a small piece could be salvaged for a meal.

Disappointed that the supper he had hungered for was out of the question, he went outside and checked the rest of his meat. One package of hamburger and the bacon seemed good, but he hadn't dug to the bottom. He had already eaten some meat that had turned light green, cutting it in strips and cooking it well, figuring if it were cooked long enough to kill the spoilage, it would be safe. But most of the steak, pork chops, remaining hamburger, and roast were all too spoiled to chance even thorough cooking.

"I guess it's hamburgers for supper," he told Misty and Spuds who stared at him expectantly. "I know; I'm disappointed, too. Seems all we eat is hamburgers. But I don't need to be cleaning up after sick dogs — or a sick me.

We'd better use the hamburger before it turns bad, too."

Misty and Spuds sat opposite each other on chairs pulled close to the small square table Dan had built for camping, looking at him as though expecting him to take their order. "I know you're hungry. So am I. But you can eat your own food until I get these hamburgers cooked."

Puzzled as to why his meat would spoil in below-freezing temperatures, Dan turned to his journal that evening to relieve his frustrations. Meat was expensive; too expensive to throw away. But nothing could be done about it, so there was no use whining. It was bad enough eating his own cooking when all winter his hankering had been for Billie's. Now he would have to be satisfied with meatless packaged meals until he left the mountain; unless he could get someone to bring him a new supply of meat. After the chewing out he'd gotten from Billie several days ago, he wondered if he dared ask.

How the hell can it go bad when it's been this cold is beyond me. It's warming up a little every morning, but not enough to spoil meat. So guess I'll live on pancakes and soup for a while.

That night, Dan's dream about spoiled meat and Billie chastising him for not planning well enough when he was packing up supplies in the fall disturbed his sleep. Restless, he stared at the tree shadows that, helped by a partial moon, created motionless patterns on the tent walls. "Must not be cloudy tonight," he thought. "And the moon must be nearly full. That would make it a good night for a walk in the moonlight. But by the way it feels in here, it's going to be too cold a night for that."

Unable to fight his restlessness, he got up several times and fed the fire, then lay listening to Misty and Spuds snoring until he drifted off again. He was sleeping dreamless and sound when a sudden noise woke him. It wasn't an ordinary noise like a shoe dropping, or a lamp tipping over. It was a noise that aroused in him an emotion bordering on terror. Quickly untangling himself from the sleeping bag, he sat up, his heart pounding. He lit the lantern, and listened. Misty and Spuds were awake, their hair standing on end. They, too, were frightened. Misty stood alert, listening, while Spuds quickly dived under the bed, thinking herself safe from a scary invader attempting to get her.

Dan's brain kicked in. It was a scream they had heard, a horrific, terrifying scream, as though coming from a woman being brutally murdered. Suddenly it came again, sending chills down Dan's back. Something was suffering a horrible torturous death, too horrible to fathom, and it was much too close. He had heard it once before, long ago, and he knew what it was. He scrambled out of bed, grabbed his rifle hanging on a nail near the door, made sure it was loaded, and settled back into his sleeping bag. His rifle would be his companion and sleeping partner the rest of his days on the mountain, he vowed. At night, he would be ready if anything forced its way through the tent door.

    Though the night turned silent, except for a light breeze pushing pine branches into a low whisper, Dan could no longer sleep. He lay down and pulled his sleeping bag to his chin, careful not to obstruct his hearing, his hand on the rifle, straining to remain alert, listening in case that horrible scream pierced the black silence again. But all he heard was the sound of his heart pounding.

    Nevertheless, he dared not sleep in case the predator decided to make him and his dogs the next victims. Misty kept watch a while longer, then hearing nothing more, settled into sleep. Spuds opted to remain under the bed safely hidden, leaving the protecting to Misty, unaware that her occasional snores revealed her hiding place. Though he managed to fight it successfully for a long while, sleep eventually overcame Dan too, leaving them all vulnerable to whatever ghosts haunted the prairie.

    Daylight crept in peacefully and without event. All scary monsters had melted away with the blackness of night, and all was safe. Hearing friendly sounds of life in the tent as Dan sat up, yawned, and left his bed to fill the stove, Spuds slowly crawled from her hiding place, poking her head out and looking around first, and with a wagging tail, pushed her way to the tent door where she paused, cautiously checking for intruders, then ran off to join Misty in a morning romp.

    When Dan stepped outside that morning, he checked the cleared paths and a huge circumference around camp for tracks, but found none other than his own and that of the dogs. He stayed close to camp that morning cutting and chopping wood, looking up from his work often to scan his surroundings, his rifle within grabbing distance, the feeling he was being watched haunting him. In the daylight, the night's terror seemed unreal, a dream. Had he really heard what he thought he had heard or had the night's boredom caused him to imagine it?

    But the terrifying sound of that horrific scream wouldn't release him. It wasn't a dream. Couldn't have been. The danger was real, and close. It was somewhere on this prairie, and he was determined to find out where. That afternoon, his work done, he grabbed his rifle, and with Misty and Spuds close behind, hiked toward Wolf Creek, looking for tracks that would nail the culprit.

Chapter 7

THE ENCOUNTER

Morning had dawned cloudy that day, but by early afternoon, when Dan was finished cutting wood, the sky had cleared, leaving an opening for the sun to throw color onto the prairie's pure unmarked blanket, unmarked except for the shadow patterns that danced decoratively across it. Stories of days past now lay buried beneath layers of new snow. Erased by the recent storm, they were stories of life's wanderings through the prairie, of humans and animals struggling to survive a brutal winter. Birds and small creatures such as squirrels, mice, and chipmunks marked days of scurrying on the snow in search of food, evidence that told Dan which ones had been there, and that he really wasn't as alone on the prairie as he often thought. Farther out, mule deer, moose, and elk tracks pressed deeper into the snow, one track often indistinguishable from the other, especially if it appeared the animal had been in a hurry.

On days cutting trees and shoveling weren't urgent tasks, Dan followed large-animal tracks, curious to see where they emerged and where they disappeared, keeping a record as he had promised the game warden he would. As temperatures began to warm with spring's closeness and the sun focused its warmth with purpose, tracks would melt into lower layers, leaving behind no history of what had transpired over the winter and of which animals wrote the story. Now, Dan's snowshoes would write a new story in the snow as, rifle in hand, ready for an encounter should it happen, he searched for evidence left by the source of the previous night's unforgettable experience.

Unsure of the direction from which the blood-rendering screams of the previous night had come, he and the dogs turned toward Wolf Creek, a two- to three-mile hike, the dogs occasionally sniffing the ground like bloodhounds as though they knew what Dan had in mind. Besides some fresh moose tracks down the hill by Quartz Creek, he found no trace of the tracks he was searching for. He could tell by the depth and position of the tracks and otherwise disturbed snow around them that the moose was merely foraging among the willows, unthreatened by predators.

It was mid-afternoon, and tree shadows were already becoming stretched and distorted patterns on the prairie snow, as the sun made its slow fiery descent to the horizon below the mountain. After examining and making a mental note of the moose tracks by the creek, Dan stopped and searched the sky for a sign of incoming weather, then whistled for Misty and Spuds to follow him back up the hill to the trail.

"We'll go just a bit farther. Then we'd better head back," Dan told them. "We don't want to be caught out after dark. Especially if weather drifts in. It looks good now but, up here, that can change in an instant," he reminded them, though it was more an unpleasant reminder for himself.

The dogs wagged their tails in agreement, then they set to chasing each other in circles, seeming to forget the serious purpose for the walk. Soon they reached Wolf Creek where Dan scanned the prairie and the woods for tracks, but the snow lay pure and unbroken.

"No luck. It's hard to tell where the sound came from on these damned mountains because of the echo. We'll try a different direction when I get a chance," he said, more to himself than the dogs, as he turned toward camp. The dogs followed close behind, occasionally running into the woods when they thought they had spotted a small animal worth chasing. It had been a fairly mild day, but now, as he faced into the intermittent breeze, he could tell the temperature had taken a significant fall.

"It's going to be a cold one tonight," he thought. "I'd better pile more wood into the tent before supper."

As they approached camp, Dan was relieved to find that the tree he had tried to cut down a few days before had finally fallen. It had stubbornly held on, refusing to let go, and he wasn't going to argue with it. The memory of his accident told him it wouldn't be wise. But he also realized a forceful wind would be persuasive in sending the tree to its final resting place, making a quick end to an unlucky animal in its path, and he didn't wish that kind of end for either of his dogs. Until the tree gave in, he would avoid going near it and, in the meantime, do his best to see nothing wandered into the path of its lean.

My big tree right here at camp finally fell over. I cut it a week ago but couldn't get it to fall at that time. So I'll work at cutting it up tomorrow. That should keep me pretty busy getting all of that in.

That night, Dan reluctantly reached over and turned off the light. He lay listening to the silence, broken only by the occasional hoot of an owl in a nearby evergreen, eyes open wide to ward off sleep, his rifle beside him. On the mountain, a windless night's silence was so deep, a whisper traveling through it from a distance sounded like a shout. Though its source might be on the other end of the prairie or high on She Bear, the scream he feared would sound like an ax murder happening beside the tent. He shivered at the thought and fought to shove it from his mind. It was a sound he never wanted to hear again and hoped he wouldn't. He tried to comfort himself with knowing Misty and Spuds were close by to warn him, and his rifle within inches to protect all of them, for Misty and Spuds together were much too small to win against an animal of that size if a fight ensued. With that thought, his eyes forced him into sleep.

Overnight, the fire went out, leaving not even a small red coal to birth a new fire, and by morning, it was 36 below. Except for the cold, it had been an uneventful night. Misty and Spuds were huddled in front of the stove rather than in their bed, waiting for it to throw some heat and most likely wondering why it wasn't when Dan reluctantly crawled from his warm sleeping bag and stepped into the subzero cold, shivering.

Before he could open the stove door, he needed to get the dogs out of the way. "Go on," he told them with as much authority as he could muster. Unmoving, they stared up at him, deaf to his command. Dan poked them with his foot, and Misty surprised him with a low growl and a showing of teeth.

Dan stepped back. "Well I'll be damned," he said. Stunned by their stubborn crabbiness, he concluded they were merely expressing a long winter's bitter cold wearing on them. If they had been in charge, they probably would have voted to exchange their thin-walled canvas tent for a warm house surrounded by a lot less snow.

Regaining his composure, he looked them in the eyes and, raising his voice, said, "I can't get a fire going if I can't get to the stove, so you're going to move whether you want to or not. Remember, I'm alpha here, not you." His voice was stern, demanding, rising in volume with each word.

Damn coffee pot is froze up, and all the rest of my water. The damn dogs are right in front of the stove to where I can't get to it without stepping on them. And when I told them to move, Misty actually growled at me, and that's the first time that has happened. But I did manage to get to the stove, and I'm still in front of it.

Misty and Spuds stared back defiantly, something in Dan's tone telling them that he was indeed alpha and that it would be best to comply. But they didn't move far. They stood close to him and the stove as he crumpled some paper, tossed it into its open mouth, threw in a handful of kindling and a match and watched as tiny flames grew into big ones, gobbling the paper and picking on the kindling. Once the kindling caught, Dan threw in a couple of small logs and shut the door. They faced a long wait before the little stove, belly bulging with wood, gave off enough heat to raise the inside temperature to comfort level and thaw his coffee pot and water. It was a lesson in patience for all of them — patience they were growing tired of needing.

"There. Now you can have your place back," he told Misty and Spuds as though he were still angry with them for disobedience. "I'm going back to bed until it warms up in here."

The sun finally came out, and it was 13 above at 10 a.m., so I went out and spent the day cutting wood and dragging it to camp. Got my tree cut up and dragged into camp and got some of the bigger branches cut up for fire starter when it clouded up and started to snow at 3 p.m. It was zero out then, so I called it a day after I got water. Had soup and toasted cheese sandwiches for dinner.

It's 7 p.m., and I'm bored stiff. Nothing appeals to me tonight. I'm just flat out bored to death. Think tomorrow I had better go for a long walk and get rid of this excess energy, if that's what it is, cause I don't know. It's 22 below at 7:30, so another cold morning is coming. If this continues, I'll have to get my long johns out again. But for tonight, I'll put on my PJ's.

Boredom plagued Dan that evening as he played several games of Solitaire, losing all of them. Tiring of that, he thumbed through the books he had read earlier in the winter but couldn't rouse interest in reading them again. Giving that up, he sat staring at the stove as though it might have something better to offer. Company would be nice, he thought, or dogs that knew how to play cards or carry on a stimulating conversation. They had already heard his life's story and stories of all the good times he had had with his best friend, and Dan had no more in him to tell.

"What can one person do to stay occupied during long winter nights so you don't get bored?" he asked Misty and Spuds. "Read, play games with yourself, listen to the radio. And when you grow tired of those things, you get bored. So what now? Sit and get lonely, I guess." Loneliness was the villain darkening his mood when having nothing to do brought his mind to it. It was a battle he had fought and lost most of the winter in spite of his efforts to keep his mind clear of it.

The darkening of his mood often plunged his thoughts deep into the past, the anger caused by his father's treatment of him as a child surfacing and escalating, though he tried hard to keep it from him. Most often, he didn't know where the anger was coming from. It appeared when he least expected it, over little or nothing. He hadn't yet realized that much of that anger was the ghost of anger from the past rather than from anything that was happening in the present. Misty and Spuds had learned long ago to stay out of his way when their master's mood swung toward darkness. When outside, they hurried out of sight, busying themselves with play or chasing real or make-believe varmints. Indoors, they settled into a corner not daring to move, hoping to make themselves invisible until the storm subsided and the sun appeared.

Sometimes when he was bored, his mind traveled on different journeys, many of them within the confines of the prairie. Named after an infamous man named Walker, the prairie had a dark history, a story he shared with Misty and Spuds during one of their walks. Dan often wondered about this man and the small mining village that once existed there in the late 1800s or early 1920s. Sometimes when on top of She Bear, where he could see the whole prairie spread out long and lean for miles, he would try to imagine it buzzing with human presence as men worked long and hard to make their fortunes mining precious metals.

Whisky, women, card games, and drunken brawls kept their boredom at bay. In those days, men carried guns, and Dan could imagine hearing the shot that killed Walker as it resounded through the mountains, most likely startling those who heard it but who weren't there to witness it. Stories abound regarding Walker's death, some saying it was payback for cheating at cards, others saying it was greed for more than his share of treasure that took him down. Some say he was buried there on the prairie where the sign still stands that says "Walker Killed." Others say his body was taken off the mountain for burial.

Only the mountain and the prairie knew for sure what had really happened. But reality dissolved in the silence of the prairie as mining days ended and the log buildings that proved human activity once existed there began to decay along with the bones of those who lived and died in that era. Now only the sign sits at the south end of the prairie marking the supposed spot Walker was killed and perhaps buried, his legacy a prairie, a creek, and a mountain named after him.

It wasn't as cold as Dan expected when he awoke early the next morning, the tent dim in the slowness of daylight's arrival over the mountain. He lit the lantern beside the bed, deciding to get an early start on his wood cutting and stacking, so he could head toward Rapid Creek to resume his search for the elusive animal that had plagued his mind two nights ago. It was important that he find it before the next snow buried the evidence.

The nightmarish sound that had filled the silent blackness with terror still frightened him, rendering his sleep restless since the night he had heard it. If he knew the area of the animal's prowling, he could better protect himself. His rifle still lay beside him at night, as it would every night from now on, and it was always within a hand's reach during the day, loaded and ready for action. "If anything should come through that door, I wouldn't hesitate to shoot it." Dan was emphatic. He knew what animal had made the sound, and he didn't want it anywhere near his camp, for it was one animal Misty and Spuds wouldn't be able to handle. Nor did he want to run into it unexpectedly in late afternoon twilight as he returned to camp from a long hike to the other end of the prairie.

Except for his slim stature, Dan, with his long scraggly hair hanging from beneath his cap, hair-covered face, determined black eyes, dirty worn snowmobile suit, and rifle in hand would have appeared to another human a formidable man to encounter in spite of his size. But to the right animal, he would just be a good meal, if it could catch him unaware. And that was something Dan was determined to avoid.

Rapid Creek was a long way, and off the prairie, but Dan hadn't planned on hiking all the way to the creek. He and Misty and Spuds arrived at the prairie's edge having seen only a few mule deer and small animal tracks including coyote along the way. The padded foot track he was looking for was shaped like that of a large canine, but had four clawless toes. In the deep snow where tracks often weren't clear, one had to examine them closely to determine the source.

Walking closer to Rapid Creek would be a waste of time, Dan thought. "We're getting too far from camp. The animal we heard was much closer than this. Now that I think about it, it sounded as though it could have been right above camp. But the way these mountains toss sound around, it could be anyone's guess." He turned and yelled to the dogs. "C'mon girls; let's go back."

He turned his clumsy snowshoes around, pulled out his binoculars, and retraced his steps, stopping frequently to examine rock formations higher up the hill, but more important, to look behind and all around him, an uneasy feeling that someone or something was following him growing in his gut. Dan tried to explain the feeling away by telling himself he was just being paranoid. And for no reason. That explanation calmed him temporarily, until a half mile before arriving at camp, Misty and Spuds, who had been frolicking in the snow, suddenly stopped and stood still, their gaze fixed on a speck sitting on a large rock ahead of them and a short distance up the hill.

Misty ran closer to it, stopped, pointed her ears at it, and began to bark. Spuds ran behind Dan, who had also stopped. Hair on her back raised, she parked herself at his feet and growled softly. There was no bed to crawl under and nowhere else to hide. Scanning the distance, Dan saw the speck too, and suspected it was the villain they had been looking for. He yelled at Misty to stay where she was. Misty, sensing this was no animal to entice in play, stood like a statue, hair raised. Heart pounding, Dan continued walking slowly toward the object, one eye on Misty, hoping she wouldn't run, his rifle ready, Spuds hanging close behind.

As they drew closer, the speck that now was nearly distinguishable began to move, crouching on the rock, its long skinny tail slowly moving back and forth in cat fashion, ready for action. It had spotted them. Dan stopped and pulled out his binoculars, his heart beating faster.

"Yup, that's what it was," he muttered to himself. "When you hear one, it sounds just like a woman getting her throat cut." He shivered just thinking about it. "And it's much too close to camp." He moved closer, stood as tall as he could and raised his rifle. "You jump off that rock and make a move for Misty, and that will be the last thing you remember. Come on; do it; I'm itching to pull the trigger. Your fur coat would feel nice and warm under my feet."

As though it heard and understood Dan's threats, the mountain lion stood up, stared at the man pointing the rifle, jumped off the rock and stood indecisive, his eyes holding Dan's. Dan held his breath, his finger pressed lightly against the trigger. As though thinking better of inviting confrontation, the lion slowly turned and loped up the hill and out of sight.

"You'd better hope I never see you again," Dan shouted after it. But his voice was lost in the wind below the hill, and the animal never looked back. Dan was relieved and thought the dogs were too, but he clutched his rifle all the way back to camp, Spuds never leaving his side. He hoped the animal's den was far from camp and that it would stay far away from his.

From then on, Dan felt a tinge of anxiety whenever he was concentrating on cutting wood, or walking the prairie, always suspecting hungry yellow eyes were watching him, always expecting the animal to sneak up from behind or above and pounce on him at any moment. He feared mountain lions more than he feared bears; they were sneaky predators, moving about the mountain noiselessly and unsuspecting on huge sharp-clawed padded feet. His clumsy snowshoes would be an impediment in his efforts to escape such a predator, making him easy prey. Would Misty and Spuds come to his rescue if they sensed his life were in danger? Or would they run? It was a test he didn't wish for.

Though he didn't want to use it on a big cat, his rifle was his most dependable companion when danger lurked close by, he thought. If the game and fish crew found a dead mountain lion with a bullet in it, they would expect a convincing argument for his actions since the hunting season on cats was long over. "How do you prove an imminent attack?" Dan asked himself. "It would be nearly impossible. My word against the lion's, and he wouldn't be saying much at that point. Doesn't seem fair. Seems animals have more rights than people." There were no visible tracks leading toward camp or in camp, and Dan was relieved. But he would never let down his guard, for mountain lions roamed a large territory in their searches for food and could run much faster than he could.

Snow fell steadily the next day, wiping the prairie clean once more, preparing it for a new story waiting to be written on its fresh whiteness. "Guess I found the cat just in time," Dan thought, as he trudged down the hill to his tent after having a telephone conversation with Billie.

It's been snowing hard all day. All I have done is shovel snow and sit on my ass. I did walk up on the prairie, and it's snowing twice as hard up there, so I'm back in the house again. This is good, though, for it will make it easier for the kids when they come up Sunday, I hope. It finally stopped at 4:30. I fixed a noodle casserole for dinner tonight, and it wasn't too bad. I've been reading a book all day, so I'm going to stay up and finish it tonight.

At 7:30 in the morning, when Dan awoke, daylight was trying its best to poke through the tent, but thick, brooding clouds prevented much of it from seeping through, and Dan was tricked into thinking it was much earlier than it actually was. Opening the tent flap for Misty and Spuds to exit, he stepped outdoors and examined the sky to see if it was snowing. Though momentarily quiet, the clouds appeared to be sagging under the weight of gathering moisture they couldn't hold much longer. More snow was coming. Of that, he was certain, and he was growing weary of shoveling.

I heard on the news this morning that Sheridan is to get two-to-four inches of new snow tonight. So I'm sure that I will get my share. Got everything shoveled off and another tree cut down and all of it dragged in and some of it chopped and brought in before it started in at 4 p.m. It's 7 p.m. now, and I was just out and shoveled around the door, and it's not slowing up any, so I gave up. Going to lie down and listen to the Wyoming basketball game and eat some popcorn if I hurry and get it made. 9:00: Had to go out and scrape the snow off the roof, for it was really sagging, and it's still snowing. Got about 4 inches so far.

The next morning, tree silhouettes made by the sun crawled across the tent in slow motion, pushed to life by a whispering breeze. Dan was thankful the tent was still standing and attributed the fact that it still was to his careful anchoring of it in the fall. It would take quite a wind storm to take it down, and while powdery snow wasn't much of a problem, heavy snow was something to be reckoned with. Morning, dawning earlier now, was most obvious on days the wind scrubbed the clouds from the sky, allowing the sun to prove its continued existence. Misty and Spuds were up early, pointing themselves at the tent door while barking incessantly.

Dan reacted quickly to a situation he thought urgent, his hand grasping his rifle as he jumped out of bed, his sleeping bag landing on the floor in his haste. "Couldn't be a mountain lion. If it was, Spuds would be under the bed," he reasoned.

He opened the tent door carefully, the dogs climbing over each other in their haste to get through it. Stepping into the sunshine, his anxious gaze followed the dogs until they disappeared into the woods.

"Guess I'll just let them handle it," he said to himself. Seeing no cause for alarm, he stepped back inside, fed the stove, put on the coffee, and climbed back into his sleeping bag until the tent warmed and the dogs had finished their run and told him they were ready for breakfast. That afternoon, he decided to hike the prairie in search of tracks that would lead him to the source of the dogs' morning unrest. "No sign of snow," he thought, examining the cloudless sky. "It's a good day for exploring."

He and the dogs were barely out of camp when he spotted animal tracks stretching ahead like a long chain in the new snow. Misty and Spuds already had their noses in the tracks when Dan knelt down to examine them. "Moose. Now I know what you two were so excited about." The dogs paid no attention. They were too busy being trackers. Though he knew moose were the object of his search and not a big cat, rifle in hand rather than over his shoulder, he decided to find out where the tracks would lead him.

I followed her tracks for an hour or better until she went into the timber. Besides, it was snowing like hell up there. I forgot how protected the camp is by the trees and the hill behind me. So, I was really surprised to see how much snow had fallen up here.

The snow grew deeper the farther up the hill the entourage hiked, making travel increasingly difficult. So Dan decided to give up the search and turn around. Realizing they were heading back to camp, Misty and Spuds raced ahead of their master, each determined to be the first in line for supper. Dan trudged behind them, his rifle now over his shoulder, taking his time. As he approached the trail at the edge of the hill, an uneasy feeling came over him. He stopped and looked back, searched the hill above him and the stream below, but could see nothing. Yet the feeling wouldn't let go. He slid the rifle off his shoulder, held it ready to fire if needed, and continued on, stopping occasionally to look behind and around him. But nothing jumped at him from a rock or behind a tree or bush or the tent. There had been nothing to justify the feeling in his gut. And he admonished himself for it.

Back at camp, Dan added a description of the moose tracks and where they led to the accumulating information he had written down for the game warden. Besides moose, he had spotted fox, coyotes, rabbits, and a mountain lion in the past couple of weeks, though the moose had no collars, he reported. Black bears roamed the prairie in summer, searching for raspberries and other fruit produced in good growing seasons, but usually were unseen in winter. Early in the season, Dan had strung a row of tin cans in front of the tent to sound an alarm in case one ambled by in search of a good meal, lured into camp by the aroma of whatever Dan was cooking at the time. But not once had he heard them clang.

"I'd be surprised if they liked anything I cooked," he had told Spuds and Misty. "They would probably just tear the camp apart looking for something good . . . like you, maybe," he teased.

His record keeping done, he checked the last package of hamburger he had retrieved from his outdoor freezer and set on the stove to thaw. Disappointment covered his face as he unwrapped it to find more than half of it spoiled beyond saving. There was only enough left to make a Hamburger Helper meal, which he intended to share with Misty and Spuds, who sat at the table watching Dan hungrily until supper was ready.

"At least, supper isn't a total loss," he told Misty and Spuds, as he spooned a portion of the hot dish into their dishes. Then he sat down to enjoy the rest of it. Later in the evening, as he sat reading, his insides seemed a bit queasy, as though something he ate didn't agree with him. So he put down his book and turned out the light, hoping sleep would make him feel better. But sleep came lightly, restless tossing and turning, the growing turmoil in his insides keeping him from falling into it deeply.

In the early morning darkness, serious stomach cramps woke him. Hurriedly untangling himself from his sleeping bag and putting on a jacket, he grabbed the toilet seat and ran out the door and down the path to his bathroom. He hadn't time to grab his rifle, and Misty and Spuds slept on, unconcerned. Should an animal stealthily approach, he was on his own, but he was too sick to think about it. Returning to the tent, he grabbed a pan near the stove to catch remnants of last night's supper he hadn't yet gotten rid of and climbed back into his sleeping bag, which had grown cold in his absence.

Spent most of the morning up sick. Don't know what is wrong. Had stomach cramps, throwing up, and I'm just down right miserable. Finally got to sleep about 4 a.m. and I started feeling better around 2 p.m. I'm just going to have some broth and toast for dinner and lay down and see if I can keep that down, for I don't have any kind of medication up here. Hopefully, this little bug I got will go away on its own. I did manage to keep a can of soup down, and the cramps are easing up a little. It's 11:30 p.m., and 8 below. I'm going to try and get some sleep.

Whatever had held Dan's insides prisoner finally let go; his appetite returning along with his spirits. "Glad you two didn't get sick from whatever it was," he told Spuds and Misty.

The next morning, his energy restored, he decided to retrace his last route up the prairie, curious about what he would find, the memory of that uneasy feeling of being watched still gnawing at him. He fastened his snowshoes, grabbed his rifle, and walked to the top of the hill above camp, Misty and Spuds following in happy play, occasionally catching a ride on their master's snowshoes when the going became more than they could handle.

At first, all he saw was his own tracks, and he was relieved. But approximately a mile down the trail, Dan began to see animal tracks on top of his, and his heart began to race. They had come from the back of She Bear, but the snow was too deep for him to follow without a great deal of muscle and energy he wasn't up to expending. Perhaps when the sun decided to shrink the snow blanket to a depth and consistency he could stay on top of with snowshoes, he would try again.

At first, he couldn't tell what had made the tracks, but he was sure it wasn't moose or elk or even the dogs. Stooping to examine them more closely, he determined them to be tracks of the animal he dreaded most, mountain lion. Couldn't be anything else, he thought, as he stood up and scanned the prairie. What made him uncomfortable was that he could tell from the position of the tracks that the animal had been stalking him, perhaps considering him an easy meal in a winter when food was scarce. Though there were enough mule deer and other varmints on the prairie to keep mountain lions fat through the winter without considering a human for a meal - unless they were hungry for a change in menu, Dan thought. But the cat had not followed him into camp; at least, not yet. And, if it ever did, there would be one less cat on the prairie.

Dan whistled at the dogs, who had gone farther up the trail, and turned his clumsy snowshoes toward camp. Just above the hill, Dan, imagining he had seen movement, grabbed the binoculars and searched the prairie for a sign of life, then fearing walking into a surprise lurking behind a tree or the tent, aimed them at camp below the hill. But he saw and felt nothing as he continued cautiously down the hill, through the trees, and into camp.

Knowing he had been stalked, whether inside or outdoors, he wouldn't let down his guard as he worked. And he would make sure Misty and Spuds and his rifle were close at all times. The rest of the day proved uneventful as he cut and hauled more wood into camp, stopping occasionally to scan his surroundings. Uneasiness and cat paranoia would plague him the rest of his stint on the prairie.

March had finally arrived with full sunshine but temperatures in the minus figures. He knew the cold wouldn't last long now, for temperatures were already beginning to moderate. Spring wasn't far off and, in a day or two, Billie and the kids would be up for a visit. Knowing that gave him renewed energy. There was much to do to prepare, and he knew that if he kept busy, the day would pass more quickly, closing the gap between his waiting and their arrival. He had no trouble finding things to do, for wood needed stacking, and his bachelor home looked like a disaster of some sort had ripped through it. His visitors would be cold and hungry when they arrived, needing food and hot cocoa to warm their insides. Just by observing her, Dan had learned from Billie how to be a good host, how to make their guests welcome and wanting to return at another time, though he admitted there were some guests he would rather not invite for a return visit.

By the end of the day, everything inside the tent was in order, room prepared for a number of people to sit and eat or just sip a hot drink, plenty of wood to keep the stove well fed and the tent comfortably warm. It would be a long cold ride up the mountain on snowmobile, and Dan wanted these visitors to stay a very long time, for he knew the day would pass much too quickly. And if they left too soon, he would have to fight temptation to pack up and go with them.

Chapter 8

THE VISIT

    March had come in quietly during the night with no belligerence, but cold at 21 below under a blanketless sky. In spite of it, that morning, Dan kept himself busy outdoors chopping wood, for he knew he would be bored and restless with anticipation if he stayed inside staring at the four drab windowless tent walls, checking his watch every half hour, wondering what to do next. Though he worked with deliberate slowness, by noon, he had enough wood neatly stacked outside and inside with no more room to put it, to last at least a week, and several day's supply of water sitting beside the stove as well. The tent was neat and cleared of debris, some of it invisible under the bed or temporarily stored in tubs. He was ready for Billie and the kids.
    When lunch was over, he put his feet on the table, lit a cigarette, took a deep draw, and blew smoke rings into the air. There was still a long afternoon and evening with nothing to do but sit and speculate on things that would be talked about during his family's visit and the good feelings that would result from their presence. Misty and Spuds had settled in for a nap, and Dan thought about doing the same. He pressed his cigarette stub into the ashtray and had just set his head down on the pillow and covered himself with his sleeping bag when suddenly he changed his mind.
    "C'mon girls," he said, throwing his sleeping bag aside. "I know I won't be able to sleep, and we're not lying here all afternoon getting bored. We're going for a walk."
    The dogs weren't as eager as he to give up their warm bed and a long nap for a romp in winter's arctic indecisive mood. Unmoving, Misty and Spuds stared at him while he put on his snowsuit, as though to ask, "Do you know how cold it is out there? You go for a walk. We're staying right here by the stove."
    As their eyes drooped into sleep again, Dan brought his leather gloves together hard in a resounding slap that brought Misty and Spuds to attention. "C'mon! Let's go!" It wasn't a choice; it was a command, and the dogs recognized it as such because they had heard it many times, and they knew his tone of voice meant trouble if they didn't obey. In protest and with deliberate slow-

Photo courtesy of Danny Longwell

The dogs weren't eager to give up their warm bed and a long nap for a romp in winter's arctic indecisive mood.

ness, they got to their feet, stretched, yawned, and hesitantly followed their master into the crisp afternoon sunshine. Sometime during the afternoon, the temperature had risen to 10 above, the best it would get three weeks from the first day of spring, but Dan didn't mind as long as the wind kept silent.

Though he carefully examined the snow for tracks as they hiked toward the Big Goose River bridge, he saw none that would make his heart race. As he and the dogs traveled, he was alerted by the sound of a gentle wind trying to make music with the pine branches, alerted to the possibility it wasn't the wind but a large animal pushing its way through thick evergreen walls in search of food. He stopped to scan the area for the source of the sound, then realized that the animal he feared moved with stealth on padded feet, crouching, creeping, eyes and body focused on its prey, silently hoping to take it by surprise. One lightning strike of its huge paw would dispatch an animal or man to the ground, choking, piercing, blood quickly flowing. He shuddered at the picture painted in his mind by the cat's scream.

Then he got to reasoning his fear away. "I can't let that cat push me into paranoia. I can't shut myself in the tent all day allowing a gun to grow into my hand. How boring would that be? Besides, I have trees to cut, outside work to do. I can't be looking over my shoulder like I'm a wanted man, either. That would make me crazy for sure. Then I may as well leave the mountain and stay home because lots of other dangers lurk here, too."

As they approached the bridge, a red fox, hurrying across the trail as though he were late for an appointment, stopped long enough to look in his direction, then disappeared up the hill. As Dan stopped and stared back, admiring his red coat, pointed nose, and long bushy tail, he suddenly envied the freedom enjoyed by wildlife that inhabited the mountain, traveling where they wanted, when they wanted, and with no rules to govern them, no concern about leaving no trace they had been there.

In the woods, a number of squirrels scampered busily over the snow and across fallen logs searching for hidden treasures they had planted in the fall. Spotting Misty and Spuds, they flew up the nearest tree, scolding them loquaciously from the safety of high branches. Misty and Spuds knew from experience that, except for an occasional stupid one, catching them was only a dream and ignored them. Squirrels were too common to waste energy on a futile chase.

On the way back to camp, Dan spotted a pine martin clinging to a tree as though frozen to it, and envied a large hawk, wings spread and still, floating lazily in the indigo sky to where ever the thermals would take it. But there were no large animal encounters that day. No elk, no moose, no cat. And, though his rifle was ready for a cat, Dan was thankful he didn't have to use it. An occasional snow machine was known to travel through the prairie as well, and Dan hoped one would appear when he was out for a walk. But today the prairie was painfully devoid of human sounds and presence.

Though it was late afternoon and the sun had already begun to rappel down the mountain to meet the horizon far below, pulling the daytime moon with it as though it were a lopsided kite on a long invisible string, daylight hung around into the early evening, tricking Dan into thinking suppertime was a long way off. It was 6:30 with a sky growing into twilight when the entourage returned to camp, Dan wondering why he was so ravenous. The moon hung around a bit after dark, lingering on the treetops as though peering over the edge, afraid to jump off the mountain but knowing it was a necessary part of its around-the-earth journey.

It's 8:30 p.m. and zero degrees outdoors. So it's a lot warmer out tonight than it was last night. Time to lay down and play video poker for a while.

More bored than tired, Dan soon put his video game away and contemplated reading for a while, but changed his mind and, instead, fed the stove and turned out the lantern. The sooner he got to sleep, the faster morning would come bringing Billie's arrival, he reasoned. But though he tried to sleep, he was unable to turn off his anticipation and lay awake for a long while listening to the dogs' occasional snores and the gentle hooting of an owl in the distance before falling asleep sometime around midnight. During the many long winter nights when he had trouble sleeping, Dan found those sounds and even the coyote howls comforting. They were pleasant reminders that he wasn't alone, the mountain wasn't mute, and that all was well.

Overnight, the temperature rose rather than fell; it was 8 degrees when Dan awoke at 6:30. There had been no wind to rattle the tent that night, but after breakfast and morning chores, he heard the wind gently playing with the tent flap, lifting it and setting it down repeatedly in an annoying sort of way. It was the second day of March at last, and he wondered what kind of day it would be, hoping the weather wouldn't keep his family from coming up. If that should happen, disappointment would lay heavily upon him, lasting a long time, for another opportunity for them to come up may not offer itself. He had put a lot of effort into preparing for their visit, making sure everything was perfect, anticipating their every need and a long afternoon of re-acquaintance.

When the sun had risen enough to bring full daylight, Dan got up, opened the tent flap and peeked at the sky, examining its mood. Thick clouds rolled intermittent and lazy across the sky, telling him the sun might not be out long enough to play today. But they didn't appear threatening.

"Billie and the kids will be here," he told Misty and Spuds, putting on a positive mood. "We'll go meet them a little later." The dogs thumped their tails lazily against the floor, then got up, yawned, and stretched. They were ready for their morning run.

I'm going to walk up and meet Billie and the kids, but I won't do that until 10:00. In the meantime, I have to make sure that things are ready so they can have something hot to drink when they get here.

Misty and Spuds had been restless and full of energy from the time they woke up, and Dan knew they were aware that something special was going on.

He had told them about the visit many times during the past week, but it was his mood and cheerful tune whistling that conveyed the message rather than his words. Now, as he pulled on his boots, the dogs pushed and shoved, each eager to be first out of the tent. Dan couldn't sit in camp idle waiting for his family to arrive. He would stretch their time together by meeting them at the Buck Camp.

Dan arrived at the cabin at 11 expecting them to be there. He stopped and listened, expecting to hear the sound of their machines within minutes. Hearing nothing but the quiet of the prairie, he began pacing the trail when, finally at noon, he heard snowmobiles in the distance growing closer, and Misty and Spuds, ears pointed at the sound, began to bark. Dan stopped his pacing as they came into view. They arrived a little later than he had expected, surprised to see Dan and the dogs waiting for them, their snow machines laden with packages. To Dan, it was Christmas all over again. Now there was nothing he should need or want before spring arrived signaling that it was time to leave the mountain. He took off his snowshoes and climbed onto the back of Billie's machine content in his closeness to her, while the kids held onto Misty and Spuds, who had begged a ride.

The kids got here around noon, and damn, was it good to see them. They brought all kinds of goodies with them: hot cereal, meat, canned goods, parts for my chainsaw, candy, whiskey and tobacco. It was just like Christmas.

At camp, Dan set the packages on the bed and motioned everyone to sit on a chair, the bed, or a tub. Then he fed the stove, made sure each person had a hot cup of cocoa or coffee to warm their hands and insides, and set to making sandwiches for lunch, all the while participating in a lengthy conversation about people and local happenings and a sometimes heated debate about recent decisions made wisely or unwisely by the county commissioners, and then about the health of today's world, not solving any of the controversial issues brought up for discussion.

With food before them, conversation slowed, punctuated by intermittent silence as everyone left politics alone and concentrated on satisfying hunger. But it soon picked up again, this time focusing on weather, as Dan put away the food, tidied his small kitchen, and poured himself another cup of cocoa, reveling in their presence and the liveliness that broke the monotony of months of silence.

Billie wore a concerned expression as she watched Dan put more logs on a fire that was already burning hot. "I think that stove has just about had it," she said, looking at it closely. "Looks like it's wearing a little thin. And look at the chimney; it's on the edge of redness."

Dan looked at the stove, then at her, reading her thoughts. "You're right; it's probably time to replace it," he agreed.

"Do you know where there is one you can use?"

"Further down the line, I think. I'll look for it tomorrow. In the meantime, I'll burn a little less wood," he assured her, noting the skeptical look on her face. "It's hard to keep warm on those machines. Wanted to keep my guests comfortable."

Billie had unzipped her snowmobile suit to the waist before lunch. "We're not cold. In fact, it's getting a bit too warm in here."

Turning his attention to the packages he had set on the bed, he picked them up, sat down, and set them by his feet, then began to open them. It was better than a birthday party. "Oh, tobacco. I was running out. And food. And whiskey. Didn't expect all of this. Can't remember the last time I had a drink, and there have been times I could have used one or two."

Billie smiled. "We thought you'd find a use for these things. Now maybe you won't need to call and ask to have someone to bring something up that you forgot."

Dan looked at her and shook his head, remembering the painful ragging he received the last time he had called her with a request. "Thanks, everyone. I really do appreciate it."

In the middle of expressing his gratitude, Dan suddenly became quiet. "Shhhh. Listen. Do I hear snowmobiles?" The room became quiet as the purr of a snow machine grew to a roar and seemed to hover above camp, idling. Misty and Spuds, whose ears were up and listening, pushed their way out the door and began barking incessantly. "Who could that be?" he asked no one in particular. "I thought they were just passing by, but I think they stopped."

"Don't know," Billie said. "Were you expecting someone besides us?" His question was answered as the roar of engines became quiet and the crunching of boots on snow could be heard between dog barks, letting them know someone had walked down the hill and was approaching the tent. Dan got up and walked jacketless into the cold, yelling at Misty and Spuds to quit their barking; it was someone they knew.

It was about 1:00 when Kenny Clemens and a couple of his friends showed up. So we had a total of six people here. It was great.

"Sounds like you have company," Kenny said, his hands holding a small box.

"Good to see you. The more the merrier." Dan had been waiting for his arrival for several days and wasn't about to let him go so quickly.

"I brought you some supplies."

"Thanks. What is it?" he said, taking the package and leading the way inside. "C'mon in and join the party; it's just Billie and the kids."

"Oh, it's just some things I knew you needed," Kenny said in answer to Dan's question. Kenny and his friends sat on the edge of the bed as directed and took off their helmets and gloves, while responding to friendly greetings from Dan's family.

"Coffee or cocoa?" Dan asked.

"A little coffee would be fine if you have it, but we can't stay long," Kenny said, looking at his watch. "Brendon is quite sick; running a fever; so I don't dare leave him too long."

"Sounds serious. Is it the flu?" Dan asked. Kenny nodded. "I think so."

"I heard it's going around in town. Usually does this time of year. One good thing about being up here, flu bugs can't handle serious cold, and I'm thankful for that."

Kenny looked up at Dan. "Well that's one good reason for being here, I guess. But I can't think of any other." Dan only smiled.

"We have to be going before long, too," Billie interjected quietly as she reached down and scratched Spuds' ears. Misty and Spuds lay at her feet, enjoying the attention and an occasional bread crust.

Dan looked at his watch and then at Billie. "It's not even 2 o'clock yet," he said lowering his eyes to hide his disappointment. "You just got here, and there's a lot of afternoon left."

Billie gave Dan a don't-argue-with-me look, which he immediately understood and said nothing more. No use arguing; Billie was usually right. "But not that much daylight. There's a good chance of weather coming in late this afternoon, and we don't want to get caught in it. Besides, some of us have to go to work tomorrow," she reminded him, a hint of sarcasm in her voice.

Dan had hoped to hold on to everyone at least until late afternoon. There was too much to talk about, too much need for human voices to fill the silent void of months without anyone to talk to. For a moment or two, he sat quiet, listening to the chatter that filled the tent, savoring it, hanging on to it so it still would be there after everyone left. But it seemed no one was aware of the vast void these moments were filling, or of his desperate need to stretch them into hours in hopes the memory of them would cancel his chronic loneliness - a disease worse than the flu Dan thought - at least for a little while beyond the day.

Billie noticed his silence and, in his expression, recognized signs of the storm brewing inside him, though she said nothing. His family's ties were to the world below the mountain, and Dan had to understand that. He had made his choice to cut them for the winter months, to be here alone, as though he were staying as far from civilization and re-supply as the North Pole or Antarctica. Having visitors wasn't his purpose. Especially visitors who brought gifts, helped him stay supplied so he would survive another month or two. Survival had been his responsibility at the beginning of his confinement. It wasn't fair to pass it on to others.

Everyone left at 2:00, and that was the really hard part for me. I didn't want anyone to leave. So I felt more alone tonight than I had in a long time.

Dan reluctantly put on his snowmobile suit and walked up the hill with his company. He watched sadly as they climbed on their machines, and waving, pointed them down the trail. Stood motionless, watching as they disappeared into the end of the prairie, the muffled sound of their engines quickly dissolving into silence, as though they had never been there. He stood listening for a long while, not wanting to deal with the reality that they were gone, wishing to pull back the moment of their departure, then sadly walked back down the hill to camp, Misty and Spuds sensing his mood and seeming as disappointed as he.

Days of preparation for time passed too quickly, he thought sadly.

Though supper time was hours away, he had no energy to fill the afternoon with cutting or stacking wood, nor was there a need. Sometimes he worked outdoors, though he had more than enough wood, just to keep from being bored. But not today. Instead, he went inside, took off his boots, hung up his snowmobile suit, and looked at the dirty cups that covered his small table, the only evidence that people had been there that day. Though he wanted to leave them there for the memory, he knew it was work he couldn't ignore because he needed the table to make supper — if he decided to make one — needed something to do to keep his mind in control. So lethargically, he gathered, stacked, and washed the dirty cups, swept the snow and dirt his company had dragged in out the door, and made grilled cheese sandwiches, though he didn't feel much like eating and shared half of it with the dogs.

After supper, Dan sat at the table staring at the bottle of whiskey the kids had brought. Seeing it as the perfect cure for loneliness, he picked up a glass and filled it half full. Though he had never made a habit of it, it had been a long time since he had had a drink, and now he was on his second one and thinking it wouldn't be his last at this sitting. As he allowed the whiskey to relax him and go to his head, the day's conversations floated in and out of his mind like ghosts playing on his vulnerability, and he began to wonder if he would have been better off not having company at all.

I had three or four drinks and just moped around feeling bad. Then I lit up my pipe and was going to have a nice smoke, but it made me dizzier than hell, for it was the first I had had in a month. But I soon got used to it, and now it tastes good. I should have never touched it to start with. Well, it's 11 p.m., and it's snowing pretty hard, but I think I'll try to go to bed.

Unlike the mountain lion, loneliness was a persistent faceless enemy with no substance that had stalked him since fall when the last hunters left the mountain. He couldn't grab it, slap it, wrestle it to defeat, shoot it, or stab it. He couldn't even run or hide from it. He was its prisoner, and disappearing into a bottle wouldn't make it go away. His only cure was to give in, pack up, and leave the mountain. But he had learned better than to quit. Learned that from his father. If he did, the voices of defeat would haunt him for a very long time, and he would never forgive himself.

"You should never have done it, Longwell."

"I knew loneliness would eventually get you. It's a formidable enemy - much worse than the mountain lion."

"I had a feeling you would succumb."

"You're weak and undisciplined."

"Feeling sorry for yourself, eh, Longwell?"

"I didn't think you had it in you."

"Why aren't you down here working like the rest of us."

With those thoughts recycling in his brain, Dan fell into dreams that repeated and distorted the day's happenings, the whiskey most likely making its contribution, as though randomly drawing pieces from a puzzle of his life's story and putting them together haphazardly. When he tried to remember his dreams in the morning, he searched for the good scenes, intending to discard the bad ones, but he couldn't remember much of either, and he was left with an empty feeling in his gut.

It was fairly warm and snowing when Dan stuck his head out the door the next morning to find four inches of new snow on the ground and his tent roof sagging dangerously with the weight of it. "I'd better get out there and clean off the roof before it comes down," he told Misty and Spuds as he hurriedly zipped his snowsuit. "Then we'd have a bigger mess to deal with."

It took most of the morning to clear the roof and pathways of snow. Heavy with moisture, it was still coming down, the weight of it seeming to pull it to the ground fast, the sky dismal and brooding, showing no signs of stopping its uncontrolled weeping.

"May as well quit until it stops snowing or I'll be out here all day trying to keep up with it. I'll just watch the roof and shovel more later, before bedtime maybe." He scanned the distance for Misty and Spuds, then spotting them, he yelled, "C'mon girls. Let's go in and have lunch and rest a while." But the dogs were too busy romping playfully back and forth along the cleared paths and either didn't hear him or didn't care. "Okay, I'll go have lunch myself then."

Dan was comfortably full and deep into a good book a couple of hours later when he heard the dogs barking excitedly at the roar of snow machines approaching above the hill. "Now who would that be," he thought. "I'm not expecting anyone that I know of."

He got up, hurriedly put on his snowsuit and boots, and stepped outside just as two men were approaching his camp. Suddenly his mood brightened. He didn't know either of them but feeling in a social mood, he invited them in for a cup of coffee anyway, something he might not have done while camping in summer or at home when he wasn't hungry for company.

Due to neglected grooming the past few months, Dan's appearance was that of a bum who had been living in and walking the streets most of his life, never coming in contact with soap and water. The two men stared at him briefly as though trying to determine whether he were a mass murderer or just a person whose permanent home was on the mountain far from modern conveniences, then apprehensively accepted his invitation. They entered the tent behind Dan, took off their helmets, exposing partially bald heads ringed by varying lengths of rumpled, short gray hair, unzipped their suits to the waist, and sat on the two chairs Dan had offered near the stove.

"Possibly retired with nothing better to do than dig into other people's business," Dan thought, hoping his expression didn't betray his thoughts. He later admitted to himself that his mood that day hadn't been the best and that he really was happy that company had arrived to break the monotony of the afternoon even though he had regarded the men as curiosity seekers.

"I'm John," said the rounder of the two men, accepting the cup of coffee Dan handed him. The other man offered his hand, taking Dan's dirty, oil-stained one in a firm handshake. "I'm Lloyd."

"If it hadn't been for the dogs, we wouldn't have seen your camp," John said.

"Judging from all the chopped wood, it looks like you've been up here for a while." Dan recognized it as more a question than a statement.

"All winter, since the end of October," he answered proudly, handing a cup of coffee to Lloyd. "Take sugar?"

"You don't say. No thanks. I drink it black and strong."

John looked at him for a moment as though wondering whether to ask the question that was on his mind, then chanced, "What are you doing up here?"

"What he meant was why am I doing this," Dan thought. "Why am I not in Sheridan, working? Am I not sane? It's none of this man's business, or anyone else's for that matter." He had tired of answering questions like this long ago, was tired of defending himself. In spite of it, he patiently tried to explain that spending a winter on the prairie was something he had always wanted to do, and that he decided to do it before he became unable or too old.

"Lots of people have dreams," he said, reading the man's skepticism. "Most never get a chance to live them, either because they die before getting around to it or because they never take the opportunity. This was my dream, and I'm not sorry I'm doing it."

"Aren't the winters pretty tough up here? I mean, how can anyone survive in a wall tent against such cold temperatures? And the winds must be horrendous at times." Lloyd's eyes roamed the tent, noticing the full jugs of water near the stove, the neatly stacked cans of food, and the sleeping bag laden log bed occupied by Misty and Spuds, who occasionally surveyed the men with wide suspicious eyes.

No doubt the man was wondering how Dan got all those things up the mountain to his camp, wondered how a man so slight of build would have the strength to cut so much wood and survive the brutal cold. But Dan felt no obligation to explain. He had seen John's expression many times on others and knew what he was thinking.

"Sure winter is tough. But you learn to deal with it," was all he was willing to say.

"Have you had any close calls?"

Dan hesitated, then casually, "A few, but nothing I couldn't handle."

The inquisition seemingly over, Dan took advantage of a momentary silence to change the subject. "What are you two doing here? Just up for the day?"

"Oh, we're from Sheridan, just up for a ride, hoping to track down some elk." John responded, his eyes betraying the lie. "Have you seen any?"
More likely curious about me and my camp, Dan thought. "I haven't seen any on the prairie lately. But I've seen moose, and I know there's a mountain lion up here. I've seen him. Huge tracks." He studied the men's faces as he said it, reading their reactions.

"Yeah?" Lloyd's eyes fastened on Dan, waiting for more.

"He's been stalking me."

"Is that right?"

"Must be pretty hard up for food. Sorry to say he wouldn't get much off of me. But, I'm not about to let it come to that. If he comes around here, I'm ready for him. In fact, anyone who comes into my camp had better announce their arrival, because if anything comes through that door unexpectedly, I'll probably shoot first and ask questions later."

John looked at him skeptically. "Isn't that a little risky?" he said politely. Then carefully, "That would be considered murder in a court of law. You could end up in jail for the rest of your life."

"I suppose you're right. But what would it be considered if a damned mountain lion attacked and killed me and my dogs? Pure bad luck, that's what," Dan insisted, answering his own question. "Why should a cat have more rights than I do? Evidently by law, I'm dispensable, but the cat is not. But if any man is dumb enough to break into my tent . . . Well, I guess that's just his bad luck."

"And it could be yours," John was thinking, but thought better of saying it. "Well, there's a good chance it won't happen anyway. They're shy animals. Just like black bears, they really don't look for human encounters. The mountain feeds them well."

He set down his coffee cup and, looking at Lloyd, who was taking a last sip of coffee, said, "I think we'd better be on our way while it's still daylight. Enjoyed visiting with you, Dan. Thanks for the coffee, and good luck with the rest of your winter up here."

While they had been engrossed in conversation, it had finished snowing and the sun had begun peeking through a hole in the clouds, brightening the tent walls with patches of yellow light. The three men stood up and walked toward the door, Lloyd and John walking out first, squinting at the sudden splash of bright light reflecting off the snow and urgently digging in their pockets for their sunglasses.

John pulled a camera from his pocket. "You mind taking a picture of us by your tent? Want to show our friends how deep the snow gets up here."

"Sure," Dan said. "Then, if you don't mind, I'll take one with my camera."

John and Lloyd stood posed in front of the sunlit tent, minus their helmets, their snowmobile suits still unzipped to their waists as though it were a balmy day. Then Dan handed his camera to Lloyd and asked if he would photograph him against the tent and the six-foot snow bank on the opposite side of the rail fence. That done, they shook hands with Dan, zipped their suits, fastened their helmets, and headed up the hill to their machines, sometimes sinking knee deep into the snow.

Dan snickered in amusement as he watched them struggle to keep their balance in the snow depth. "Guess they found out it's kinda hard to walk in this stuff without snowshoes, wouldn't you say? From their machines and the new appearance of their suits, I would guess they had plenty of money. Seemed nosy, but friendly enough, though, didn't they?" Dan said to Misty and Spuds, who looked up at him and wagged their tails, waiting for a pat. "More curious than friendly, though. Like someone in town had told them about a crazy man staying the winter on Walker Prairie in, 'can you believe it, a wall tent'," he mocked.

"Don't believe it?" they probably said. "Go check it out for yourself."

"Why would he do that?" these guys probably asked.

"Don't know. Why don't you ask him? A death wish perhaps? Maybe he wants to die up there; let the starving animals pick his bones clean."

"From the looks of him, not a very satisfying meal."

"After seeing me and my camp, these men are probably convinced I'm crazy," Dan muttered to himself as he finished shoveling snow off the roof, then called the dogs in for supper. "But why do I care what they think?"

The words of his deceased friend popped from his mind's depths as though he were communicating from the grave. "Dan, you concern yourself too much with what other people think of you. You let them influence you because you want them as friends. Forget them. What's most important is what you think of you. You know who your real friends are."

Later, after he had had time to relive their conversation, he got to thinking that perhaps the game warden knew John and Lloyd were coming up to Bear Lodge to do some snowmobiling and had sent them to check on him. "It's a possibility," he thought. "The game warden knows trouble follows me, and he's worried he may have to haul my dead ass off the mountain. Not a pleasant thought. Then again, maybe my imagination is making up stories to satisfy my suspicions."

Had a couple of snowmobilers show up late and said hi. I've never seen them before. They would have never known that I was here if it weren't for the dogs. Haven't had any company forever. Then in the last two days, there have been eight people here. But none stayed for very long. It's going to be another cold one out. It's 9:30 p.m. and already 13 below and clear. I shoveled the snow

I got this afternoon, so now I'm going to lay down and start another book and mark another day off the calendar.

What Dan hadn't realized was that the continuous gray column of smoke rising from camp high above the evergreens looking to join the real clouds above it, revealed his location to John and Lloyd and anyone else passing through the prairie. It was visible from a distance, especially from high above camp as either a small forest fire or a campfire, in either case having human origins.

It was a restless night for Dan, waking periodically to coyotes howling from somewhere nearby, perhaps from high on She Bear, Misty and Spuds woofing in reply, trying to imitate their howling but not succeeding. Finally, Dan climbed out of warmth and strongly encouraged them to go out, hoping they would head up the hill with their barking, allowing him to get back to sleep. But the dogs kept running in and out, hair raised and barking. There would be no sleep until the coyotes or the dogs tired of the game.

Misty took out after them, and Spuds went out, barked a few times, then came back inside and climbed on top of me. I made her go back out, and she did for maybe a minute and came running back in and straight under the bed. I don't know what she would do if one turned on her. I hope that never happens.
It's still 11 above, so it's a nice evening. The high today was 24, so it was very nice out, all but the wind. It blew off and on at probably 30 miles per hour.

The next morning, Dan fed the stove before going outside, picked up the new chain Billie had brought for his chainsaw, and began installing it only to discover it was the wrong one. "Oh, well, no biggie," he said, talking himself out of disappointment. "It's a good thing I have a used one for a spare. I don't know how sharp it is, but we'll soon find out."

The chainsaw ready to go, he picked up the rest of his supplies, and with Misty and Spuds romping close behind, walked into the woods behind camp in search of trees to cut. It wasn't so much that his supply was running low as that he needed something to keep his mind from sinking into boredom and loneliness. He found a couple of medium-sized lodge poles a little more than a mile back of camp on the other side of Walker Creek and made a note of their location. Dan was happy to find they weren't widow makers. They were straight, tall, and uncomplicated, and should fall with ease, he thought. Cutting one tree and hauling it back to camp in sections would keep him busy at least until his stomach told him it was time for lunch. He would get the other one later.

As Dan approached camp with his first load of wood, he noticed an intense smell of smoke, more intense than the usual odor emanating from the stack when small flames were happily gnawing at a few small logs, slowly turning them into hot red coals that would keep the stove from cooling for a long

Photo courtesy of Danny Longwell

The stove and its pipe were weary from hard continuous labor over a very long and cold winter.

while and offer a start for a new fire when Dan returned.

"Oh, no! That's all I need, my house burning down!" he exclaimed, panic rising in his voice. Misty and Spuds ran and hid as Dan urgently dropped his load and opened the tent door to a greeting of thick smoke that brushed his face and filled his nostrils on its way out into the cold, as though eager to be free of confinement. Coughing, and in near panic, he pulled his handkerchief from his pocket, placed it over his nose and mouth, and hurried to the stove hoping to find the smoke's source and that the tent had not caught fire, at least not until he knew he could put it out. To his relief, as he fought smoke to get to the stove, he found little flame in it, just thick black smoke flowing out a good-sized hole in its side — a hole that had been growing unsuspected for weeks, like a cancer that develops and spreads silently with ill intent.

The tent hadn't caught fire. He opened the door, took a deep breath of fresh air, coughed urgently, and fastened the flaps to the tent sides, then filled a pan with water and threw it on the remaining coals, generating a column of thick black smoke, its pungent odor penetrating everything in its way before escaping into the prairie. There was nothing he could do to remedy the situation until the stove had cooled enough to handle. In the meantime, he had to decide whether he could patch the hole or would have to replace the stove and its pipe, both of which were weary from hard continuous labor over a very long and cold winter. Examining it, he determined that the stove in its weakened condition rendered patching the hole futile and that a good section of pipe and stove had burned dangerously thin, though some of it was still functional.

"I should have listened to Billie," Dan thought. "She's always right; I should know that by now. I didn't realize the stove was getting that bad. Guess I've been negligent."

That problem solved, Dan's brain raced on to the next one. Until a remedy was in place, he and his companions would be without a source of warmth, and the fixing could easily take the rest of the day and most likely into the evening. To begin with, fixing it meant hiking down the prairie to a distant hunting camp. Though rare, abandoned camps were scattered on the mountain, existing as virtual stores where tents, stoves, and other equipment lay free for the taking or were on their way to rotting into the topsoil.

The Forest Service had only begun scouring the mountain of these camps that littered the otherwise pristine landscape as though awaiting discovery by future archeologists in their search for primitive human presence. Dan's scavenging of them would lighten the Forest Service's load as they hauled stuff down the mountain to the already overloaded dump, he reasoned.

"C'mon," Dan shouted to Misty and Spuds, who had crawled from their hiding place. "We're going stove shopping." He fastened his snowshoes, picked up his rifle, and headed toward Wolf Creek closely following the Quartz as it ambled in lazy horseshoes along the edge of the woods, most of it frozen.

Though he knew approximately where it was, the camp he was looking for would be hidden in the trees, easy to miss if he didn't watch for it. The tent was gone, but he remembered the rail fence was still standing, and barrels and other equipment were scattered in the trees. When he was up for hunting season earlier in the fall, he remembered seeing an old stove and its pipe he thought to be in fairly good condition partially hidden behind a tree, perhaps tucking that information into his memory for future need. If he were lucky, it would still be there, patiently waiting to be resurrected from its graveyard and put to use again.

Misty and Spuds, playing tag in and out of the woods, were the first to notice the camp, suddenly ending their play to sniff rusting tin cans, bottles, and cooking pots lying half buried in the snow, their sensitive noses perhaps recognizing a remnant aroma of something good having been in them long ago. Dan followed the dogs and began searching the woods.

"This is disgusting," he muttered as he knelt in the snow and uncovered a pile of empty beer bottles and food cans. "Why are people such pigs, littering the forest like this? They need a hefty fine and then they shouldn't be allowed to come up here." He stood up and scanned the camp. "Now where did I see that stove? I sure hope no one took it, or we're in trouble. Don't have time to search this whole prairie for stoves."

As he searched the woods, coming up empty, his stomach began to knot, his mind coming up with what ifs: what if I don't find it; what if I find the stove but no pipes; what if it's damaged beyond fixing. Even if they found it, by the time they dragged the stove to camp, installed it and brought a fire to full flame, it would be well into the evening before heat-producing coals beneath the flame brought the tent to comfortable warmth. Without a stove, surviving a sub-zero night would be a questionable challenge.

His imagination fired, he began to berate himself for not being more careful with his stove, for not inspecting it often for developing weakness, for overloading it. His mind delved into a number of grim consequences, playing them like a suspense movie: smoke slowly leaking out a growing hole in the stove during the night, suffocating them; he and the dogs suddenly awakening to a tent beginning to flame and barely escaping; or the tent fully engulfed with himself and the dogs in it, their charred bones their only remains.

As he walked along the river, Dan tried to remember where he had seen the stove. "Maybe a little farther down," he thought. "I think it was leaning against a big tree, where not many people would notice it. It's probably buried in a ton of snow by now." But he had already searched close to camp and had found nothing. The sun was beginning to lower itself into mid-afternoon, but Dan wasn't ready to give up the search, couldn't give up just yet.

A short distance down the river, the dogs were digging in the snow. Seeing something black sticking out of a drift piled against a thick-trunked evergreen, Dan hurried to it and began digging with his hands.

"This is it," he yelled to Misty and Spuds. "You found it. Now I just have to dig it out. Should have brought a shovel, but I guess I'll have to do it the hard way."

To his relief and surprise, the stove and pipe, though a little rusty, were intact. He cleaned them of snow, then wondered how to get them back to camp. "Rope." he said. "We need to go back to camp and get a rope."

He whistled at the dogs and turned toward camp, his mind cleared of worry but filled with a promise to himself and the dogs that he would watch the stove more carefully now, not allowing it to burn so hot and fast, cleaning the ashes and pipe more often. He would also clear a good space around the stove to reduce fire danger. It wasn't just his own life that was at stake; he was responsible for the safety of his dogs as well, and he wouldn't wish them a fiery death, or any death for that matter.

"This couldn't have happened on a better day," Dan thought, unzipping his snowsuit to his waist to allow the comfortably crisp air to cool his body, which had warmed to a sweat. "Not that I wanted it to happen at all. It must be near 30 degrees today, a heat wave. It could have been 20 below with a 50-

below wind chill, and that would have made life very miserable.

Back at camp, Dan took the roll of rope off the fence post and the trio headed back to the abandoned camp at a fast pace and with purpose. He turned the stove on its side, looped one end of the rope around it and the other end around his waist, and tugged. But the stove wouldn't move.

I thought it would be easy dragging it over the snow. But when the snow is three or four feet back up in there, it's really hard to pull this thing.

Not only were there deep drifts in the woods, but while they were in the shaded forest, the warm sun had been working its magic on the open prairie loading the snow with moisture. As he slowly made his way up the hill pulling his precious load behind him, Dan noticed an increased difficulty managing his snowshoes. And now its stickiness held his feet to the ground like a magnet and forced the stove to resist his efforts, slowing his travel even more. Though camp was barely a half mile away, the trip would be long and difficult. Resigned to his dilemma, he took off his glove, pushed up his sleeve, and looked at his watch. Mid-afternoon, and the sun would soon be hitting the horizon. "I hope we make it to camp before dark," he thought, as he struggled with his load.

I finally did get it back to camp, and it took me 1.5 to 2 hours to get the stove there. By the time I got it set down on the stove I was using, put my good stove on top of it so it would put more heat out on top, especially where my feet are, it was beyond dark. That's where I keep my eggs and my batteries and everything in my sleeping bag, too. So it kept everything pretty warm that way. I was hoping anyhow. So I don't know how that's going to work, but we'll find out as the days go by. Up here, you learn something new every day. Some days you think you're a complete idiot. Other days, you think you're pretty damned smart. I can guarantee you one thing; there ain't anybody smarter than this mountain or whoever is raining down hell on you every day.

Chapter 9

CHAINSAW TROUBLES

It seemed to Dan that winter had forced on him an endless chain of problem solving, that when one problem appeared and subsequently was solved, another quickly presented itself. Especially during those small chunks of time when he became too comfortable, too relaxed in his life on the mountain, taking too much for granted — times when his mind took a vacation and slipped into depression or down the mountain to relive past events with family and friends.

It was as though these problems had stood in line, invisible, waiting, their intent to test him, to keep him focused on his fight against winter's brutal attempts to destroy him, and to keep him occupied until winter reluctantly gave in to the warm sweetness of spring.

But when he thought about it sensibly, the voice inside his head admonished him for complaining. "What did you expect it to be, a life in the Bahamas? Up here, every moment is about survival because there's always the unexpected waiting to get you. You should have known that before you even considered this little vacation. The easier decision would have been to stay in Sheridan and work 40 hours a week, bring home a paycheck, and not have to worry every minute about what's going to get you next."

To that, Dan had to admit he had no reason to complain. He had made his choices and now he had to live with whatever consequences they brought, doing the best he could to turn the insurmountable into the surmountable. And when he thought about it, he had actually done very well against the worst winter had delivered so far — the worst winter of his life for that matter.

On mornings when the sun, nestled comfortably in its deep blue softness, had the sky to itself, which was happening more often now, it peeked over the prairie early, laying a warm yellow blanket on the tent, poking its brightness annoyingly at Dan's eyelids, insisting it was time to get up, though the hour on his watch told him it was not. The sun climbed the mountain earlier each day now, as the earth tilted closer to the spring equinox.

It was 10 above at 7:30 on March 7 when Dan was forced from his overly warm sleeping bag to begin his day. Barefooted in his pajamas, he stuck his head through the tent flap and scanned his surroundings, Misty and Spuds shoving their way between his legs and out the door for their morning run. The trees and their shadows were statues in the air's stillness. The prairie had no breath, and as such, offered no challenge to the sun's warmth, which by 11 a.m. had brought the thermometer to 30 degrees, a warm summer day to Dan, whose blood had thickened over the past months to keep him warm in sub-zero temperatures.

The imminence of spring on his mind, his mood rose with the sun's warmth as he dressed, had breakfast, and hummed his way through beginning-of-the-day chores. Perhaps because they sensed their master's sunny mood, perhaps because of the sun's warming presence, Misty and Spuds were more energized than Dan had seen them in a long time, romping outdoors with unusual vigor, occasionally barking at nothing in particular, just each other.

Breakfast over, Dan sat at the dining room table sucking on the pipe Billie had brought him, savoring the tobacco taste, content to watch the smoke curl into the air and saturate everything in the tent with its sweet aroma, all the while planning the day's activities but in no particular hurry to begin them.

It was too nice a day to waste sitting inside, but though his energy levels were high, he wasn't eager to work, either. A long walk would have been his first choice for the day, for as yet, there were many places he hadn't been; he had been too occupied with surviving the cold to allow time for exploration.

Cutting and splitting wood and hauling water had long ago become mundane, but he never tired of exploring the prairie, hoping to discover hidden secrets he liked to think would be revealed to no one but himself. This was his home, his prairie, his mountain. He knew it better than anyone else, had become its best friend, and in a sense had earned ownership of it. Its secrets were his, and he would never share them with anyone, except perhaps Billie.

By the time he had finished his smoke and tucked his thoughts deep into his memory to be coaxed out later when he needed them, the sun had caused the snow to warm beyond walking quality, leaving Dan no choice but to tackle the mundane task of wood splitting. It was either that or sit inside and allow his thoughts to turn down paths he didn't want them to travel. Perhaps plunging him back into the evil blackness of depression that sometimes stalked him as stealthily as the mountain lion he knew was out there.

I was going out for a walk today, but changed my mind, for it got to warm, and I would just sink to my knees, even with snowshoes on. So I'm going to chop some more wood. Hell, it's only 11 a.m., and already it's 30 above. So it's one hell of a nice day - t-shirt weather as long as the sun is shining on you.

By the time he had split what wood he hauled into camp days ago and cut the previous day, Dan had exchanged his snowsuit for a jacket, and later, as the sun burned hotter, his jacket for a t-shirt and bare arms. There was some mysterious ingredient in the sun's warmth that arrived each year only in spring that had altered his mood for the better, for his spirits hadn't been this high since he had anticipated spending the Christmas holidays at home with Billie. But soon after finishing his wood splitting, what had begun as a good day, deteriorated as quickly as it had arrived.

It was a perfect afternoon for cutting another tree and Dan, his energy far from spent, was up to the challenge of felling the one he had marked several days ago for that purpose, then cutting it into five-foot pieces and dragging them a quarter mile through the woods back to camp. If he tired of it, or ran out of time, he thought, he would finish another day. He set the chainsaw down on a log and, after feeding it with gas and oil, he revved it into action only to have it suddenly zing, snap, and stop before he could make the first cut.

"Damn," he shouted into the woods, as he examined the near-fatally injured saw. "I knew things were going too well. My luck just isn't that good."

What had started as a good day turned to shit in a hurry. When Billie came up last week she brought a new bar and chain for the saw. I found out it was the wrong chain, and today, I found out that it was the wrong bar, too. But to find this out, I had to use it. The chain caught on the power sprocket of the bar and that tore the hell out of my chain sprocket and strained the clutch. So now I need all kinds of parts. The only good thing out of this is that I will have a new chainsaw when I'm done. But the way my luck is going today, I think I'd better stay damned close to camp, for something might happen to me next.

Billie wasn't to blame; Dan recognized that she, like most women, or even a lot of men, for that matter, wasn't a chainsaw mechanic. She had followed his instructions without deviating, even writing them down in detail, explaining to those at the store she supposed knowledgeable what she needed. "They told me that what they gave me would work for this type of saw. I don't know how, but they must have misunderstood," she complained toDan when he called her that morning.

Not doubting that, but needing someone to blame, he directed his anger at the store clerks who, according to him, should have known from her explanation what she needed. It wasn't that difficult.

The stores she went to don't know jack shit about what they are selling. So now what should have cost me $40 is now costing me $100. And that is crap.

Now, because of their ignorance, bringing the chainsaw back to life would require an expensive fix, one he hadn't counted on or budgeted for, but that was necessary if he were to remain in his winter home, for though March had turned momentarily gentle, flaunting snippets of spring, it wasn't finished with its meanness. It had come in like a lamb and, because of that, was expected to go out like a vicious lion. And even after its roar settled into tameness, winter's reluctance to give in was likely to continue in spurts through April and May, refusing to leave the field until Mother Nature called the game, its angry tantrums causing serious damage to the forest and anything or anyone in it.

Disgusted, Dan picked up his chainsaw and equipment and trudged wearily toward camp, weary not from the day's work, for he had done little of it that day, but from discouragement and wondering why a such a promising day had gone bad and how much worse it would get now that it had begun to go that way. This morning, he could have tackled anything, anyone, but now the problem of getting parts to do the fixing and the expense of it lay heavy on his mind, leaving nothing to stop his mood from falling further.

"Just my luck," he thought, picking up the damaged saw and chain. "Never seem to have much of it. That's the story of my life."

Dan's eyes were fixed on the ground as he negotiated the deep drifts through the woods, climbing over and around fallen logs frozen into the snow and low tree branches looped just above the ground that were always ready to grab his snowshoes or a boot and send him face down in the snow.

"There's always something waiting to get you," he mumbled to his feet. But he had long ago become wise to the tricks of the forest and knew how to avoid its traps. Crossing the river, he noticed that a thin layer of water lay on its frozen surface, warning him to proceed with caution.

"Oh, great. Now I'll have to figure out how to keep snow melt out of my tent," he said, as he cautiously put pressure on the ice with the toe of one foot before stepping onto it with his full weight. "I wonder how big a lake I'll be stepping into in my yard or, more likely, inside the tent if this weather continues."

As he approached camp, Dan scanned his front yard, which he kept shoveled nearly to dirt, piling the snow on the other side of the fence in a growing six-foot wall, and found it buried under a couple of inches of water trickling with ill intent toward the tent opening. Though he wasn't surprised, its presence and likely destination kept his spirits on a downward trend. To him, it was like a rattlesnake lying in wait, intending to seek refuge in his living quarters, doing harm to everything it touched.

The snow is melting out front, and the only place it has to go is right to the front door. So I have three inches of water just about ready to run in, and there's no place to put a ditch to get rid of it because of the drifts around me. So it hasn't been a good day at all, and it's only 2 p.m. I think before it's all done and over with, I will have water running through the tent. Then it's going to get interesting.

But the day was turning into late afternoon, distorting tree shadows stretching like a rubber band, darkening and cooling the prairie. Already, the water was working toward solidifying and would be ice by morning as the temperature dropped to well below freezing overnight. And as the snow melted and thawed again during nature's roller coaster ride into spring, a thin crust of ice would form over the snow as well. But Dan had little objection to that; a crusty surface would keep snowshoes on top of the drifts, although at the same time make travel over its slipperiness tricky. Seemed to him everything that had an up side also had a down side and that there were more down sides to life than up sides.

Sloshing through the thickening water, he set what was left of his ailing chainsaw on the table outside the tent and climbed a short distance up the hill to place his parts order with Billie and have her ask Kenny to bring them up by snowmobile as soon as he was able. His wood supply would likely last two or three days at most. That is, if the temperature didn't plunge too far down the thermometer, for though recent days had been what Dan considered unseasonably warm, temperatures habitually dropped significantly with the sun's disappearance each evening. The longer the chainsaw sat nonfunctional and, as he watched his wood diminish, the more concerned he would become in spite of his efforts to talk himself out of it. He could only hope the weather stayed fairly warm and that there would be no unforeseen delays keeping Kenny from coming up.

As he waited for Billie to answer the phone, his apprehension grew, for he supposed she would be angry with him for needing assistance again. "You're not supposed to be having people bring things up to you all the time," he expected to hear.

"This wasn't my fault, and I hope Billie sees it that way, too," he reasoned with himself. "I wasn't negligent. It was the sales people. They're supposed to be familiar with the products they're selling. Know something about how they work. But these days, they're not."

As he explained the situation to Billie, his apprehension disappeared. Billie considered Dan's request legitimate. There were no harsh words for him, just apologies.

"I spelled it out for him; didn't know what else to tell him, but I guess he didn't understand. So tell me again what you need and what was wrong with what I got you, and I'll draw him a picture this time."

"Then can you call Kenny and have him bring up the parts as soon as he can?"

"I'll go to the store this afternoon and call Kenny tonight," she assured him.

With a better feeling than before he had made the call, Dan concluded the conversation and made his way down the hill, satisfied that, with effort, he would soon have a working chainsaw, but the cloud that had parked itself over him that afternoon wouldn't move on, his thoughts delving deep into rewarding conversations with his best friend and the grief resulting from his loss. It seemed he was thinking that, as long as his mood was grim, he might as well fall farther into it, for there was nothing at the moment to pull him out.

That evening, he did his best to poke his grief beneath his mind's surface and divert his attention from his problems by listening to the boys and girls basketball tournaments on the radio. Soon he was absorbed in them, even cheering loudly for his favorite team, as scores hovered near a tied ending. It was 11 p.m. when Dan turned off the radio and sent Misty and Spuds out for their final run before settling in for the night, hoping his mind would clear enough to allow him a restful sleep free from worry.

"It's out of my hands for now," he thought. "Just have to wait until Kenny comes up, and hope it's soon."

But when he stepped into the late starlit night to call the dogs, Misty refused to come in. Though he heard nothing, he knew there was an invisible something out there holding her attention, keeping her yapping incessantly into the darkness. Dan grabbed his rifle and stood for a long while, listening, expecting to hear what he hoped he wouldn't hear. But the only sound breaking the night's stillness was loud barking followed by spurts of silence.

"You just stay out all night, then," he yelled into the black night after calling her one last time. "It's 11 o'clock, and Spuds and I are going to bed." Then to Spuds, who was at his feet wagging her tail, "If she won't come in, there's nothing I can do to save her from whatever is out there."

Reluctant to go in and leave Misty vulnerable, though knowing he could do nothing unless she willingly obeyed his calls, he stepped back into the tent. Spuds hesitated, then followed, curling up on the floor next to her master's bed, expectantly eyeing the tent flap until the light was extinguished. Even then, Spuds was restless without her companion by her side, frequently getting up and standing by the door, then lying down again, sometimes uttering a barely audible "woof."

"It's all about choices," Dan said to Spuds in resignation. "And staying out at night asking for trouble is a bad one. You made the right choice." He hesitated. "Come to think of it, I've made more than my share of bad choices. And I pay for them later. I just hope Misty doesn't have to pay for hers."

Dan had just settled into his sleeping bag alongside his rifle and was drifting off when a chorus of coyote howls drowned the silence, soon followed by Misty's responsive barking and Spuds offering sporadic yips. Back and forth like questions and answers, their conversation continued at length. To Misty, it was a game — perhaps a filling of need for social interaction with her kind, much like Dan's unconscious need for human presence. Spuds, more selective in her social pursuits, was content to leave the coyotes to Misty, joining in the conversation from the safety and warmth of the tent, her hiding place at hand should the conversation go bad.

Misty is out raising hell with the coyotes. Now she's trying to howl like them instead of just barking, and it's driving me nuts, and she's not listening to me. And now Spuds is starting in, and she's right here by the door. God only knows when they will quit.

Much of the night was like that: howling and barking; Dan yelling at them to shut up so he could sleep; silence; more howling and barking; more yelling; silence. Seemed to Dan there was more howling and barking than silence, and when he awoke early the next morning, his brain was cloudy from lack of sleep, his body unwilling to begin the day, his mood angry.

Damned dogs woke me up again howling at the damn coyotes. Be damned if I know when they sleep, for I didn't get much. Called Billie this morning to see if she got the things that I needed, and she said yes and that they tried it all on another saw. So I should be in business when Kenny gets it up here either today or tomorrow.
Billie asked if it was cloudy and snowing, and I said no that it was clear. And now it is 10 a.m. and snowing like hell, big old wet flakes. Didn't even know it was snowing until the dogs came in all white. It looks like I could get a bunch of it.

Snow kept falling throughout the day, accumulating to nine inches, carefully measured by Dan at 3 p.m. when he decided he had better put his shovel to work in case it continued into the evening and possibly overnight, collecting heavily on the tent roof. And from the sky's grim appearance, grim as his mood had been the day before, his speculation was more than a possibility. So he was pleasantly surprised when he stepped outside after supper to see a slivered moon dropping its light from between cloud holes, and no precipitation. Before settling in for the night, he walked over to his shrinking woodpile and counted the pieces.

"Not much left," he told Misty and Spuds who were comfortably curled up in their bed looking disinterested. "Sure hope Kenny gets here tomorrow or I'm in trouble."

Daylight crept in late and unwilling the next morning, keeping Dan asleep beyond the time of his normal waking, the sky overcast, but lacking snow threats. His first thought before he was out of bed was that Kenny would be coming up sometime during the day as Billie had said.

"Sure hope he gets here or I'll have to start cutting wood the hard way, and I don't know how long I'll be able to keep that up. Forty pieces of wood will barely last the day."

When he comes, I will be cutting and chopping lots of wood again. But until then, I won't be doing much of anything. Maybe I'll go for a short walk while I'm waiting, but I don't know yet. Damn. Just caught another mouse. That's the third one this week, and I haven't seen or heard a mouse in over a month. Hope I'm not getting another run of the son-of-a-bitches, for I thought I had got rid of all of them. But I guess not. Called Charlie down at the Legion yesterday. Sure was good to talk with her for a minute.

"Guess I can't do much without a chainsaw, and the snow isn't sticky," Dan told Misty and Spuds. "So how about a walk?" Their tails wagged excitedly as though they knew from his tone what their master had offered. Normally his walks took him down the trail to Wolf Creek or to the Big Goose River and the bridge. But today, he decided to hike a distance behind camp and explore places he hadn't been. He fastened his snowshoes, slung his pack over his back and his rifle over his shoulder, and turned toward the woods.

"Hey, you two; we're not going that way," he called after Misty and Spuds who romped up the hill toward She Bear Mountain. But they weren't listening. A high, sharp whistle rent the crisp air, causing the dogs to stop and look for the source.

"C'mon you idiots. We're going this way." Dan turned toward the timber-clothed hill behind camp, the dogs running to catch up.

Several paces from camp, Misty and Spuds beside him, Dan was startled by a twig snap and something approaching from behind the evergreens, their branches set in motion by something invisible, and it didn't seem like the wind's doing. The dogs turned their attention in the direction of the sound, while Dan stopped to listen and ready his rifle, wondering whether the wind was playing tricks or something was preparing to spring at him. Misty and Spuds, ears forward, growled softly but didn't approach.

"Shhh," Dan ordered. "Let's see what it is before getting all excited." The trio watched intently as a huge, nearly black, gracefully curved nose pushed the branches aside, allowing the rest of its large head and matching body through the opening between the trees. Startled by Dan's presence, but not fearing him or the dogs, the long-legged animal stared at him momentarily with beady brown eyes as though trying to determine what kind of creatures were confronting it. Then, suddenly lifting its head and legs high, it trotted effortlessly into the woods as though floating above an uneven ground and deep drifts that didn't exist.

Dan, sure his heart had stopped, lowered his rifle and breathed deeply as he stared after it, admiring the ease and grace with which the animal moved its large body through the forest. "Just a cow moose," he told Misty and Spuds.

"Am I getting jumpy, or what?"

Deeper into the woods, Dan stopped to examine a set of tracks. As he suspected, they belonged to a very large cat that had been in the area and wandered off to the left of his path. Misty and Spuds merely sniffed the tracks and turned their attention toward their destination, though unsure where that was, assuring their master the cat wasn't in the vicinity. It was a long trek through the woods, up a hill, and onto a high meadow where he could take in the whole panoramic prairie, Dan too busy keeping track of where they were going and watching for tracks to realize how far they had traveled.

"Wow!" he exclaimed, as they reached a high open meadow. "What a view! See that tiny string snaking along the mountain way over there?" he said to Misty and Spuds, who appeared to be admiring the view as well. "The forest road is over there somewhere — about ten miles away. Most likely buried in six feet of snow so you wouldn't recognize it. You just have to know where it is by looking at your surroundings. I imagine snowmobilers frequently travel that road. Not many hikers or snowshoers would know which direction to go to get out of here and off the mountain if they had to. The mountain closes highways and forest roads in the winter, so you probably couldn't get off it that way anyway. At that time of year, you have to know what you're doing or stay off the mountain if you don't want trouble."

Dan had come to a oneness with the mountains, a similar oneness he had felt for his good friend. But his love and admiration for the Bighorns exceeded what he had ever felt for any human. He drew comfort from knowing that, unlike humans, at least the mountain would never leave him. He could sit alone for hours admiring the beauty of its wildness, exploring its hidden places, gazing over a cliff's edge into a steep, rocky canyon, awed by the wonder in the making of it and the rugged danger that lay beyond its edge.

Those who knew and loved the mountain knew its personality has endless facets: it's protective; it opens doors and closes them; it's punishing, rewarding, moody, comforting. There would be no end to his love affair with the mountain's unsurpassed beauty and unpredictable nature: its closeness to heaven, its offer of solitude, soothing sounds of whispering winds and rushing water, bugling elk, howling coyotes, and owl hoots softly breaking the night silence.

The mountain knew his thoughts, his triumphs, his failings, and shared his grief, listening, consoling, but without comment or criticism, without judgment. Its punishments, dealt mainly to the foolish, were harsh but, if you knew and respected its rules, heeded the lessons it offered, the mountain was kind, rewarding. The mountain accepted Dan as the human being he was, never expecting him to take on someone else's ways or thinking, never admonishing for merely being himself, and he respected the mountain for that.

In his wandering, absorbed in deep thought and admiration, Dan found himself farther from camp than he had planned. But the mountain rewarded his effort by laying out miles of panoramic peaks, meadows, rolling hills, and vast woods for him to admire and photograph.

After snapping several shots, he tucked his camera back in his pack, picked up his rifle, which he had set on a tree stump, and turned toward camp, carefully following his snowshoe tracks. A few yards down the trail, he discovered his weren't the only tracks in the snow. Bending down to examine them, he noticed the four clawless toes and padded impression of a feline turned toward the hill he and the dogs had just come down. A predator lurked nearby, invisible, most likely watching them, considering them prey. Dan again readied his rifle and picked up the pace, nervously searching the woods behind him and on all sides as they traveled, watching the dogs' behavior as well.

Though the tracks soon disappeared, he couldn't relax. The cat was roaming quietly, stealthily somewhere in the woods, but there were no more signs of it. As he and the dogs neared camp in the growing shadows of late afternoon, he noticed snowmobile tracks stretching through the prairie above camp. But no tracks indicating someone had stopped and walked toward his camp. He returned to his tent tired from the two-mile uphill walk, shed his snowmobile suit, fed the fire, and lay down. But his rest was soon disturbed by the sound of snowmobiles approaching, luring him outside to determine who was driving through his prairie. But whoever it was hurried by without so much as a wave and disappeared, leaving Dan to wonder.

I was just dozing off when Misty took off. Two more snowmobiles went through, but they didn't stop. Don't know if they were going over to Bear Lodge or if they were headed down. I didn't see them, just heard them. Called Billie, and Kenny's not coming up until late this evening. Can't believe he's coming up in the dark.

The sun had lowered itself behind the timber, taking the temperature down with it by the time Kenny arrived at 5, earlier than Dan expected, carrying the supplies he had nervously anticipated. By the time Kenny and Dan finished supper and had checked the supplies to make sure they were correct with nothing lacking, it was dark, and Kenny was shivering with cold.

"Where's your jacket?" Dan had asked when Kenny arrived without it.

"I forgot it. It's in my truck."

"Well, you'll freeze to death before you get down, and I don't want that on my conscience." Pulling a heavy jacket from a large tub and thrusting it at Kenny, he said, "Here. I have more jackets up here than I can wear. I won't miss this one."

Kenny and Dan exchanged expressions of gratitude after which Kenny fired up his machine and headed into the darkness. Dan picked up his chainsaw and disappeared inside and, though it was late, set to work on it, figuring on a fairly easy fix. But, as much of his work with the saw had offered, he was wrong.

I finally got my chain saw put together, then broke the pull rope on it. And when I took it apart, that damned spring came unwound. I finally got it put together and running at 11 p.m. I thought it was around 8. It's still pretty warm out tonight at 8 degrees above. I'm going to eat a couple pieces of candy Kenny brought, then head off to bed, for I'll be cutting and chopping wood all day tomorrow.

Morning blessed Dan with a warm 24 above zero and an overcast sky. But his stove had become cold as ice some time during the night, and he had no wood left with which to feed it. After dressing, he put on a jacket and fixed himself some oatmeal and coffee to warm his insides, then went outdoors to test his chainsaw. It coughed and sputtered, hesitated, and stopped, then took off and purred effortlessly on the second pull, for which he was grateful. So he spent the day urgently replenishing his wood supply, and when enough to keep the stove happily fed for a day or two had been cut and split, he took a short break to clean the stove of ashes and return heat to the tent.

The chainsaw works so good that I got carried away with it, and now I have over 70 pieces to chop up. Got some of it chopped up by 1:30 and decided it was time for lunch. So I'm fixing a big pan of spaghetti, and there's a lot of it. Put new batteries in the radio, and they lasted maybe 20 minutes and are dead. Oh what the hell; I'll just put on my snowshoes and run down to Wal Mart and get some more.

Dan finished cleaning his kitchen and set the leftover spaghetti in a cool corner of the tent where it would neither freeze nor spoil. He and the dogs would have the rest of it for supper. Inside chores done, he put on his jacket and boots and stepped outside into mid-afternoon semi-darkness. During his lunch break, thick gray clouds had met the mountain and decided to rest at ground level before lazily moving on. Since there was little wind to push them, the sleepy clouds would linger indefinitely, unable to find their way off the mountain until the wind gathered enough speed to nudge them on their way.

Hardly able to see two feet ahead of him, the prairie seemingly vaporized into non-existence, Dan decided it would be unsafe to persist in his woodcutting chores. He had enough to last the rest of the day and perhaps tomorrow, too. This time, the thought of spending the rest of the day in idleness didn't bring down his spirits; he was content with the opportunity to sit with his feet up, watch the smoke curl decoratively from his pipe filling the tent with its sweet aroma, and think about the last few days' happenings and his conversation with Kenny.

"I'm using the fog as an excuse to come back in and drink this one lonely beer that Kenny left me last night," he told Misty and Spuds, as he popped open the can. "You can stay outside if you want. Don't go too far, and make sure you can find your way back." Then to himself in a mumble, "Later, if the fog lifts, I'll go out and cut more wood."

Later in the afternoon, higher clouds moving in brought wind, which began pushing the fog from the mountain, the clouds dropping snowflakes a handful at a time, as though trying to decide whether to get serious in their efforts or remain mildly threatening. Not trusting their intent, Dan took advantage of the fog's absence and the weather's indecisiveness to split and haul more wood into the tent. Though she may try to catch him off guard, trying to fool him into thinking winter had left for good and that he was safe from its grip, Mother Nature wouldn't catch Dan unprepared if he could help it. She had tried it many times during the long winter and hadn't succeeded. And, he knew as long as he was on the mountain, she would keep trying.

Winter's cold and the need for wood had kept Dan's explorations to a minimum since fall. Now that spring was hovering behind winter's skirts, occasionally persuading temperatures to moderate, and that he was well supplied for warmth in case a blizzard shut him indoors for a day or so, his thoughts increasingly turned to exploring the prairie's nooks and crannies he hadn't yet ventured into.

If it does drop a lot of snow, I'm ready, for I have enough wood inside to last two weeks. I'm going to spend the rest of the week playing around. I have lots of places I want to go and see, just look around and take pictures. The high today was 32 degrees, and I'm off to bed.

Chapter 10

GNATS IN THE WATER HOLE

Snow that had fallen softly the past few days lay like powder over the old, flaunting its unblemished sparkling white beauty, as yet unmolested by anything living, even by the wind. It lay quietly, unmoving over the prairie like a sheet of pure white paper waiting for the artist's touch, the story told in footprints, or for the wind to arrive and play in it, sculpting it into fancy designs or anything the imagination could conjure up. But this morning, the wind hung back, absent, letting the sun have its way, something in the air hinting at the coming of spring but reluctant to promise an arrival date.

"A perfect day for exploration," Dan thought as, clad only in his pajamas and bare feet, he thrust his head through the tent flaps into the sunshine. "Oh, it's going to be a beautiful day," he said cheerily as Misty and Spuds pushed their way outside to take care of their morning duties and do their own determining. "How about a nice long walk?" he shouted after them as they trotted nonstop into the woods.

"Sounds like a good idea to me," he shouted even louder.

The dogs either didn't hear him or didn't care. They had more urgent business to take care of. "We'll discuss it when we come back," they seemed to say, as they disappeared into the woods.

Misty and Spuds had become more complacent during the past few weeks, as though winter's bitter cold had slowly, unobtrusively, eaten their energy. By now, even the warm sunshine didn't seem to energize them. Dan noticed they didn't run, play, and wrestle as much as they used to, but contented themselves instead to lie inside and nap more often much as when the temperatures and accompanying winds were too arctic for anyone to go outdoors and warmth was their main priority. Concerned, Dan hoped spring's coming would recharge them, plant in them a new spirit, a semblance of their puppyhood.

Nearly blinded by the sun's rays dancing on the diamond-studded snow, he pulled his head back in the tent, set to dressing, and fixed a bowl of instant oatmeal and a cup of hot coffee, a quick breakfast he could devour in a hurry and then get more quickly to enjoying the day. After finishing breakfast, Dan threw his oatmeal package into the stove and emptied yesterday's burned tobacco from his pipe. With fresh tobacco in its bowl, he struck a match and puffed until he could taste and satisfy his olfactory nerves with the tobacco's sweetness. This is much better than a cigarette, he thought as he sat back, feet on the chair next to him, and directed his thoughts into deciding what would keep him occupied outdoors for most of the day. His love affair with his pipe had become routine the past several days when neither urgent chores nor inclement weather pushed him to action. And it seemed he was most indecisive when the weather beckoned him to play than when it threatened to close him indoors.

Now the climbing sun penetrating the tent with its warmth suddenly brought Dan to realize he was wasting a perfect day and that he needed to get outdoors to enjoy it before it was gone. "Made that mistake before; not going to do it today. Guess I'm getting as lazy as the girls," he told himself, as he quickly extinguished his pipe, set it on the table to light after supper, and stacked the dirty dishes, intending to wash them that evening. His growing pile of burnable trash could also wait until later when he would be around to keep an eye on an outdoor fire. Not that it would go anywhere set inside a ring of snow. But unattended fires in the forest always made him nervous. Too many fires had turned into big ones when no one was watching.

Bypassing his snowmobile suit, he put on a light jacket he pulled from a tub that stored his extra clothing, a cap, and a pair of dark glasses, and stepped into the bright sun still undecided about where he would go, just knowing he had to get outdoors and let his sun-deprived body bask in its spring-like warmth, for knowing the mountain, the next day could bring a return to nastiness.

When Misty and Spuds, returned from their romp in the woods, saw him put on his snowshoes, they knew adventure lay ahead, and they intended to follow whether they felt like it or not. But Dan only made it to the top of the hill above camp with his walking stick and a great deal of effort before deciding to give it up. No matter which way he turned, his snowshoes kept sinking deep into the powdery snow, his legs quickly tiring with the repeated effort of pulling his feet up and setting them down. He knew his legs would cause him pain later on if he continued to put that kind of stress on them, for it had happened many times after walking up and down the mountain or after long walks on the prairie, and he didn't need the pain persistence would bring.

The going proved as exhausting for Misty and Spuds, who had stopped half-way up the hill and stood looking at him as though to say, "This is too much work for us; we're going back. You can go ahead if you want."

"Seems the snow is either too sticky or too powdery, and that keeps me in camp as much as cold stormy weather. So now what do I do?" he asked himself as he trudged back down the hill and removed his snowshoes.

Oh what a boring day. Started to go for a walk, but the snow is so soft you sink clear to your butt. So I gave that up and came back to the house and sat outside and got some sun on my arms until the wind came up.

As the day wore on, painfully slow, it became more pleasant, even with the lazy intermittent wind that arrived in the late morning to (purposely, it seemed) raise goose bumps on Dan's bare arms and send him inside for his jacket. A half hour of bare skin exposure was the best that could be expected in early March before the Solstice arrived to announce that spring was taking over.

But there would be even better days as the earth tilted deeper into spring bringing comfortably warm air that was clean and pleasant. Better than summer when the prairie winds sometimes blew hot and dry and even the creeks dwindled and slowed, too lazy to move on. He just had to be patient. Dan settled himself in a lawn chair and lit a cigarette. But he could only sit a short while before becoming restless, needing something to occupy him.

Officially, spring was three weeks away, and he had grown weary of months of cutting and splitting wood, weary of his race against nature to stay alive when it seemed it would rather have him dead, weary of winter's imprisoning hold on him.

The past few days, the sun had become warmer, only the wind, when it was present, feeling like it had raced in after gathering cold from the icebergs in Alaska or Antarctica. But, absent the wind, the sun enticed him to forget that the battle had not yet been won, luring him to play, but limiting his activities. It seemed a fickle sun, warm and welcoming but at the same time punishing — giving and taking away.

Now he sat studying his camp, wondering how he could improve it, or more likely, planning outdoor projects that would occupy his remaining time on the mountain. Overall, the camp was in good condition, except for the horse corral, which, with its downed rails and leaning posts, had suffered through a number of hunting seasons and hard winters. He would have to repair it before he brought Kenny's horses up the mountain again, for he didn't like to tie them to trees or even a tether rope, which he had sometimes done. But did he want to repair it or move it to a different spot? Repair seemed the most logical option, but moving it would consume more time otherwise spent in boredom.

"How about over there?" he asked Misty and Spuds, pointing to an open patch on the edge of some tall lodge pole pines just outside the fence that encircled his tent. "They'll have shelter from the wind and rain under those trees. And they'll be far enough from the creek to please the Forest Service." But Misty and Spuds were too busy napping in a patch of warm sun to pay him heed and, besides, what did they care where the horses were housed or if they had protection from the weather. Neither the horses nor the Forest Service was their concern.

"Okay, don't answer me. I'm going to walk it off and mark it so I'm ready to start on it as soon as spring thaws the frost from the ground and I can get the posts pounded in. Until then, I can start cutting the rails and gather wood for the posts, though some of the old rails will probably do as well. And I don't need your help."

The decision made with no objections from Misty and Spuds, and corral boundaries walked and marked, Dan stood thinking about whether to tear down the old corral now or wait. Doing it now would give him something to do, and he really wanted to, but he couldn't. If he tore it down too soon, there remained the problem of where to keep Kenny's horses when he brought them up before the ground had thawed to pack equipment down the mountain. He thought for a moment. What had begun as a good idea had just turned sour.

That settled and nothing else to do because Dan had talked himself out of it, he went in, made himself a peanut butter and jelly sandwich, took it outside, and while eating it, pondered how to keep busy the rest of the day. Preferably outdoors. The aroma of peanut butter and jelly brought the dogs to life. They quickly trotted to his feet where they sat wagging their tails, staring up at him with hungry eyes in hopes he would share his lunch with them. Dan peeled off the crusts and tossed them on the ground. The dogs quickly gobbled them and went back for more.

"You have your own food in the tent," Dan said, stuffing the last of his sandwich into his mouth. "You don't need my lunch, too." Misty and Spuds sniffed the ground for crumbs then lay down near his feet disappointed. Dan's thoughts turned to the problem of boredom and how to keep from it during his final weeks on the mountain. He had worked too fast, too efficiently, and that efficiency now left him with little work to occupy his time.

If he sat unoccupied too long, his thoughts free to roam, they would turn corners leading to paths he wished to avoid. He had been down those paths and the dead-end paths that branched off of them until they were worn, looking for solutions to problems he wasn't sure he could define. Traveling there only brought him to loneliness and a sadness he wished to forget. A walk would have sent his mind on the right paths, paths that filled his spirit with admiration and wonder for the mountain and of winter beaten into oblivion by spring's impending arrival and the victorious conclusion to his stay on the mountain.

His thoughts spent, and tired from boredom, he went in, took off his boots, stretched out on the bed and fell asleep. When he awoke a half hour later, a cloud still hanging over him, he decided to wash his dirty dishes from breakfast and lunch. He picked up the water jug closest to the stove and, turning it upside down, emptied a cup full of water into the pot. Checking the remaining jugs, he found he had used all he had hauled in a few days ago.

"How did all of them get empty so fast," he asked himself as he put on his jacket and boots and picked up the empty jugs. "It's a good thing I checked or I wouldn't have had water for coffee in the morning." Now he had something to do out of necessity, and he would take his time doing it, for a long evening stretched ahead of him like an endless deserted road.

During the afternoon, the temperature had climbed to well above freezing, and much of the snow in camp had turned to puddles. Eager to find out how much snow had succumbed to the day's warmth, Dan dropped his water jugs by the fence and climbed up the hill to open land to find that the sun had directed its intensity onto the upper prairie as well, exposing large patches of bare ground.

"Wow. It's going fast," he said to himself. "Spring can't be that far off." He made his way down the hill, picked up his water jugs, and hiked slowly and deliberately to the creek to discover that, even though most of it lay in shade, the sun had worked its magic on the ice as well, but not for the good. The stream that all winter had provided him with clear spring-fed water had very suddenly become a polluted nightmare.

"What in the hell is that?" he exclaimed, kneeling in the watery snow to get a closer look at the huge clump of tiny black specks floating on the water's surface. "Yuck! Gnats! Millions of them. I've never seen so many of them in one place. How will I ever get rid of them?"

Dan saw them as an insurmountable problem. This was his only source of drinking water. But, like the mice, Misty and Spuds didn't see them that way. Without hesitating, they stepped onto the ice and lapped up the water as though the bugs weren't there. Dan wasn't as adventuresome in his tastes, nor was he that desperate for food. He quietly walked back to the tent, picked up a cup, which was the best he had for straining and scooping, and headed back to the creek. But each time he dipped the cup into the water, the more agitated the water and spread out the gnats became. And the more he scooped, the more they seemed to multiply, the chore becoming more difficult and time-consuming, and Dan increasingly angry and frustrated.

Though he thought about tapping into another of the prairie's many springs, searching for a different water source wasn't an option, for it would mean a walk too far transporting so many heavy, water-laden jugs by hand. And those springs weren't as prolific and operable as this one.

There were 10 million little gnats in my water hole. I scooped for 10 minutes trying to get them out, and they just kept coming to the top. Finally got all I could, but I know there's still a bunch in my drinking water. I guess that's what I'll have for supper tonight, coffee and gnats or gnats and coffee. Maybe a piece of bread if there's enough of them.

Well, supper was good; had a juicy hamburger and macaroni and cheese. The coffee was less desirable, but drinkable as long as there was a little whiskey in it.

It was early evening and suppertime by the time Dan had finished filling his water jugs and hauling them back to the tent. And even with all the effort he put into the straining, he couldn't completely rid the water of the troublesome bugs. But he had nothing better to do that day than try. Besides, gnats in his coffee gave him good reason to pour a little whiskey into it.

"I hope I don't have to strain the gnats off my water every time I fill my jugs," he said as he set the last jug on the floor near the stove. While finishing supper dishes, he reflected on the day, thinking he was glad he wasn't able to take a walk that day.

"I thought about walking down to whiskey rock and getting my glasses, if they're still around," he confessed to Misty and Spuds. It was the second time he had left a pair of glasses at Whiskey Rock. "But I know if I got down that far, I would have just kept going to town. The man on the radio said we're supposed to get snow the rest of the week. Maybe I'll feel more at home then."

Misty looked up at him at mention of the word "home" and gave a slight wag of her tail and a soft "woof" as though she, too, was eager to end this harsh winter and go home. Not wishing to delve deeper into thoughts of home, Dan picked up a book from his stack and lost himself in someone else's life struggles until the hour grew late and his eyelids fought to close against his efforts to stay awake. Losing the battle, he put down his book, settled into his sleeping bag, and hoped his closed eyes would take him into warm sunshine, green grass, flowers, and horseback riding on the mountain with Billie. "No nightmares, please," he begged softly, as he drifted into sleep.

Dan expected to awaken the next morning to gray skies and falling snow, but was surprised to open his eyes to yellow splashes of light heating the tent walls. The thermometer read 22 degrees early in the morning, the sky had become an uninterrupted indigo ocean, and the breeze gently caressed the pine branches, promising not to turn to roughness.

"So where is all this snow we're supposed to be getting?" Dan asked himself as he put on his snowshoes and headed up the hill toward the prairie hoping the snow had turned to a more cooperative consistency overnight. "No, I'm not going to Whiskey Rock," he told Misty and Spuds, who were wagging their tails and running circles as though excited about going home. "We're going to look for moose for the game warden. Let me know if you see any, especially if they're wearing collars. But don't chase them away, or you'll be in trouble. You're only allowed to do that with coyotes." The dogs looked up at him as though to say they understood but that there would be no promises regarding the chasing.

At the top of the hill, Dan turned toward Walker Mountain looking for tracks. They had gone approximately a mile when he saw long-legged black specks in the distance. "Shhh! No barking," he warned the dogs. "Let's see if we can get closer without spooking them." As they moved slowly toward them,

Dan was able to determine that there were five in the group. But he would have to get closer to see collars, if they were wearing them.

"Spring must be coming," he said. "That's the most moose I have seen here on the prairie all winter."

As Dan and the dogs moved closer, the moose lifted their heads and turned to stare at the advancing entourage. Finally, Dan was able to determine that they were wearing collars, but he couldn't get close enough, even with binoculars, to determine color. Though moose didn't shy easily, neither did they desire closeness with humans. Over time, they had long ago become used to summer tourists gawking at them, pointing in jest at their awkward paddles, roman noses, and long, gangly legs. They were used to the occasional ignorant human who thought it fun to try a face-to-face approach, daring to attempt petting a baby moose, the animal most likely finding such stupidity hard to believe.

The moose were used to it, but not tolerant of it.

As he stood admiring them, Dan remembered someone telling him about a woman who approached a cow moose and her baby one summer so her husband could get a shot of the three of them being cozy. Dan shook his head. "I can't believe the stupidity of some humans. That cow showed her coziness all right," he said to Misty and Spuds. "She knocked the woman down with her nose, then walked away. That was a kind warning from a tolerant moose that could have trampled her into the ground. That woman was lucky to walk away with minor bruises. But the story goes that she threatened to sue the Forest Service."

Dan laughed at the thought. "Some people have no respect for moose, or any animal for that matter," he said, as he reached down and scratched Spuds behind her ear. "And they deserve what they get when they're not respectful."

There are people who consider moose giant masses of ugliness, animals good for nothing but hunting. But others, including Dan, saw in them magnificent, graceful animals, that could trot effortlessly along the prairie and into the woods, the antlered bulls with heads held high, unencumbered by their heavy headgear, which for some of the more magnificent animals were destined to become a hunter's trophy.

Now, he stood and watched as though transfixed, as the animals moved off down the prairie in search of food, their legs cooperating beautifully even in the deep snow, and he was pleased that his walk had been fruitful.

"Couldn't tell what color the collars were, but I'll probably see them again. The game warden needs the colors so he can determine which moose are still up here," he explained to Spuds and Misty, who had sat obediently by his side watching and seeming to admire them as much as their master did but not caring about the collars.

The temperature didn't seem to rise much that afternoon, and by the time Dan and his canines turned back toward camp, he could feel a chill in the air and see gray clouds beginning to gather in the west. "Maybe we're going to get snow after all," he said.

It was early evening and turning to dusk when they returned to camp, and Dan, checking the thermometer, found it was 8 degrees and knew from the direction and feel of the wind, the temperature would drop further during the night. Fog was now stretching fat fingers into the prairie, gradually dropping into the low lands, playing its hide-and-seek games, growing to obliterate everything that wasn't within a couple of feet of human eyes. Dan was thankful he wasn't still a distance from camp having to deal with it. It was a good night to settle inside, the well-fed stove chasing away the chilly dampness brought by the fog.

It's already 6 p.m. and it really cooled off in a hurry. But there's hardly any snow at all from She Bear half way down. It's all melted in the last two days, and all I have heard on the radio is snow and more snow. And all I'm getting is more sunshine and more sunshine. But as the old saying goes, you just never know what the weather will be on the mountain.

Had a one-pound hamburger, macaroni, and cheese and corn for dinner. Waiting for some coffee to get done, then back to my 1300-page book.

As he sat reading, Dan could feel the temperature drop, chilling his nose and ears, and hear the wind playing annoyingly with the tent flap as it often did. At 10 p.m., he marked his place in the book and set it on the table, then stripped down to his long underwear, fed the stove, and climbed into bed, waiting to turn off the lantern until Misty returned from her night run. Spuds was already settled in when Dan heard Misty howling a distance above camp.

What she is howling about, I don't know, for I haven't heard a coyote all day. I think she's just letting everyone know that she is here and to stay away from here.

"Don't worry. She'll come back when she's ready," he told Spuds, who sat watching the door expectantly. "She did the other night when she stayed out so long. I don't hear anything out there. But that doesn't mean there isn't something. If not coyotes, then possibly . . . hmm. I hope not."

The memory of that blood-curdling scream popped into his mind again. He didn't want to say it, didn't want to think about it. Just in case, he got out of bed, grabbed his rifle, and after making sure it was loaded, he climbed back under the covers, set the rifle beside him, and turned off the lantern, his eyes unwilling to close for a long while.

When Dan awoke the next morning, Misty was huddled next to Spuds. She had come in quietly and undisturbing during the night, for which he was thankful, for sleep sometimes didn't come easy, especially when worry wouldn't let his senses rest. He sat up in bed and forced his breath into the frigid air where it lingered momentarily, then evaporated. It was 22 below, and the stove was icy.

"And to think, everything was melting a couple of days ago," he said, pulling on his jeans and a warm sweater. "Don't think it's going to warm up much today, girls. Make your run in a hurry."

Five inches of snow had fallen during the night, not as much as Dan had expected judging from the weather report. Though the pouting sky was quiet for now, he expected it could drop more moisture before the day was over, so after breakfast, he shoveled the roof and his crucial paths, then, fingers freezing, resigned himself to being closed inside for the rest of the day. He passed the afternoon and evening in conversation with Misty and Spuds, and when they fell into sleep, he picked up his book and opened its pages, thankful he had his stack of books and magazines to occupy his time, though he had read nearly all of them at least once.

Before he began to read, his eyes rested momentarily on the dogs sleeping peacefully on the floor next to him, an occasional twitch betraying a dream.

Over the winter, Misty and Spuds had become his closest friends with whom he could share secrets he had never shared with any human. They were dependent on him, and he was equally dependant on them. The sound of his own voice kept his vocal cords from growing stale and broke the silence, a quiescence that in the past, he had often longed for but which, alone on the mountain for an indeterminate amount of time, could become unbearable, fueling the loneliness that often crept in. It was a loneliness that could drive a person mad if he succumbed to it. And he expected Misty and Spuds were sometimes lonely, too, needing the comfort of a human voice or perhaps even another canine voice.

"They listen without being judgmental, without criticizing," he later told Billie. "I can yell at them, and they're still my friends. People are a lot less tolerant of your shortcomings."

That night, unaware of the temperature's intent to fall deep into the thermometer, Dan intended to wear pajamas to bed. But before putting down his book and settling into sleep, he felt a chill and checked the temperature before rousing the stove to flame.

Right now it's 10:30 and 34 below, and I'm about froze. I have been chucking wood in this stove every 20 minutes, and it's still cold in here. I do have my long johns out and warming up, and they are going on in a few minutes. To hell with light pj's. I will keep the fire going as long as I can.

The fire went out some time during the night, and when he awoke, Dan discovered two dogs huddled on the bed next to him. It was 25 below. He pushed the dogs aside amid protests, wiggled his way out of the sleeping bag, and put the stove to work warming the tent. Then he climbed back into his sleeping bag, which had lost its comfort, and settled in until the stove began producing warmth and the small amount of water he had left thawed so he could make breakfast and wash the dishes that had accumulated the previous day. After that, he didn't know what the day would bring.

Days of confinement in the tent's stale air, its dingy blue windowless walls, and the clutter of a bachelor's small quarters were beginning to close in on him. Solitaire bored him, and he had nearly exhausted his reading material. It was too cold to wash clothes or take a shower, something he hadn't done for at least a month and hadn't planned on doing now until he left the mountain and could stand in a hot shower in a modern bathroom inside a warm house. In the meantime, any humans he encountered would have to keep their distance or put up with the odor.

"It's a good thing no one is with me," he told Misty and Spuds one day. "They wouldn't be able to stand the smell. Taking a shower isn't something you want to do in below zero weather in a tent. So you just live with yourself without it."

I need to do these damn dishes, for they're all dirty. Then I can dirty them again when I have lunch. Don't know what that will be, but probably soup of some kind, for I have lots of that. Damn, you talk about bored. I'm about ready to go crazy, and so are the dogs. The snow is either too soft to go tromping around or it's snowing and it's driving me up a canvas wall. Can't even take a nap, for every time I do, the dogs jump up and try to lick me to death. And now, since I'm up there sleeping, I have run out of books to read. Guess I'll start re-reading them.

This would be another day trapped inside the tent, the weather cold enough to quench any desire to be outside, except for the necessity of filling enough water jugs to get him through the next couple of days. Cabin fever, boredom, and a desperate longing for spring were sending his spirits further downward. He needed warmth only the sun could offer, fresh air that wasn't biting, and a brisk walk in the open where there were no walls to close him in. He needed to stand on the top of a hill and take in the great expanse of prairie where he could imagine all of it belonging to him and to no one else. The challenge of winter and his meeting it successfully had made it his.

Though the temperature never climbed to zero that day and the wind, though not strong, bit his exposed skin, Dan's loneliness forced him to put on his snowmobile suit and climb to the top of the hill to call Billie. Long after the conversation should have been over, he continued on in an endless stream of words about not much of anything. His loneliness made him hang on in desperation and wouldn't let her go. Billie, recognizing the conversation was going nowhere, tried to end it politely, but couldn't. She had no choice.

"She had to literally hang up on me to get me off the radio. I don't know what got into me. I never talked so much in my life at one time," he told Misty and Spuds as they walked down the hill together. He had been talking in steady streams to the dogs lately, too, but talking to Billie was different. There was so much to tell her and so much he wanted to hear about family and friends. It had hurt that she had hung up on him, but he understood.

Finishing supper, he made a large batch of popcorn, then spent much of the evening sitting at the table, playing their conversation in his head, telling Misty and Spuds all that was said. "She asked when we were coming home. I've been thinking about it, too, but I didn't have an answer for her."

Misty and Spuds looked up at him, more interested in the popcorn he crammed into his mouth between words than in what he was saying. "It's the middle of March. Too early yet. What would people think if we quit now? Winter's not even over yet." He tossed the dogs a handful of popcorn, stuffed a bunch into his mouth, crunched on it as though he hadn't eaten for days, and thought for a while.

"Come to think about it, why should we care what people think?" The dogs gave him a strange look and begged for more popcorn. "It's none of anybody's business what I do. They're not running my life. Winter is nearly over, and if I want to quit now, I will. I've already done what I said I would do," he said, pulling the cribbage board out from under a pile of magazines, while the dogs fought over two pieces of popcorn that had escaped from Dan's fingers and plunged to the floor.

I guess I'll play some cribbage. But that gets boring too, for I haven't lost a game all winter. But I imagine myself playing H. Wayne, so it's no wonder I haven't lost a game yet.

There being no challenge to the game after an hour had passed, Dan put it away and stepped outside to aim his flashlight at the thermometer. It was 27 below with a biting wind that quickly sent him back inside where he fed the stove, stood close to it until the chill wore off, then stripped down to his long underwear and lay in bed, the sleeping bag pulled to his chin, listening to the basketball game until it was over. Trying to convince himself he was tired, he turned out the light, but his eyes refused to close in sleep, his thoughts stirred by boredom and loneliness. His conversations with Billie only increased his loneliness; they didn't satisfy it. They only made him long to be home.

Billie's words came back to him more than once. "Winter is almost over; have you thought about when you'll be coming home?"

"After a couple more weeks, anyway. Spring isn't here yet."

He had been careful not to sound too eager, not to reveal in his voice or words how lonely and tired of winter he really was, for that would be admitting weakness. Nor did he ever want to admit what a horrible, energy sapping experience it had been, and that he just wanted it to be over. Now, as he lay staring into the darkness, he wondered what sense there was in staying longer. He had battled the worst of it and won, had done what he had set out to do and what he had told others he would do. Spring was nearly here, and winter couldn't get much worse now than it had already been. So what was the point? he asked himself.

"This cold spell is probably the last we'll see for this season," he said to the darkness. "Heck, this is nothing compared to the 50-below zero nights when the damned wind tried to tear down the tent, and I fought to stay awake and keep the fire going all night. That was the worst of it, and I survived." Then as his eyes began to close, "Would I want to do it again? Would I ever do it again? What would people think if . . . There I go again. Why can't I stop thinking that way? From now on, I'm going to be careful what I tell people, careful not to shoot off my damned mouth."

Soon only the dogs' occasional snores broke the night silence. And when Dan finally drifted into sleep, his snores joined theirs in a rhythmic intermittent pattern that would have been heard beyond the tent walls had there been anyone to listen, until deeper sleep that, other than an occasional owl's hoot from a nearby tree, brought a peaceful quiescence to the night.

Chapter 11

THE DRAW

Dan's conversation with himself dissolved into sleep in mid-thought, to be continued the next morning while he split wood in the frigid sunshine, the light jacket he had worn a few days ago replaced by his worn snowmobile suit and a cap with flaps that covered his ears. There was something in the air, though it was still crisp, that foretold spring's imminence. But, though it would try to arrive in late March as promised on the calendar, spring wouldn't happen until winter was willing to let go, and the past day or two, it seemed to be hanging on with a firm grip.

Tired of the enduring repetitiveness of it and seeing no need, except for diversion from boredom, Dan soon gave up splitting wood. Nearly enough to last another winter already filled his yard and tent, and he was certain there wouldn't be another severe sub-zero spell this season. At least not with enough duration to deplete what filled his camp and tent. Now, what wood he burned on weekend visits to the mountain would be minimal, leaving much of it still sitting there, tempting anyone passing through who needed fuel for a campfire but was unwilling to work for it. But Dan didn't mind. "I'm not going to spend another winter here," he said with determination, "so someone ought to use it."

Surely by the time April arrived, spring would be well on its way, greening grasses, sprouting early flowers and buds on the aspens, and giving Dan permission to leave the mountain. At least that was his hope. Come to think of it, it had been his hope and the hope of others as well who, by every winter's end, had become tired of living in a black and white world and longed for color, warmth that brings shedding of clothing, the long-missed energizing cheeriness of sunshine, geese honking overhead, songbirds filling the forest with music, and the exciting birth of animal babies.

Lifting the ax well over his head and bringing it down hard, he sank it deep into a tree stump to rest there until it was needed again, piled and covered the remaining wood he had split, and walked into the tent with purpose. Misty and Spuds followed, wondering if it was time to eat.

With lunch far from his mind, Dan sat down at the table and, ignoring the dogs, who sat looking at him expectantly, set his pen to paper, listing everything he could think of that cost him money during his five-month vacation from work. Food, ammunition for his rifle, chainsaw and its fixings, mouse traps, snowshoes, storage tubs, horse feed, meat (much of which had spoiled), personal items, dog food, and many miscellaneous items such as batteries. Then there were all those months he could have been gainfully employed but wasn't.

Money earned that could have helped pay the bills that had accumulated during his absence. Now, though Billie had a job, the income column was seriously lacking, and money was running short.

Dan got up, poured himself a cup of coffee, and sat down again, deep in thought. Since the night before, monotony had caused him to ponder every reason he could think of for leaving before March was over, since Billie had put the thought of ending his stay on the prairie in his mind, as though to remind him of his responsibility but unwilling to say it. To stay on the prairie five months had been his goal from the start, the goal he had made public, and he had nearly completed it.

"I could leave now, or I could wait two more weeks," he said to himself as though giving himself a choice but already knowing what the answer would be. "What difference would it make; two weeks early is close enough. Besides, by the time we get out of here, it will be closer to the end of March anyway.

The first day of spring is close, and I said I'd stay until spring. So there." Then looking at his canine friends, he said, "I think the winter has been hard on you, too. And it's beginning to show."

As he sat there, another side of the argument presented itself, that his loneliness was causing him to look hard for reasons to leave, fantasizing that there was need and that the need was urgent. Loneliness and a long hard winter far from civilization can work on a person's brain, twisting and distorting reality, rationality all but gone. Regarding work, two more weeks wasn't going to make that much difference. Was the word from others that he was on the prairie to escape the responsibility of supporting his household producing a mountain of guilt he couldn't overcome in spite of his efforts to disallow such thinking?

He brought his fist down hard on the table, instantly bringing Misty and Spuds to their feet barking. "What do I care what other people think? Why is that so damned important?" he said angrily.

Sensing that their master was preoccupied and that lunch wasn't going to happen any time soon, Misty and Spuds had long ago crept quietly to their bed and lay down to take a nap. But now they were fully awake, wondering what they had done to cause their master's anger and not wishing to get in the way of it.

Dan sat staring at the paper in front of him, ears attentive to the silence. He looked reminiscently at his piles of wood, his kitchen with its stacks of pots and pans, the bed that had kept him warm on arctic nights, the small stove that had worked so hard to warm the tent, the dogs lying comfortably on their bed.

This had been their home for five months. The prairie in its winter harshness had worked him hard but, at the same time, had offered a meditation-encouraging quiescence devoid of the logic-prohibiting clutter of civilization. He had made good use of it, had become one with the mountain, had solved or at least come to some understanding of his confusion about life and his place in it.

Perhaps now he was ready to go home. But what would it be like to live in a house that would stay warm without need to cut wood, to listen to a telephone ring, watch television, visit a crowded store, be surrounded by people expecting things of him, to be tied to a job, to give up his freedom? But here on the mountain was he really free, or was freedom something the mind dreams of but that is never attained? Come to think of it, winter hadn't given him much freedom, had instead tied him to a job, had dictated his daily activities. But that was something more to think about, something for another day. For now, he was becoming weary of thinking, and it was all becoming fuzzy and confusing.

After a while, Dan put down his pen. He had made up his mind. He looked over at Misty and Spuds, who were beginning to stir, and said, "How about a Spam sandwich." Tails wagging as though to say "We thought you'd never ask," they got up, stretched, climbed onto the dining room chairs and stared at him while he busied himself in the kitchen, determined not to miss the offering of anything that would fill their bellies. Dan was used to their begging, sometimes even encouraged it. They were the company he could never have lived without, the loyal friends that had stuck with him when humans would have left him long ago.

"How about we pack up and go home next week?" he asked, as he spread mustard on one slice of bread and lay Spam slices on the other. "I'll call Billie this afternoon and tell her we're going to call it a winter. How does that sound? I think you're as sick of being cold as I am."

He broke apart a half sandwich he had made just for them and offered it, reminding them to take it nicely without chomping on his fingers. Taking a bite of his own sandwich, he continued his speech to Misty and Spuds while they sat staring at him in hopes he would share some of his lunch, too, since theirs was gone in a gulp.

"Besides, I think you're as bored as I am. The days are dragging, no more wood to cut, no snow to shovel, no challenge to winter any more. Soon the tent will be filled with snowmelt, and I'll have to put everything on the bed to keep it from getting wet. It will be like living in a lake." He paused to shove the last of his sandwich into his mouth without sharing, after which he lost his audience. "I've had plenty of time to sort things out, to find my purpose in this world, and to realize how stupid I was to do this, and I'm satisfied with that."

Taking a last sip of coffee, Dan stomped on the Spam can to flatten it, put on his snowmobile suit and boots, grabbed the radio off his nightstand, and after throwing the can in the garbage, trudged slowly up the hill to call Billie. "I've given it a lot of thought, and I think it's time to call it a winter," he told her, relief that it was over obvious in his voice.

"It's March 15, and winter is on its way out anyway. Not much to do here anymore, either, and I'm bored as hell. Before coming down, I need to get things organized here and pack up what I need to take with me. I'll come up and get the rest on weekends. There's a lot of money tied up in this camp." He rattled on without pausing to allow Billie room for comment.

"Depending on the weather, I'm thinking of coming down on Tuesday. If it snows, I'll stay up, and if not, I'm coming down and find a job so I can pay for this vacation. It cost me a lot more than I thought it was going to, what with the chainsaw problems and all."

When Dan finally took a breath, Billie agreed that the winter had been costly. She gave him no argument, didn't tell him it was about time, either, just wanted him to let her know which day she could expect him so she could give him a ride from PK Lane.

Now Dan had purpose in his last days on the mountain. He decided to split and haul more wood into the tent for use on weekends when he came up to pack and haul equipment down the mountain that he would no longer need for two-day stays. That chore done, he busied himself planning his next day's activities and made a list. If the weather allowed, he would go down to the Goose River and pick up the fishing pole and gear he had hidden under the bridge, an all-day outing.

That evening he stepped into a 22-degree night with a starlit sky and a moon that appeared to have a large bite taken out of it. A cool breeze reminiscent of winter whispered through the branches as though to say, "I know I've been hard on you, given you so many life and death choices but, when you leave, I'll miss you. The prairie will miss you. You're much wiser and stronger now for having survived all the grief I gave you."

It was almost an apology, and Dan could feel melancholy creep in as he stood in the starlit darkness for a long while deeply breathing the fresh mountain air, admiring the sparkling canopy above him, committing to memory the silence that enfolded him so he could draw on it later on when he needed it to keep his sanity, all the while thinking he really wasn't alone. There were all kinds of living things somewhere in the night, things he couldn't see but that somehow he could sense because he had become part of their world. This was their home, and he had been allowed to share it.

When he awoke the next morning at seven, it was 26 above with fluffy clouds decorating the sky, occasionally floating over the sun as though playing hide and seek, and a warm Chinook wind tugged playfully at the tent but with no mischievous intent. Expecting it to be a long trip, Dan hurried through his morning coffee and breakfast, put on his snowshoes, grabbed his rifle and gear, and climbed up the hill to the trail headed to the Goose River. Half way there, he stopped to unzip his snowsuit to his waist and sip from his water flask. Then whistling at Misty and Spuds, who had ambled a distance into the woods in search of small critters, he continued on.

It was several miles to the bridge, an approximate two- to three-hour hike in summer and a much shorter one on horseback. But it was at least a half-day hike on snowshoes when the trail was snow covered to varying depths.

Now, though, the snow was losing its depth, was even down to exposing patches of grass in some spots, which made the going easier than in the depths of winter.

When they arrived at the bridge, Dan found his fishing pole and gear under the bridge where he had left it, found a large rock to sit on, and pulled the two peanut butter and jelly sandwiches he had made for himself from his pack, giving Misty and Spuds their portion along with a treat of dog biscuits, which deterred them from begging for the rest of his lunch.

In a pensive mood, he sat for a while, staring down the twisted white river, reflecting on the winter that would soon be memory, the winter the prairie had shared with him, though unwillingly, it seemed. But the mountain had been honest with him, had not held back its moods, hadn't sugar-coated the truth about the way things were up here. The mountain had mercifully allowed him to live, when one wrong move on his part could have turned it otherwise.

"Dishonesty is a people thing," he said softly, half to himself, half to the dogs resting in the snow. "Most people don't say what they really think, either because they're trying to be too polite, or because they prefer to say one thing to you and another behind your back to someone else."

He sat reflecting on those thoughts for several minutes, then got up off the rock, slung his pack and rifle over his back, and stared into the distance as though he had spotted something.

"It's still early. How about we go back a different way?" he asked Misty and Spuds, who were now on their feet, tails wagging as though to ask, "What next?" Then pointing to a dark line on a distant hill, Dan said, "There isn't as much snow over there, and I think the walking will be easier. We'll just approach camp from a different angle. Besides, then I won't need these damned snowshoes." He put down his pack and rifle, knelt down, unfastened the snow-shoes, and tied them together for easier carrying, relieved to have lighter, less cumbersome feet.

As he made his way up the hill, seeming in no hurry to get there, the dark line grew into a wire fence running east and west on a gradual slope that was well enough exposed to the direct rays of the afternoon sun so that much of it was bare of snow.

"Easy. We'll just follow the fence line and hit the prairie up high," he said. "Much better than fighting deep snow."

What Dan hadn't figured on was that when eventually he would have to come down again, for his camp was below the hill by the river, the snowless area would eventually end, and that could mean trouble for someone without snowshoes. As he left the fence line, the bare ground he had seen from a distance disappeared, and he now saw a patch of snow he estimated at 20 yards wide that would have to be traversed. Thinking the snow depth had diminished significantly under the warm sun and that he could make it across without snowshoes, he carefully stepped onto it, was able to walk several paces, then suddenly found himself falling endlessly into icy darkness.

Only the realization that his head wasn't far below the surface and that the snow was fairly soft, kept his fear from growing to panic. Anger at himself became his only emotion, anger that gave him the strength to free his head from its icy sepulcher. As soon as he could see daylight, he rested his arms a short while and took a deep breath, then resumed digging, resting between efforts, hands and arms growing tired and sore, until he was finally able to wiggle the rest of the way out of his predicament.

I forgot I still had to cross a draw. I started across it and fell through clean over my head, and it took me 20 minutes to get out. After I was out, the snowshoes definitely went back on.

Exhausted from exertion and wet from the moisture-laden snow and the perspiration that saturated his inner clothing, Dan sat on the ground catching his breath and considered what had just happened. Luck, or something else, had been with him. There were many draws on the prairie, some much deeper than this one — death traps when covered with snow. It could easily have been one of those he had fallen into, one that could have left him buried much deeper, the panic and exertion from trying to dig himself out killing him. That was why it had been crucial for him to memorize the location of every draw in summer and fall, for if he hadn't, hiking the prairie, especially without snowshoes, would have been like walking through a mine field. It wasn't that Dan hadn't known about this one. That hadn't been his mistake.

"My mind was on something else and I forgot about the draw," he admonished himself. "I should have known better." As he sat catching his breath and contemplating the seriousness of it, he heard the prairie whisper, "It's not over yet, Dan. Don't be cocky and quick to let down your guard just because you're leaving in a couple of days and think you've already won."

When rested, he stood and fastened his snowshoes on his feet and considered the distance he had left to travel. Now he still had a stretch of timber to hike through and another hill to climb before heading down the other side to camp, and he wondered whether his energy spent body was up to the challenge. But he had no choice, for here he had no shelter for the night. An hour-and-a-half later, he was through the timber where deep snow, fallen tree branches, and tangled half-buried brush tried to trap his snowshoes in their grip sending Dan face down in the snow, struggling to free himself.

When he emerged into the open, the wind, which had picked up strength and grown bitter during the afternoon, turned against him, trying to push him back into the woods. He pulled up his collar, covered his ears, and braced himself against it as he and the dogs started up the hill beyond the timber. Suddenly Dan looked up from watching his feet and noticed water trickling down the hill in a would-be river. He stared at the running water for a minute, thinking about what had caused it. Now climbing the hill should be much easier without snowshoes, he thought. "And I know there's no draw up there."

He thought about it for barely a minute before a snippet of wisdom struck him like lightning, spurred on by his legs telling him they wished he were back at camp, and his arms letting him know they were sore from digging. "It's tempting, but I'd better not chance it. I don't have the strength to dig myself out again. And the next one could be fatal."

The entourage climbed the hill slowly, stopping every few yards or so to rest. It was a difficult, wearying climb, not because of the hill's steepness but because Dan and the dogs were already tired and sore and because the mountain's low oxygen levels caused stress from exertion to happen more quickly than at lower elevations.

Relieved to have reached the top, Dan stopped and rested heavily on his walking stick, wishing there was a rock to sit on, while Misty and Spuds, panting, lay down in the melting snow. The trip back had been hard on the dogs as well. As he rested, he scanned the distance. From here, he could take in a good chunk of the prairie, recognizing landmarks he had memorized over the years. It would be fairly difficult to lose him on this section of mountain. Admiring the great expanse of it gave him a sense of exhilaration, like a rancher looking over his spread and thinking, "This is all mine, as far as I can see, and then some. How awesome."

Suddenly the faint sound of an engine broke into Dan's daydream, the wind carrying the sound his way. As it grew nearer, Misty and Spuds became attentive. "It's definitely snowmobiles. I wonder if they would give me a ride to camp." He wished it desperately, but with not much hope behind it.

Listening as the sound grew closer, he saw four machines become visible and walked toward them as fast as his snowshoes would allow, shouting and waving wildly to catch the riders' attention. But he couldn't get close enough, and they sped off, oblivious to his existence.

Here came four snow machines. I got within 50 yards of them, but they didn't see me, and they were stopped. So I sicked the dogs on them.

Watching from where he stood, too tired to walk any farther to hitch a ride, Dan was sure he had seen one of the riders stand up on his machine and stare in his direction. But instead of turning their machines toward him, they rode off in the opposite direction. Tired and disappointed when the dogs didn't bring the riders back looking for their owner, Dan continued on, eager to get to camp where he could rest his aching legs.

"I guess I don't blame people for not stopping," he said to Misty and Spuds, as they came running back. "I'd be afraid of me too, looking like a grizzly mountain man with my messy beard, moustache, and long hair. And I haven't had a shower in months. I must smell pretty bad by this time." The dogs wagged their tails. "You don't have to agree with me," he told them.

Resigned to walking the remaining distance on legs that were already punishing him, he once more leaned heavily on his walking stick and continued on, his steps deliberate and slow. As he approached a mile from camp, he stopped again and listened to a hum in the distance that was growing louder. This time, it was coming toward him.

"Go get 'em," he yelled at Misty and Spuds, who took off running toward the loudening sound. Determined not to miss them, Dan stood on the trail wildly waving his arms, hoping they wouldn't run him down. This time, the riders saw him, stopped, and lifted their helmets so he could see their faces.

Dan seemed surprised. "Well if it isn't Jerry and Gene. What are you two doing up here?"

"We just came from Bear Lodge," Jerry said. "We're on our way home. What are you doing out here this late in the day? You look exhausted."

"I hiked to the bridge to get my fishing pole. Fell in a damned draw on the way back and had to dig myself out. So I'm pretty sore right now."

"Those draws can be tricky; swallow you in an instant if you aren't aware of them."

"I knew it was there; just wasn't thinking."

"Would you like a ride to your camp? I think we have room."

"I'd appreciate that."

"You can ride with me. I think Gene can manage the dogs," Jerry said as Dan climbed on behind him.

I'll be damned if it wasn't Jerry Pelesky and Gene Gonger. So Jerry gave me a ride to the house while Gene went pretty slow bringing the dogs along. Thank God for good people or I would still be walking.

Back in camp, Dan invited the men in, started a fire, and heated water for coffee.

"I see you're getting a little melting in your tent," Gene said, noting a small puddle on the floor near the entrance.

"Yeah, that's going to be a big problem when the temperatures get warmer. But there's no place else for it to go. No drainage ditch around the tent, and I can't make one. So I just have to live with it. But not for long; I'll be off the mountain in a day or two."

"You're calling it a winter, then?"

"Yup. Need to find work. This vacation has been pretty expensive. Besides, this old stove is nearly as worn out as I am, and I don't think there's another one up here I can salvage."

Gene and Jerry, who hadn't seen Dan since before winter began, were full of conversation lasting more than an hour, their cool hands warming around steaming coffee cups as they sat near the fire seeming to enjoy Dan's company as much as he was enjoying theirs. It was coming onto late afternoon and, though there was much more to be said about life and winter below the mountain and adventures on top of it, Jerry noticed daylight was beginning to wane and mentioned getting off the mountain before twilight.

"But first, while we still have a little light, I'd like to take some pictures, if you don't mind," he told Dan as they zipped their jackets and walked into the grayness that announced the sun's imminent disappearance and, with it, evening's cloud-covered arrival with no stars or moon to brighten it.

The photo session over, the men put on their helmets and started their machines. Dan sighed as he waved goodbye. It was a sigh that echoed his body's fatigue and a willingness to just rest the evening away. It wasn't a sigh of lonely sadness like he had always felt after visitors left, for the next day or two would bring him off the mountain, leaving loneliness well behind him. Then, if loneliness should return, it would be for the mountain, its quiescence and the solace it had offered when he was in need of it.

"I did enjoy that part of the day," Dan wrote in his diary that evening in reference to Gene and Jerry's visit. The rest of the day had been hard on him, and he was glad it was safely over.

Now I'm just sitting here with two very sore legs and two sleeping dogs. It's still 34 degrees at camp, but a lot warmer on the prairie, and the wind has died down, for it was blowing earlier 30 to 40 mph.

Sleep came easy that night, his body crying for recuperation, his legs wishing to be left alone, and Dan all too willing to comply. And he knew Misty and Spuds felt much the same, for they never moved in response to a coyote's intermittent howl during the night. The wind that had blown with serious intent during the day, adding to the misery of his walk, backed off during the evening, and with the calm and moderate overnight temperature, the tent stayed comfortably warm, adding to the ease of sleep. When he awoke the next morning, his legs, though still a little sore, were good enough for the easy work he had in mind for the day.

Well, today I'm going to get everything stored away and put up on the bed, for I have officially called it spring.

Dan took his time over breakfast, listening to the radio while enjoying a hot cup of coffee before tackling the cleaning and packing he needed to do before leaving his winter home. Things had to be organized according to urgency of need. Sorted by value and usefulness off the mountain, some things would be brought down on the first trip, some on the second, and so on. It would be a slow process until he could bring Kenny's horses up to do the hauling, and that should be soon, barring a serious snow storm.

Once Dan had figured out how and what he planned to pack, he took the sleeping bags off the bed and hung them over a rope near the tent's ceiling so they would be out of the way as he packed the tubs for hauling down. Then he placed a row of empty tubs on the bed so they wouldn't sit in water when the snow began to melt, and began filling them. When he was finished packing, only the pots and pans and dishes he needed for weekend camping were left, and he would pack them in his leave-behind tub after supper chores were done.

That evening, after everything had been organized and packed, the bed invisible under its load, and floor that he hadn't seen since fall now exposed, Dan sat down at the table and contemplated with sadness the emptiness he had created in his winter home. And suddenly he realized that packing wasn't just something he invented to fill an otherwise boring afternoon. Their leaving was real, and he was beginning to wonder if he were ready for it after all. But now it was too late to stop what he had begun. He was committed. Billie would be expecting him, he needed to find work, and the dogs needed a respite from the cold. A respite he needed as well, but not as urgently as Misty and Spuds, for he sensed in them an increasing weariness that needed to be addressed.

"Got everything put away, and now I really don't want to leave. Got some really mixed emotions about it. I just got a gut feeling that I'll be kicking myself for coming down this early, but I do have to find a job to pay for all of this, and that's the main reason for coming down.

A loud crunching of freezing snow broke the evening silence as Dan stepped outdoors to check the weather and send Misty and Spuds for a run. "Another cloudy night," he said to the darkness as he lit a cigarette and took a deep draw. Just then he felt something wet on his cheek. He directed his flashlight toward the sky. "It's starting to snow," he exclaimed. "But it doesn't look like it will amount to much. But just when I say that, Mother Nature will prove me wrong."

Just then Misty and Spuds came ambling up to him. So far, the night had been silent, the wind conspicuous in its absence, the snow, what there was of it, falling straight down. "Our last night here, and the coyotes aren't even going to show up to say goodbye. And neither are the stars, or the moon. I'm sure going to miss this place. In a lot of ways, I wish we didn't have to leave." Spuds and Misty looked up at him sadly as though to say they agreed, and Dan reached down and patted their heads. He took a last draw on his cigarette and put it out in the snow, then looked up at the sky. It had finished snowing. "That short little spurt must have been a goodbye - the best it could do for a last snowstorm."

Suddenly the thought came to him that the prairie might have a sense of consciousness, an awareness of his presence and of his thoughts and mood. But was that the prairie or was it something else? Something more powerful that he hadn't experienced before and that he had suddenly become aware of.

Something seeking him, even protecting him when he wasn't aware. His thoughts scanned his winter memories, stopping at all the times he was inches away from dying, but hadn't. He stood in the inky darkness for several minutes, mesmerized by the recalling of it, his mind far away, trying to make sense of it.

When his mind was jostled back to the present, he whistled for Misty and Spuds, who he thought were still in the woods or up on the hill. But they had been sitting near the tent door for a long time, waiting for their master to go in.

"Oh there you are. Time for bed," he told them as he motioned them through the door. "Tomorrow we go home, so we need to get a good night's sleep." There was melancholy in his voice, but Misty and Spuds were too tired to share it.

Though it would be a mild night, Dan piled wood in the stove and set his alarm clock for 4:30, planning to get an early start down the mountain before weather moved in or the snow became too sticky for travel. After making a final journal entry and placing the journal in his back pack, he found a spot on the ground that was fairly level, pulled down his sleeping bags and set one on the damp floor for a cushion and the other on top of it. Then he turned out the lantern and climbed into the top sleeping bag, and tried to settle into sleep. But the ground was cold, hard, and uncomfortable without a mattress, and sleep wouldn't come.

It didn't help that his mind wouldn't shut off, kept reliving the day's accident that could have killed him, all the other accidents that had happened through the winter as well, and along with them, imagined death scenes resulting from each one. Then his mind went on to reprimanding himself for his carelessness.

"It was stupid of me. One careless moment. That's all it would take. I've been damned lucky, thanks to something or someone, but I'm not off this mountain yet."

Chapter 12

HOMEWARD BOUND

Sleep finally came, but tossing and turning on lumpy ground made the night seem much too short, and Dan was surprised when, in the gray dawn, he shined the flashlight at the alarm clock, which hadn't gone off. "Six thirty! I thought I'd set this damned thing! No wonder it's so light in here."

Dan had yelled loud enough to scare away any wildlife that might have been hanging around, and by this time, Misty and Spuds, who had been snoring peacefully, were suddenly awake and stretching, looking at him as though wondering what the clamor was about. Dan quickly untangled himself from his sleeping bag and turned on his side to roll out of bed, his body complaining of soreness brought on by lying all night on the cold hard ground.

"Oooh, aahh," he grumbled in pain as he tried to get his stiff joints to cooperate. Grasping the bed frame, he pulled himself to his feet and urged the dogs outdoors for their morning run. "No more sleeping on the ground for me," he mumbled. "Getting too old for that." He picked up the ill-intended clock and examined it closely, hoping to discover the cause of its disobedience.

"Wouldn't you know. Not the clock's fault. Human error. Forgot to push the damned button. Could've slept until noon. Then we might as well have waited until tomorrow."

While the dogs were out, he dressed for a mild day, hung the sleeping bags on the line near the top of the tent, then made a quick breakfast, which he ate while he opened his last can of Spam and prepared sandwiches for the trip down. By this time, Misty and Spuds were back in the tent noisily chomping on dog food while Dan quickly picked up their bed and whatever else on the floor that was in danger of succumbing to a flood, and piled it on the bed, working fast in an attempt to make up for the two hours he had lost to sleeping when he should have been well down the trail by this time.

"Hurry and finish your breakfast or you'll go without," he ordered the dogs in a commanding tone of voice. But Misty and Spuds weren't listening.

They were too focused on filling their bellies. Having given warning, Dan began putting on his snowmobile suit and sat down to work on his boots.

"If you don't finish soon, I'm putting the rest of your dog food back in the tub and hope the damned mice don't take over the tent while we're gone. There's a lot here they could chew on besides your food."

His boots on, pack and rifle in hand, he scanned the tent one last time to make sure he hadn't forgotten anything. "Well, if I did forget anything, I'll be up next weekend if the mountain will let me." Misty and Spuds were still chomping on a few morsels of breakfast that Dan in his haste had left in their dishes, torn between following their master outdoors and leaving their dishes clean. But Dan wasn't going to wait.

"Let's go," he urged impatiently. The dogs sensed his eagerness and reluctantly followed him out the door, soon realizing they were going home.

As the entourage prepared to set out, the sun was making its way up the mountain preceded by a yellow haze in the eastern sky, which had turned cloudless during the early morning hours when Dan should have been awakened by the errant alarm clock. It seemed the mountain had put on a happy face, the prairie and mountain glad to see him leave, happy to be left alone, at last free from human presence. At least until the snow's disappearance, stormless warm spring days, and a longing for relief from cabin fever lured people back.

Hunters would soon be back for sure, curious to discover how the winter had treated their camps. But some of them would wait until the spring storms were over, bringing chainsaws to clear fallen trees and debris that littered trails and camps, for when winter finally turned over the helm to spring, it would not be without a violent temper tantrum. The wind would race through the mountain, blowing harder and faster on the prairie, and hundreds of huge trees that had stood solid for eons would be forced to release their grip on the earth, innocent victims in the war for supremacy.

Dan, too, was concerned about his camp nestled among aging lodge pole pines that could come crashing down on his tent, smashing everything inside. That, alone, gave the wise hunters good reason to clear their camps immediately following hunting season, for those who foolishly decided to wait, chanced destruction. He would be among those returning to the prairie early to haul things down as quickly as he could. He had spent too much money equipping his winter home to leave it to Mother Nature's sporadically destructive moods.

"Twelve above and sunshine," he said cheerily, as he checked the thermometer for the last time. He overlapped and tied the tent flaps, securing the entrance as much as possible, then sat down and put on his snowshoes. "Going to be a warm one, but if we make time, we won't get caught in sticky snow. It's going to be close now that we got a late start."

Pausing to tell himself he was thankful there were no storms brewing and that it wasn't likely winter was going to play one more trick on him, he slung his pack over his back and his rifle over his shoulder, whistled at the dogs, who had wandered to the creek for a drink, and began the long walk to meet

Soldier Creek Trail. He paused at the top of the hill above camp, turned and stared at it for several minutes, already missing it. Then with increasing melancholy, he turned and continued on without looking back. There had been good times and bad times, times he had drawn pleasure from the prairie, and times he had cursed it. The winter, which in its bleak storminess early on seemed to drag, would now become a memory vulnerable to fading through the years, like the abandoned log cabins that would soon be indistinguishable from the earth beneath them. Dan was glad he had kept a journal, for through it, his experiences would some day live again, the reading of it bringing him much pleasure and a sense of accomplishment.

It was still cool enough that the snow hadn't become sticky yet, and Dan was certain it wouldn't be deep as he neared the face where the sun shone warmer than on top. Spring should be further along at lower elevations, making it an easy trip. But as he neared Soldier Creek Trail, he discovered he was wrong. Snow drifts still covered the trail and, though they didn't appear deep, when Dan thrust his walking stick into the first one, all but the handle disappeared in the snow. Hesitant, he stepped onto the drift, but even with snowshoes, he sank approximately a foot.

"I sure hope it's not going to be this way all the way down the mountain," he said, recalling the extreme pain he had suffered when he walked down at Christmas. Now he struggled for more than a mile, his legs growing tired of lifting his heavy snowshoes, stopping often to rest. At each stop, Misty and Spuds lay down, panting. They, too, had tired of winter's cold, the long hikes up and down the mountain and across the prairie, and navigating the deep snow, and Dan was concerned about their increasing lethargy. Finally, after a little more than a mile, the snow lost its depth, beginning to show ground and even to disappear in spots, and travel became much easier.

Coming down, the going was really good until I hit the trail. There, the snow was really deep and soft, so it was hard going for a mile and a half.

That the difficulty didn't last all the way down the mountain relieved his concern. They would make it with no problem. The going had become so easy that for a moment Dan was tempted to remove his snowshoes, but an instant's reflection caused him to think better of the idea. Besides, that would be one more load to carry down, a load more conveniently carried on his feet than on his back.

When he arrived at Whiskey Rock, he stopped to rest and search for the glasses he had forgotten there early in the season. "Maybe they're somewhere under the snow," he said hopefully. "Guess I'll just keep looking for them every time I come up after the snow melts." He sat for a while staring at the towns spread out like intermittent groupings of tiny dots below the mountain, imagining them full of traffic and activity. It would be difficult and even strange getting used to city life again.

"Been too long on the mountain. I feel like a hermit, someone who doesn't belong in society, doesn't fit in anymore. Guess we're just damned misfits," he told Misty and Spuds. "But we have no choice. Might as well head on down and join the other idiots down there."

When Dan and the dogs got to PK Lane, they found the road clear of snow and no one to greet them, for he had told Billie he didn't know what time he would get there. So they walked the three last miles to home, arriving at 12:30 in time for lunch, Billie happy to see they had made it without incident.

Though he was happy to be home, the next few days, Dan moped around the house as though he was lost, and though he quickly found a job, he seemed to exist in a trance, his mind absorbed within the mountain's secret folds. His conversations with Billie focused on the winter, his stories never ending. Other than work, he made no effort to see friends, for his absence from them had made him less tolerant of people than he ever had been. Most of his conversations now were directed at Misty and Spuds and Billie.

"Your friends have asked about you," she told him one evening at supper. "They heard you were off the mountain. Wondered why you hadn't been to see them. They're anxious to hear how your winter went."

"They're probably surprised to hear I'm still alive," Dan said sarcastically. "Well I'm sorry to disappoint them, but I'm not up to answering a lot of questions right now. So they'll just have to wait until I'm ready."

He was adamant, and Billie didn't pursue the matter further.

The next weekend came with a promise of fair weather. That after living through a few days of rain and snow mixed together as though the clouds couldn't make up their minds which season they were in. During those days, Dan had stood at the window looking up at the mountains through the raindrops, their tops shrouded in gloom, while wondering how his camp was faring the storms, part of him wanting to be there, the other part glad he was warm and safe in a house with a solid roof on it.

"If the weather clears up, I'm going up this weekend," he told Billie. "Gotta check camp and bring some stuff down. Think I'll ask Kenny if I can borrow his horses. Keep Misty and Spuds here. The long walk up and down is getting too hard on them."

Dan got up before dawn that Saturday morning and, happy to be leaving his snowshoes behind, saddled the buckskin and put the panniers on the appaloosa, then trotted down PK Lane to meet the mountain at Soldier Creek Trail. The trip was much easier on horseback, and it seemed his legs thanked him for the respite from a long, difficult uphill walk. The week's storm hadn't deepened the snow significantly, especially at camp, but Dan found that one side of the tent had fallen, most likely the work of a mischievous wind, the same wind that had played with it and threatened him all winter. The problem wasn't serious; it was an easy fix. Just annoying. The worst would have been a tree lying across the tent. But after examining his camp, he was relieved to find no trees had fallen anywhere.

    Satisfied with the camp's condition, he tied the horses, set to fixing the tent, then went inside to start a fire. Once it began to flame, he went back outside and removed the panniers from the appaloosa and unsaddled the buckskin, setting the gear near the tent door. Then he untied the horses, put them in the corral, and gave them some feed, which they happily set to gobbling as though they hadn't eaten in many days.

    "Looks like everything in the tent is just like I left it," he said as he looked around for something to eat. "Sure miss having Misty and Spuds up here with me. But they would just be in the way," he reasoned.

    Dan had just finished packing one of the panniers and was thinking about what he would put in the other to even the weight when he thought he imagined the faint sound of voices in the distance. He quit what he was doing and stood listening, but the sound had vanished, so he set to work again. "Just my imagination," he mumbled. "Maybe I'm going crazy. A winter on the mountain will do that to a person."

    A minute or two later he heard it again. This time it was louder, and it was definitely voices, and then a horse whinnying. The appaloosa and the buckskin stood like statues, ears pointed toward the top of the hill, and uttered a long deafening reply. Following their cue, Dan directed his attention to the top of the hill where two riders soon emerged from behind the trees and headed toward Dan's camp.

    "Hey Dan," one of them shouted. It seemed more of a taunt than a greeting. "I thought I heard you had come down the mountain to stay. Was that just a rumor?" They brought their horses to a stop just outside the fence that encircled his camp and faced Dan without dismounting, easing up on the reins and leaning casually on their saddle horns.

    Dan stood watching them without approaching the fence. He resented their closeness. They were trespassing. "I did leave the mountain. Just packing things out. What are you doing here?"

    "Same, if the storms left anything to haul down."

    "Well there's still a lot of snow in the woods yet."

    "Yeah. We see that. So how was your winter? I see you survived it. Hadn't seen you at the Mint Bar lately, though."

    Dan stared at him, not caring if his contempt showed, remembering that day in early November, when they had hurriedly left their camps, fearful of being caught in the developing blizzard. "Heck, that was just a wimpy storm, and they ran from it," he said to himself, but replied tersely as he continued packing, "Been busy. Got a job now."

There was an awkward silence, the men leaning on their saddle horns, their horses standing quiet, eyes half closed in the afternoon sun as though to take advantage of the conversation to catch a short nap while their riders waited for Dan to say more. Then, sensing he wasn't in the mood for conversation, the men shifted their weight in the saddle, picked up their reins and turned their horses toward the hill. "See you later, Dan," they called after him.

His visitors' resentment of him was obvious. They had expressed their disapproval of Dan's actions to each other many times, wondering if he did it for the attention it would gain him if he lived through it. And possibly even if he didn't. People weren't supposed to live in the national forest in winter, let alone survive it. They had heard the Forest Service prohibited it for safety reasons.

Who would be responsible if he severely injured himself and had to be airlifted off the mountain? Anyone foolhardy enough to attempt staying the winter at this elevation in a wall tent didn't deserve rescue. In fact, deserved to die or have some other ill fate befall them. Besides, the Forest Service mandated vacating all hunting camps and equipment at the end of the hunting season each fall. What or who gave this man special rights? What they had conveniently forgotten was the camp they had left in the fall and were just now coming to rescue.

Dan knew different, but he didn't owe anyone an explanation, especially these troublemakers. "Curiosity seekers," he muttered to himself as he carefully placed his chainsaw and whatever else would fit into the other pannier. Then he chuckled as he watched the rear ends of the men's horses disappear up the hill. "And they thought they would find my body up here. Guess I fooled them. I hope they're not too disappointed." He thought for a while. "I wonder if a winter stint on the mountain would humble those arrogant hypocrites."

When Dan had packed everything he determined needed taking down this trip, he emptied the panniers, careful to keep everything from the left pannier separate from things he had taken from the right pannier so each of them would be evenly weighted when he packed again in the morning. Then, with a few hours of daylight left and the weather conducive, he decided to saddle the buckskin and ride up the hill to the other side of She Bear Mountain, just for something to do until the sun's steady drop behind the mountain brought its usual evening chill and confined him to the cozy warmth of his tent and a happily crackling wood burning stove. The appaloosa pawed the ground, as though protesting being left behind, then whinnied a goodbye to its companion as Dan rode up the hill and out of sight, Dan happy to be on horseback and able to make more distance in a shorter time than he would on snowshoes. If only it could have been that way all winter, he thought.

That evening, he sat puffing on his pipe, attempting to read one of the books still sitting on his nightstand. But after reading the last two paragraphs several times and not remembering what he had read, he closed the book and let his mind wander into reminiscing about his winter adventure and all the work that had gone into preparing for the long cold months ahead.

August 11: Got up at 8, got the fire started and coffee brewing, then crawled back in bed until it warmed up. Watered horses and then the dogs and ate breakfast. Now I'm heating water for doing dishes, then I'll go cut wood for a while. If the chain will cut. It's awfully dull. I plan on going back down around 2 p.m. Well, it's noon. I've been cutting wood for three hours now, and I still don't have much. Just looked at the temperature. It's already 88 degrees. Think I'll sit down and drink some ice tea and then fix lunch and head down. Today, Misty and Spuds spooked three head of elk here at camp.

In some ways, he was happy to be on the mountain again. It was like visiting a good friend in better times. And he was sure his best friend's spirit roamed the mountain as well, for they had had many good times exploring it together. Even so, he missed the joy and companionship Misty and Spuds had offered, realized that the winter would have been unbearable without them. They had shared his adventure, had played a big part in it. But the winter had stolen a chunk of their spirit and perhaps a chunk of their health as well, and now they needed time to recover.

This night, there was no one to talk to except himself. Regardless, he was glad the other hunting camps were far enough away that the men on horseback weren't likely to be back for a visit. They would ask questions he wasn't ready to answer, looking to criticize, looking for reasons to tell him, "We could have told you it would be like that. Now aren't you sorry you did it? You're lucky to be alive, Dan."

"No, I'm not sorry. Will never be sorry. It's none of their business; they don't need to know," he often told Billie when people tried to pry open his private thoughts.

It was coming onto April, the daylight lasting longer, the sun growing warmer. Dan always looked forward to spring with its emerging new life. Life that was so conspicuously absent during winter's long dark months. Before long, rain would replace snow, bathing the mountain in readiness for the long summer that lay ahead and the many visitors that would come to admire it. The aspens would soon be dressed in their new mint green attire, and small early flowers splashing color randomly over the greening prairie grasses, feeding butterflies and bees searching for nectar. Animal babies would soon be brought into the open by their mothers to show off to the rest of the world, wishing admiration, but at a distance. Streams would soon pick up speed, pushing and shoving in frothy busyness as snowmelt from the high country deepened them, scrubbing the rocks as the water tumbled and laughed boisterously over them perhaps in anticipation of the relaxation they would enjoy when the land flattened, slowing their pace to laziness.

Dan awoke early the next morning, helped into consciousness by the sun, which was rising now at an hour that in winter found most people still sleeping. The spring equinox had arrived and gone, and April promised to bring 50-degree temperatures, temperatures that to Dan's cold-acclimated body were hot. He dressed quickly and lightly and ate a breakfast of toast with peanut butter, then stepped out into the mild, windless sunshine, the horses greeting him with a nicker and a look that said, "Where's our breakfast."

"Okay, I'm coming," he said as he approached them and patted their noses. He attached lead ropes to each of them, led them from the corral, and tied them to the hitching rail where they could eat their oats while he saddled the buckskin, fastened the panniers to the appaloosa, and packed for the trip down. That done, he secured the tent, shoved his rifle into the scabbard fastened to the saddle, mounted the buckskin and, hoping he wouldn't run into the hunters going down, turned the horses toward the trail.

A couple of weeks later, Dan and Billie planned to meet friends at the Mint Bar, friends Dan hadn't seen since before winter began. They wanted to know all about his adventures on the mountain that winter, and he was eager to catch up on their lives as well. As they walked into semi darkness, leaving the bright sun behind the closed door, several pairs of eyes followed Dan as he and Billie found a table and sat down.

"People are staring at us," Billie said.

Dan turned and scanned the room. Though he knew gossip traveled quickly, he hadn't realized that half the town knew he had been living on the mountain. And seeing him now, perhaps sooner than they had expected, fired curiosity they could barely contain. "Most likely those two men that have done all the gossiping," he thought, as they found an empty booth and sat down, joined in a few minutes by the friends they were expecting.

As the group sat talking, some of the guys Dan had met while packing supplies up the mountain in the fall and who had questioned his plans in a critical sort of way, gathered around to listen and, at first, Dan wasn't happy to accommodate them. Instead, wanted them to go away and mind their own business. But deeper into the conversation, he discovered he didn't mind talking to them about his winter. He had accomplished what he had set out to accomplish, had stuck with the worst of it, and soon found he was ready, even eager to share with them. They were a good audience, and for once, Dan didn't care if he was the center of attention, in fact, rather enjoyed it. He was encouraged by their hanging on every word, waiting for more, interjecting comments like, "Really?"

"You don't say."

"Oh, Dan, you could have died from a concussion."

"How big was that lion?"

"It's a good thing Billie came to get you."

"You kept a journal? Interesting. I'd love to read it some time."

"How did you keep from freezing to death? We had an awful stretch of subzero weather down here. I can't imagine how cold it must have been on the mountain. Those tent stoves aren't made for that, you know."

"Colder than 50 below," Dan had answered. "My thermometer only registered that far, and I know that the wind brought the temperature much lower."

Wish I knew exactly how low, but I'm thinking minus 70 anyway."

One of the men who had criticized his venture was quick to comment.

"You must have misread your thermometer. It doesn't get that cold on the mountain in the winter."

Dan shot him a look that said, "I don't care what you think; I know I'm right. I was there, and you weren't." But, not wishing to argue, especially in the presence of friends, he politely said nothing.

As he spoke, giving away his secrets for survival, telling about his near-death experiences, he thought he noticed a hint of respect, not only in his friends' voices and in their expressions, but also in the voices and expressions of those he had not considered his friends. It was a respect that hadn't been there before, and it gave his self confidence a hefty boost, the self confidence to be himself, as his deceased friend had often advised, and to hell with what anybody else thinks. What mattered now was that, from now on, he pleased himself, because trying to be what everyone else wanted him to be would be self-defeating.

From that day on, when he met people who had formerly belittled him, who had made fun of his winter plans, who had said he would never make it out alive, who said he would abort his plans after his first encounter with subzero temperatures and the first blinding blizzard, he was greeted with kinder words, words that were even cheery, welcoming. Now he wouldn't be afraid to help protect the mountain from people who didn't respect it. Now he wouldn't hesitate to approach people he saw dropping beer bottles and cans alongside the road, people he saw destroying the landscape with their ATV's and dirt bikes, and those generally making life miserable for other campers.

Dan's days had now turned to work and occasional trips up the mountain to check his camp and haul things out that he wouldn't need for the next hunting season. Misty and Spuds never accompanied him, for they never seemed to recoup the energy they had lost on the mountain. These days, they lay around more, wagged their tails less, hardly ever got excited about anything, even their master returning from work, and they turned their noses up at food they once would have swallowed a hand for.

"I think you'd better take them to the vet," Dan told Billie after a couple of weeks had passed with no improvement in their behavior. "Something has to be wrong with them."

When he returned from work that day, Billie gave him the bad news.

"It's their hearts. The vet said they both have enlarged hearts. Probably from the extreme cold and over-exertion. They might have died on the mountain if you had stayed much longer."

Dan was saddened by the news, even became remorseful. "They're too young. They're only five years old. It was my fault. I never should have brought them up with me. I should have known it would be too much for them."

He stared affectionately at Misty and Spuds sleeping soundly next to each other. "Except for the last few weeks on the mountain, they seemed so happy and healthy, like they were really enjoying themselves." He looked at Billie, who read the remorse in his voice. "How long do they have?" The words didn't come easy.

"Could be a year. Maybe less."

It seemed that the summer had flown, fall had come and gone quickly, and with the coming of spring, Misty fell ill and died. Spuds became increasingly lethargic following Misty's death, obviously grieving deeply over the loss of her companion.

"I know how you feel," Dan said in a soothing voice as he squatted next to her and stroked her head and neck gently. "I've been there, too, remember?" Spuds made a feeble attempt to thump the floor with her tail, as though to say,

"Yes, I remember. You weren't much fun to live with at that time, but I forgave you."

Spuds followed Misty two months later. With both dogs gone, the house seemed empty, a gloom had settled in, and Dan spent more time than before lost in his journal. Within its pages lay solace, a bringing to life memories of the winter when Misty and Spuds romped and wrestled in the snow, listened to his stories, and roused laughter in him as they terrorized chipmunks and squirrels and tried to howl in answer to the coyotes, Spuds diving under Dan's bed when she imagined something was out to get her. They had been his sanity and comfort in his darkest moods when grief and loneliness had threatened to claim his spirit. He turned to his August 10 entry when he was preparing for the long winter and Misty and Spuds had endless energy.

Got up late, fed the dogs and myself, staked the horses out on the prairie, and cut wood until 2 p.m. Was too hot (87 degrees) to go on, so I worked inside the tent and stacked wood inside and put a tarp on top of the tent. What a job that was. Saw lots of riders today getting camps set up for hunting season. Ate super at about 7 p.m., then walked around on the prairie. I was going to turn in early, but the dogs were playing cat and mouse with a coyote at 9:30. That went on until well after 10 p.m. Don't know who played out first. Finally got to bed.

The day after burying Spuds, Dan stared out the window pensively. "They deserve a medal for putting up with me all winter."

Billie glanced up from the day's newspaper. "I wouldn't doubt that." Dan smiled, but said nothing.

Though their deaths left an empty place in Dan's heart, he was in no hurry to replace them, for he knew they never could be replaced, no value put on them, and puppies brought home now would have too great a reputation to live up to. "Not fair," he thought. Misty and Spuds had earned a special place in his heart that no other animal could move into. Perhaps in a few years, when the healing was done, he thought. But not now.

Time came full circle to winter and Dan suddenly found himself standing at the window one morning staring at the mountain, admiring its shining pure white head set against an indigo blue sky. Something began to stir inside him, something pulling him toward it like a magnet. It seemed to whisper, "Dan, how about coming back. Winter is waiting for you. You know all the things you did wrong the first time. How about giving it another try."

He continued to stare longingly at the mountain, picturing the prairie 10 miles distant, well hidden at its top, reliving his many brushes with death, wondering why winter hadn't claimed him. There were times he would have welcomed it, but now he was glad it hadn't. Now he wondered, too, what this something was that dwelled in the mountain that drew him to it. It was as though the mountain had a spirit of its own, but was it the mountain, or was it something else?

God had never figured highly in Dan's life. Whenever he considered the possibility of a supreme being at the ship's helm, it was more with contempt than anything else, contempt born of a misunderstanding about why hardship is allowed, perpetuated, and even, it seemed to him, encouraged. If God existed, where was He when he was growing up in a loveless home with a curmudgeon for a father? Why had he allowed his closest friend to die so young, so tragically? Why were there so many people out to get you? Dishonest people full of lies and scams? People doing evil to one another?

Life hadn't made sense to him, but on the mountain, he had had all the time he needed to think about it, to figure it out. And, though he still didn't have all the answers, he felt closer to an understanding now than he had been before that winter began.

During the long arctic silences, the endless dark nights, which allowed and encouraged deep thought, he had begun to mull over the possibility that a wise and well-intentioned creator was responsible for the beauty of the world he loved so much. During much of it, he had been too preoccupied with his own misery to realize the possibility that in addressing his admiration and respect to the mountain, he was addressing his feelings to God, its creator. All his life he had blamed that creator for the world's evil, its pain and suffering, until the thought came to him that humans made their own decisions and that possibly for every decision and action there was a consequence.

"I took my chances, was even pretty stupid about some things, nearly died because of them, but I'm still here," he thought, still staring at the mountain. "Somehow I survived it. I guess I just wasn't meant to die this early in life."

Now, as he stood facing the prairie, he recognized that something in him had changed. The mountain was a living, breathing spirit that had claimed him, and he no longer belonged below it. It wasn't that he thought less of Billie or of his family. It was something different, something he couldn't explain, though he knew how he felt. Now all he could think of was going back.

A tinge of melancholy tugged at his insides. "Yes, I know what I would do different if I were to do it again. And now I know I could do it again." He thought for a moment as he watched a little white cloud float slowly over the mountain, then said under his breath, "It's mighty tempting. But would I?"